T0131617

How to Catch a Love Rat

Tales of Love & Losers, Self-Help & Self-Sabotage

Dawn Anna Williamson

BALBOA.
PRESS

A DIVISION OF HAY HOUSE

Balboa Press books may be ordered through booksellers or by contacting:

Balboa Press
A Division of Hay House
1663 Liberty Drive
Bloomington, IN 47403
www.balboapress.com
1 (877) 407-4847

Because of the dynamic nature of the Internet, any web addresses or
links contained in this book may have changed since publication and
may no longer be valid. The views expressed in this work are solely those
of the author and do not necessarily reflect the views of the publisher,
and the publisher hereby disclaims any responsibility for them.

The author of this book does not dispense medical advice or prescribe the use
of any technique as a form of treatment for physical, emotional, or medical
problems without the advice of a physician, either directly or indirectly. The
intent of the author is only to offer information of a general nature to help
you in your quest for emotional and spiritual well-being. In the event you use
any of the information in this book for yourself, which is your constitutional
right, the author and the publisher assume no responsibility for your actions.

Any people depicted in stock imagery provided by Thinkstock are models,
and such images are being used for illustrative purposes only.
Certain stock imagery © Thinkstock.

Print information available on the last page.

ISBN: 978-1-5043-6634-2 (sc)
ISBN: 978-1-5043-6635-9 (hc)
ISBN: 978-1-5043-6641-0 (e)

Library of Congress Control Number: 2016915161

Balboa Press rev. date: 10/27/2016

For all the 'Crazies' the 'Impassioned' the 'Scorned' and the 'Brave'....

And for C & C Always x

With Special Thanks to Sar aka Sasha Fierce – a girl's best sounding board

Prologue

The pursuit of love is a tricky business, it comes often slowly and leaves so damm fast. I've come to see that finding it, is a universal problem that relates all the people in the world to one another. The search for love is a common goal. We all need it, but with love comes great risk and the possibility of one of the worst kinds of pain: heartbreak. It is a wonder then, that so many of us steadfastly hold on to the fervent belief that he/she is out there somewhere and continue our quest for soul mates, fairy tales and true love.

I am Dylan Sheriden; Private Investigator, woman scorned, exhausted dater and perpetually questioning singleton. These are the stories, thoughts and lessons of my life, the lives of my clients, my friends and gathered from my own meandering, often colourful experiences. I study the often subtle nuances in human behaviour, mostly in the context of romantic relationships. I am also a person who is looking for love, but often in all the wrong places.

I spend my days exposing the destroyers of these hopes and dreams - the love rats* - and my nights trying to find someone who is not. My life is an endless quest for balance and truth. Life is full of mysteries and secrets, but there lies my playground…. unearthing those secrets and solving the riddles: the jig is up, my friends, we know who you are and we know where you live….

Love Rat: a man or woman whose purpose is to lie, cheat and deceive another in the game of love

Lipstick, Inc.

The phone rings for the tenth time that morning and it's only 10am. I glance over at the three shiny cell phones lined up on my desk: two regular and one burner. The one flashing tells me it's a work call. Instinctively I reach for my Marlboro white tips and light one up before answering. Smoking centres me - at least that's what I tell myself at minimum ten times a day. In any case, it also allows me to be a good listener, providing the speaker with enough pauses in which to bring forth their story. Don't get me wrong: I don't work for the bloody Samaritans. Oh no, my job is altogether un-holier and often more sinister than that.

'Hello, Dylan speaking, how can I help?'

The voice on the phone is female - nine out of ten calls are and she sounds nervous and unsure. Then again, they always are. I imagine it's never easy for anyone to decide to hire a private investigator, let alone make that first call. As always I try to put the caller at ease by sounding breezy and friendly; this isn't always the easiest thing for a self-professed ice queen to achieve.

'Err hello, I was given your number by a contact, she referred me. I want to hire someone to find out what my ex-boyfriend is up to… do you do that?' A pause. 'You must think I'm crazy I mean he's my 'ex' boyfriend we're not even together anymore, but its driving me crazy and I need to know.' She breaks off.

This is a standard sort of call. I get them all the time. So often people struggle with breakups because they become totally obsessed with what their ex is doing, who they might be with and if they've moved on. In my three years as a fulltime P.I. I find it's generally women who make this kind of enquiry - not always though; there have definitely been exceptions to that rule.

I've found over the years that the way men and women deal with the end of a relationship is very, very different, although I didn't need to be a PI to draw that conclusion - I am a bloody woman after all. Women cry, obsess, stalk, make repeated phone calls and texts to their ex begging and pleading to give it another go, not realising that this behaviour only further cements the decision to split in the male mind. Some men on the other hand can be cold motherfuckers - they internalise, deal with it quickly and move on. Too often they do so straight away or even more commonly they already have someone new in mind by the time they execute the breakup, allowing them to move seamlessly from one relationship to the other. The peculiar coldness that usually accompanies said transition puts a chill in my bones even to this day. *Oh crap*. I seem to have woken up on the male-bashing side of the bed.

For the record I love men, well at least the physical parts. I love their smell, their wide shoulders, those firm quads and the fact they carry no fat on their thighs, I love stubble, large hands, armpits and the obvious part of the male anatomy that makes them well, men. I couldn't live without them, but frankly they drive me round the proverbial bend.

Now I try not to have a bias when it comes to gender, apart from the fact that I am indeed a woman who has been burned on more occasions than I care to mention, because I know that in matters of the heart we are all - regardless of gender, capable of acts of damage to another person. It's not my job to further inflict damage on people, whether it's the guilty or the innocent. I get the facts, present them in a non-exaggerated fashion, collect my money and get the hell out of there. I am also not a confidante, a relationship counsellor or an agony aunt. But if I was to change careers, I know I'd make a bloody fortune.

But really, some of these guys just don't take the time to deal with their emotions and the pain post breakup, but believe me, it remains there somewhere deep inside of them and surfaces months or even years later, by which time the emotionally wrecked woman has finally moved on and is ready to start anew. *Arghhh*. The amount of times in my life I've wanted to tear my hair out about this effect. These kinds of fools always want another chance long after you've given up all hope of ever hearing from them again. You've already gone through the sleepless nights and the endless days, the not eating, the drinking to blot out the pain and the drunken texts at 3am and then: bang! Just as you start to feel bloody normal again, they 'pop' back up to give you another run for your money. There's a great name my best friend gave to an ex of mine years ago that describes this scenario perfectly: 'The Mushroom'. But more about him later.

Okay Dylan, give the guys a break. To be fair, some guys do take breakups hard and some do lock themselves in dark rooms playing Lionel Richie LPs and lamenting what went wrong. But I reckon this is almost never the case, and if it was the case, women never get to hear about it. They close ranks, those frustrating creatures! After a breakup, men and their friends become like the bloody Illuminati: you have to be one of them to know anything about them. The reality is that men move on - quick! Yes, it's utterly cowardly and damn-straight disrespectful to the relationship, but they don't want to feel the feelings so they cover them up. That's why you hear the same story a million times: Guy breaks up with girl, tells her he loves her but isn't ready to settle down yet, a month later he's shacked up with a woman he met over the water cooler at work, and is engaged and married within a year. Boy, does that cut…deep. 'Ex-boyfriends' (and I'm not saying ex-girlfriends' aren't a pain in the ass too) are all dicks, they have to be, because it's how they get rid of you in the end. They can't have you around cock-blocking them forever, can they?

I realise mid-thought that I've taken rather a long pause and I wasn't even smoking. 'Please don't feel foolish. You're not alone. I work with women all the time who just want the facts so they can deal with it and move on. You're definitely not crazy. How long were you together?'

'Almost two years. We've broken up a few times, but nothing like this. I haven't heard from him in weeks. He's blocked me from his Facebook and Whatsapp; he won't return my texts or answer my calls…I don't get it. Do you think he's with someone else?' The caller, who identifies herself as Karen, sounds desperate and on the verge of tears. Her words make her face the reality of the situation - verbalising often does that.

'Impossible to say,' I reply, even though I'm nodding my head on the other side of the line, 'but we can certainly do our best to find out for you - if you're sure that's what you want?' I know the answer will be yes. People always think they want the truth, but the truth is ugly and it hurts. The old saying 'ignorance is bliss' is so bloody true but then if everyone took that stance I'd be out of a job.

'Yes, I need to know. It's driving me crazy, my brain won't rest'.

'Okay then', I say absentmindedly doodling on my pad - it's a large heart with a dagger through the middle and a trail of blood drops dotted across the page. 'Let's arrange a meeting. We can have a chat over coffee and I can see what the best way forward is'.

I arrange to meet her at a Starbucks in central London in a few days' time. My schedule is so hectic right now that I can't manage anything earlier, so I outline my fees, say I'm looking forward to meeting her, tell her to try not to think too much, that these things have a habit of working out exactly the way they are supposed to and close the call.

How many errant ex-boyfriend cases am I working on right now? I pull up my client list, silently totting them up: one, two, three... eight! Eight pain in the ass ex-boyfriends and that's just this month. March is proving quite the month for these bastards. I'm thinking maybe it's something to do with 'snugly winter'. Okay, that's not actually a real thing, I've totally made it up. It's what I do when I can't remember the actual name for something. Anyway, I definitely recall reading a piece in a women's magazine about how men all go crazy and get girlfriends in December so they have someone to spend Christmas with and snuggle up to at home with in dry cold January and February, then Spring comes and everyone's thinking about summer holidays, so the guys break up with the women so they can be free to enjoy the single life again. *'Snugly winter' seems to happen all bloody year round in reality*, I think dryly.

I glance over the notes I've written, already forming a picture of the scenario in my mind. My private phone buzzes with a WhatsApp message and I involuntarily roll my eyes before even opening the notification screen; I never open a message without previewing it first. The invention of smart phones is frickin genius, the preview screen will tell me the gist of the message without my having to read it and alert the sender that I've even seen it. How I hate it when someone writes a long message, so I can only see the first line. In this instance, that's not a problem. 'Hi Sexy How r u?' it reads. *Urghh.* 'Sexy', really? It's not 1982 anymore, my friend.

Sean is one of about five guys currently hitting me up to 'chat'. This whole 'chatting' phenomenon is the bloody domain of the male of the species and no flipping sane woman I know can be bothered with it. Dick pics, cheesy lines trying to open up a bit of late night sexting or sometimes just plain boring as fuck chat seems like it's all in a normal day for your average single woman these days. I really hate 'the chat'. I mean why not dispense with the crap? Let's really set this out straight. The guy who's just messaged a woman and often just put a smile on her naïve little face has also sent the same message to at least three other women. Hey, it's all about the averages right? Men are just all about the numbers and I guess probability states that at least one of his targets will want to start a dialogue and, if he's lucky and good at the game, more than one will reply and his little ego will get a giant-sized boost as he flicks between messages thinking he's Don-fucking-Juan.

I'm on a roll now; my absolute least favourite of the Internet chatters is the 'serial sexter': the guy who has no concept of 'small talk' and dives straight in for the kill with a 'send me a sexy pic'. *Yeah, sure, I don't know a thing about you beyond your first name, but sure let me send you a snap.* Really, guys? I roll my eyes again. Is it too much to ask for a proper introduction and establishment of at least a basic relationship first? A girlfriend of mine sent me a great solution the other day: a text of the 'image loading' clock, so next time some idiot wants snaps send him that and then let him sit and waste his time for an hour waiting for the non-existent image to load.

Now let's say for arguments sake that you do want to exchange a few sexy pics - oh, how many times have I had to solve 'dirty photo'-related problems for clients - do you expect your sexy pictures to be leaked all over the Internet? You should. Just to tick off a mental checklist I have ready for those of you who think it might be 'fun' to send a sexy pic: first rule of thumb - and this should be obvious - try to never feature your face or any obvious identifying features like tattoos, piercings, and the such-like; second, include nothing in the photo that gives it a determinate location, like your childhood teddy bear in the background of your bedroom; and three, never send anything remotely porn like to someone you've never met and do not, I repeat, do *not* use the video function. Now, I'm totally down with sexting. Believe me I think it's a viable relationship keeper-hotter (if there was such a word) for couples and it's one of the best ways for a woman to keep her partner completely engrossed and away from some woman on the internet who's freewheeling open-leggers (don't think that's a word either) to all. But for casual dating, it may be a case of too much too soon. There is such a thing as 'giving away the farm' people. At least give them something to aim for. Now, I'm thinking of some of my best tactics: a classy lingerie shot or a flash of side-boob seems to be most popular these days, and yes the under boob is really getting hearts-a-racing the internet over.

Oh wait, I missed one fun fact, you're most likely not the only woman sending him photos right now - don't you just feel special? So why not be a little different from the rest? I'm not suggesting anyone goes frosty ice queen, but cheeky and teasing will suffice over give-it-all upfront. From my experience, you gotta leave as much mystery as you can until you're in person or you might never get the chance to meet in person. These men are a lazy bunch and will choose to sit at home wanking over yours and whoever else's photos rather than ever take you out on an actual date; it's bloody cheaper, too.

I stand up, stretching extravagantly and walk over to the giant white Rococo mirror, which leans nonchalantly against the wall in the office and examine my face for lines, wrinkles and the ever-elusive answers. The reflection staring back at me is 5.6", a hard-earned size 8, slender but curvy, long, icy blonde hair, green almond shaped eyes with long dark lashes, alabaster skin, cut-glass cheekbones and strong arched brows defined daily with my favourite 'Madison of London' brow kit. My features are delicate but strong and I unfortunately have a classic 'resting bitch face', it's lucky then that I got blessed with dimples, which soften things considerably. My style is pared back and classic and I can usually be found in head-to-toe black: my standard uniform of choice: a pair of black COH Avedon skinny jeans, black cashmere sweater worn off the shoulder, biker jacket thrown on the top and a pair of suede pointy heels with toe cleavage. A few wrist chains, a masculine vintage Rolex and one large statement ring complete the look: the YSL 'Arty' in turquoise and gold is my favourite. Oh that heady combination of blonde and turquoise, blondes look so good in cool blue tones while the brunettes get to carry off the warm reds with aplomb. I wouldn't mind a change of career: telling people what to wear instead of how their boyfriend tried to sleep with me after all of five minutes would be a nice change of pace and a helluva lot more fun, but anyway I've got distracted and so not finding any useful insights nor thankfully wrinkles in the mirror I wander back over to the desk deep in thought.

Honestly, I'm just sick of getting played. When you're a strong woman, attractive and fiery with a mind of your own, you get used to being in control of situations. Sometimes, once in a while, a man comes along that throws you through a loop: they say all the right things and make you feel things you haven't felt in so long. Then when they hook you, reel you in and have you wanting more, they just fuck off. I mean literally fuck off. They stop calling, start playing games, start refusing to read your Whatsapp messages for hours then replying eventually with something blah - and you lose control. You lose your temper; you freak out. You act like what they love to call "a typical woman". You've become the mess they want you to be: a crazy ass person. Even if it was they who drove you mad in the first place, now they can just write you off without taking any blame for their behaviour and walk away thinking they've had a lucky escape.

Some men can't deal with real emotions. If you make them feel remotely out of control, and 'feel the feel' they cut you off - it's better for them that way. They don't want the highly-strung girls they want the girls who keep their feelings nicely to themselves - the ones that won't cause them sleepless nights and unstable thoughts - those other girls are trouble and not the 'keepers' as they are way too much trouble, too much drama. Guys feel it's best to push them as far away as possible; they might just upset the applecart. Worst part is, I totally get it, but you are what you are. Boy have I tried a ton of times not to be quite so tempestuous but when I feel like I'm backed into a corner I revert to type, biting my tongue just makes me passive aggressive and I think men are as in-tune to this one as they are to the openly emotional outbursts. Hmmm this is quite possibly why at the grand old age of thirty-five I'm still single, sure I've been deeply in love a bunch of times but I could never quite get on board with the level of change and supressing of my 'Type A' personality required to make them last the distance. A fact that makes me endlessly sad.

So I have unfortunately become very adept at fucking with people, and I'm not proud of it. If I get the sense that a guy is playing me then winning becomes more important than feelings. Although that winning comes with a certain emptiness; victory, I've found, is often hollow. I've lost men that I genuinely loved, because my desire to win and come out on top outweighed my desire to retain love. Did I win? Sure, I won the battle. But what about the war? Well that is a far trickier one to call, because even though I won the moral victory, or maybe I just argued better, in the long run I was always left filled with regret and five kinds of loneliness. It's a crapshoot: you can't do right for doing wrong and in the end you always come back to you and what needs to change within yourself. I am decidedly a work-in-progress; a building and renovation project on the scale of Barcelona's 'Sagrada Familia'.

Finally, deciding to ignore this particular WhatsApp message for a while or maybe forever, I turn my attention to my full email inbox. Scrolling down, I see it's mostly enquiries from the website and a few follow-up emails from old clients filling me in on their lives and updating me on the ins and outs of their various predicaments. Being a private investigator is kind of like being a personal shopper or a hairdresser. You create a relationship with the client, they tell you their darkest secrets and share their stories with you and the time you spend with them is often one of the most difficult times of their lives, so naturally, long after you finish your work they still keep in touch with lovely success stories (always glad to hear those) or to ask advice on new loves. Sometimes, their desire is to hire me again and while my bank balance appreciates it, my soul doesn't quite so much. It's depressing but true. Once a person has hired a PI, they can get a little bit addicted - all of sudden business deals, friendships, romantic relationships and any other kind of normal human interaction comes under intense scrutiny.

People always want to know how I got here: how did I become a PI? Well, as with most people in the business, I entered this world through bitter personal experience. The misfits I have had the misfortune to meet in my life led me by the hand into a world of betrayal, short, sharp shocks and deceit. But I guess I always had a predisposition for mystery and unearthing the truths, too, a kind of deep sense of intuition for people and situations that helped. I always felt like I was in an endless quest for truth in all things and it made me an absolute demon at getting to the bottom of things. My favourite TV show when I was a kid (and until this day) was (is) Columbo - boy, did that guy always know what's up. I was endlessly entertained by how he always knew who did it right from the start - Peter Falk is my absolute hero. I'm definitely inviting him to my ultimate dinner party, along with Brigitte Bardot, Stuart Wylde (Guru and sharp shooter) and Ronan Keating (for the eye candy, naturally). I think old Columbo would be proud of some of my discoveries because some are downright legendary - at least, for the select few who know about them. Then again, they are equally downright scary to others.

I think about my nearest and dearest who over the years have gotten used to the comedy of errors that is my life and are never shocked anymore by my tales. In fact, I'm sure they enjoy living vicariously through the madness just a little bit. I envy their normality sometimes in return though, just a teeny bit. They originally turned to me to help with their own mysteries and before I knew it I was running a regular little cottage industry armed with just my iPad. It would appear that I am the person who, no matter what the situation, can empathise and commiserate (usually because I've already been there). Nothing shocks me anymore and I'll listen and advise with the patience and understanding of a confessional priest.

It only took a few years as an amateur for me to realise that I had a knack for this kind of thing and my little cottage industry grew into a fully-fledged business. I work on referrals mostly: do a good job for one and you'll have five of their friends hammering down your door for help. And so this is how it began, the iPad turned into two iPads, three laptops, a GPS tracker, night vision goggles, a 3D lens SLR, bugging software, covert cameras, car window tints and an army of loyal hackers on speed dial. My business is mostly covert. Only my close friends know what I do, hence the cover name for the business: 'Lipstick Inc.'. To the rest of the world, I do consultancy work for the fashion and beauty industry. Referrals can only be given with my express permission and clients sign non-disclosure agreements; my identity is a secret as is the true nature of my job.

Of course I don't just work on cheating cases. There's all manner of enquiries a PI gets: corporate espionage, kidnapping, insurance fraud and background checks to name a few. But I appear to have made a name for myself in affairs of the heart. I think I may just be a little bit psychic, too, and I've often toyed with training as a medium or maybe a healer, but before I can contemplate healing other people I first have to learn to heal myself.

The email enquiries in my inbox today are fairly standard; most are asking about prices and I get that a lot. Hiring a PI is less than you imagine but more than most are willing to pay. It can tot up pretty quickly. Almost all of the jobs I'm working on right now are relationship based and as a whole this pretty much accounts for 90% of my work these days. I think again (for the millionth time) that the invention of the internet and social media is damm straight the worst thing that ever happened to the evolution of romantic relationships. The sheer availability and ease of being able to contact anyone just heightens the instinct to cheat. For many people it also does a bloody good job of providing the ego boost that their fragile egos need - all at the touch of a button.

On the other side of the coin, it's made everyone their own private investigator; you can literally find anything out if you choose to look hard enough. As I so often tell my people: dig deep enough and you'll always find the dirt. No one is squeaky clean when it comes to social media; sometimes what you find isn't as bad as you've imagined, often it's much worse. Figuring out if your guy or girl is shady is kind of like a giant puzzle. It's all about patterns and the answer is almost always in the tiny details - the ones most people overlook because they are too busy looking for the obvious things, think about it: people get all obsessed with exes and don't notice when their partner is suddenly making an effort with his appearance in the mornings because actually he has a new female colleague, or they start checking his mobile phone for text messages and calls when in reality a lot of cheating starts on email, it's a 'don't check his wallet, check his glovebox' kind of situation. Me? I look at the small details first; it saves time and after all, I'm on the clock.

Private investigation is just basic psychology; it's about knowing your subject and observing their patterns of behaviour. I can't give social media such a bad time in the end; it does provide me with most of the information I need to find out whether a person is cheating or not. Gone are the days of endless in-car surveillance and trailing targets to find out what they're up to. Now I can just click onto Instagram geotagging, Facebook check-ins and the like and locate that person. I can see where they visit often, who they are with, where they are likely to be and sometimes even what they had for dinner yesterday - all from the comfort of my office.

The thing is these days with the advent of social media, everyone is under surveillance they just don't know it. In any case, I have aeons of social media stalking to do today, but I seem to be taking any distraction I can get. I'm in one of those reflective sort of a moods. Us PI's have our own demons, too, you know; we're not exempt. In fact, my job makes me more untrusting than your average Joe. I see every day the basic deceit prevalent in many human interactions and I know that even the best of us will most likely cheat or be cheated on at some point in our lives - well, at least *most* of us.

I think part of the reason I became a PI was to get out of my head and into other peoples. Since I was a little girl, my brain always travelled at 100 miles an hour, open twenty-four-seven like your local shop. I've always thought and felt too much and somewhere between there and here, life happened and I lost the magic. It just left me and with every bitter disappointment, with every betrayal and with every loss, I think I became less and less of who I used to be. Roald Dahl once said 'those who don't believe in magic will never find it' and boy, it sure is a daily battle to keep believing.

I lean back in my chair and look out of the tall sash window onto the busy London Street below: hundreds of people like little ants are scurrying to and fro, most of their heads are buried in cell phones (checking their Facebook newsfeed most likely). I read the other day that fourteen is the average number of times in a day that a user checks Facebook on their mobile and that one out of every four minutes on mobile is spent on there. Taking my eyes away from the window and the ants, I look around my stark minimalist office. It's all white with fabulous high ceilings, black and white prints filling noir frames, a white leather Sixties style sofa and Perspex table. My shiny white desk is laden with an iPad, laptop, and phones. My eyes fall onto the heading of my notepad 'Lipstick Inc.' with its pouting pink lipstick print. Fun fact: it's an actual imprint of my kiss on paper; the logo was a creative collaboration between me and a graphic designer friend of mine. My office is kind of like a home away from home with all the time I spend here - even though it's not a remotely homely space. There is nothing personal in the office of a PI. You can't afford to have clients attach themselves to you as an individual; you have to keep things simple, no distractions for them or me.

I'm absentmindedly still scrolling through mails. I've found two so far that pique my interest as both are from men, about eighty per cent of cases that come through my door are instigated by women but I am starting to see a lot more enquiries from guys at the moment. I click and scan through the first: it's from a 'Simon De Venere' - *what a great name.* I say his name out loud to myself, over pronouncing the 'Venere'. How regal. Well it's either regal or it sounds like the name of a sofa from DFS. The email itself is super polite, proper and very to the point. The signature reads 'CEO' of a large and well-known hedge fund with worldwide assets. I do a quick Google search for his name; yep, he's the first one who comes up. I quickly verify his identity and status, which all looks in order. He's clearly a high-powered and very successful professional. Now that I know he's the real deal, I read his email in full.

"Hello, I am in need of your services for a rather delicate matter that requires immediate attention. I am considering proposing to my girlfriend of six months and I would like a full background check done on her previous relations and a detailed report of her current daily activities with particular attention to her social media activity. I am a high net worth individual and I am rather understandably keen to protect myself financially in the instance I enter into this marriage."

It is insanely blunt and to the point, but not a surprise. Yes, he sounds cold and calculating and love doesn't seem to come into the equation but these sort of contractually arranged marriages are becoming more and more common, especially since divorce is a costly issue if you manage to unknowingly tie yourself up with a professional fortune hunter. London is the divorce capital of the world and England is one of the few countries where a home-maker is legally entitled to a 50:50 split of chattels - in good old England a partnership is exactly that.

I've done quite a bit of work in this specific area and over the years it's often been men who retain my services for this sort of thing. Leaning back into my large leather chair, I chew on the end of my ever-present pen and reflect on his email, thinking how prudent he's being to plan for such an eventuality. *God, Dylan when did you become such a cynic?!* But it is sadly true that I'm beginning to see more and more often that marriage is a mutual agreement between two parties entered into with full disclosure and eyes wide open rather than the romantic faith and blind trust that people associate it with. And it's not just the men who are right to be apprehensive; us women had better cotton on, too.

I turn my attention to the second email. It's from a guy named Elliot and he has an altogether different request. I scan over the three paragraphs to get the gist: he wants me to find his high-school sweetheart who it seems has vanished into the ether. His email is rather sweet. He says he's a thirty-nine-year-old man, divorced with two kids and can't stop thinking of the woman he lost touch with over twenty years ago. Locating people is another major job for any PI, whether it be a former lover who wants to reunite with someone from their past, someone who owes someone else money or missing persons. A PI can probably track anybody down for you given time and enough information. I have a quick look at Elliot online, too. A Google search doesn't bring up much social media-wise, but I find two online dating profiles for him (I scribble a quick note to tell him not to use his surname in dating profiles). So here's a man who's approaching forty, has one failed marriage behind him, is probably hating the single life and his mind has gone straight back to his first love, it's a natural leap I suppose. Hell, why do you think 'Friends Reunited' was so successful?

I fire off a quick email to both, advising them of my fees and say I'll be able to meet with them in about a week or so. I'm glad to have a few men to work with for a while; it makes a refreshing change. That done I'm ready to start on my existing caseload, so I reluctantly turn my attention back to my social media activity. I have a well-worn routine for this that gets adjusted whenever a new social media, networking or dating app is created, which seems to be a bloody daily occurrence at this point. But before I can start, I hear the door in the hallway open accompanied by an 'Only me' in Cassie's familiar voice. Cassie is my PA-come-secretary-come-general-gopher in the nicest possible way. She's here because she desperately wants to be a PI and she's the little sister of a very good friend of mine. When she found out the true nature of my work (incidentally she learned this through hacking her sister's phone), she hounded me for months to take her on as a trainee. She's an endless source of amusement and it will literally take me years to knock her into shape. She is not poised or stylish or 'together' and boy can she natter on, but then she is only twenty-two and the whole phone hacking incident showed me she has an instinct for this business.

'Oh-em-gee you won't believe what I just heard', she says as she appears in the doorway.

I squint at her quizzically in response. She's dressed rather strangely; she has on a black Fedora, which is a good start, but the outfit goes downhill from there. She's wearing large, oversized fake eyeglasses, which are a bit too Michael Caine in the 70s, and a vintage 80s full-length trench coat with a huge storm flap, which is about three sizes too big on her and I'm certain is a man's coat.

'Cassie, what exactly are you wearing?' I ask, raising an eyebrow. She's well used to my bluntness and dead-on sarcasm by now.

'Oh this. Well, I was thinking it was about time I dressed like a PI, if I'm going to be one. I'm reading a great book at the moment that says you have to live and breathe the life you want and then you'll get it, so I thought I'd start with my wardrobe. So you can expect to see me in a variety of this attire from now on', she states dramatically and strikes a pose.

Oh lord. 'Please don't', I take moment to inhale a deep breath before I continue, 'How about we start with you wearing outfits fit for a PA?'

'So, anyway', she continues undeterred as she pretends she didn't hear my question, 'I was telling you about Peter Day'.

Peter Day? That piques my interest. Peter is one of my most high-profile celebrity clients, a TV actor and one-time popstar. I helped him last year after someone set him up big time. He was having an extra-marital affair with a co-star and was being blackmailed after audio proof surfaced up from the hotel room and scene of the 'crime', Peter is unfortunately well known for his 'wandering eye' and frequent dalliances with a series of women other than his wife. Turns out someone had rigged up the room and got the whole sordid scandal on tape. I helped him figure out through extensive covert investigation, the source of the blackmail, the culprit was prosecuted but it didn't stop the story eventually surfacing in the press.

'Well he's splashed across the tabloids again this morning; there's photos of him in full-on latex-tied to a bed', Cassie continues. Lifting my eyes upwards as if I could ask the heavens for help, I groan. *Oh Peter, you poor sex obsessed fool.* 'He's saying he's been "stitched up", that he was tricked, you know? But look', she thrusts the newspaper at me, 'He looks like he was pretty into it and I'd say "tied up" not stitched up' she laughs loudly.

'Right. Well, Cas, there's a pile of case notes on your desk to type up, so whenever you're ready that would be great', sensing my tone, she quietly retreats to her desk.

As I'm left staring at the grainy photos of Peter enjoying a good old dose of S&M, I'm thinking that I've certainty had some strange cases come through the doors over the years. I reckon I'm pretty un-shockable at this point. But the trouble is that you shouldn't ever think like that, because the second you do, you can be sure that the universe will send you something to make you rethink it - it's bloody Sod's Law.

"Fake it till you make it"

Pulling up the list of active case files in the order that I need to prioritise them, I tell myself that I really need to get cracking on Erin's case. I must have said this out loud without realising before moments later I hear a shout of 'What was that?' from the other room.

'Nothing, Cas, don't worry about it - just talking to myself'.

Erin is an old client; being hired twice by a client isn't unusual, especially if you've done a good job the first time round. I first worked with Erin a few years back when she suspected her husband of having an affair. It was a cut and dry case for me; unfortunately, it resulted in her divorce being finalised less than a year later. Since then, I haven't heard from her, until now. It turns out 'once bitten, twice shy' Erin has a new boyfriend and just can't shake off the feeling he is up to no good. He's also six years her junior, which is another factor that's probably not helping her paranoia.

She told me rather excitedly when she called how she'd turned into a wannabe detective. Just from learning from me the first time around, she had already found out a good bit of information but she was struggling to figure out it was it pertinent or not. So she needed me to act without 'emotional attachment' and find out the actual cold, hard truth.

To boil it down: Erin had a hunch. Her new boyfriend, James, had been on the scene for over six months and was utterly devoted to her - I'd even call it obsessed from the tales she told me. James had proclaimed his love after four dates and had practically moved in after five. They were happy by all accounts and to be honest, it was hard to see why she even had her suspicions. But a woman's intuition is a curious thing - some ignore it, others take it too seriously, and the wise woman listens to her heart while also listening to her brain, remaining alert but not totally paranoid.

But it is nice to have an old client back. Having a previous relationship with a client makes my job easier, I don't need to spend too long psychoanalysing nor do I have to spend time sugar-coating shit. So I can pretty much get everything I need from a phone call and can get straight to work. Hand-holding a new client is tiring and time consuming, I know Erin will let me get on with it and won't be calling every ten minutes to see what new piece of information I've unearthed. From our talk I know she's concerned with his social media activity (who isn't these days) and his affinity to his cell phone (again, standard). She mentioned feeling sure he was chatting to other women online, but said she didn't necessarily feel like he was actually cheating. So armed with all his vital statistics, I open up my laptop and enter the world of cyber space...

First call: Facebook. I'm armed with the only search tool I need: his cell phone number. Gone are the days of trawling through 100s profiles for Dan Smith, for example. There is a little-known search tool that I learnt from a young and cocky guy in a bar: if you have a person's mobile number, you just type it into the search bar and voila, they appear. This is assuming of course that they have the same number registered on their Facebook account and it's up to date. Even if they don't and it's an old number, you might get a hit with an old profile. What's weird is that a lot of the men I've investigated, especially those that fancy themselves as some sort of lothario, always seem to have a second 'ghost' profile (i.e. one with their name or a variation of that, so Stephen Jones might have a second profile 'Steo Jones'). This profile won't have any details or a profile photo and they are always friends with their 'real' profile. This is something I've seen several of my shady exes do and it's a massive giveaway that they are up to no good. I'm still not entirely sure why they create these false profiles, but a few possible reasons I can think of are so that they can check on themselves and see what's visible on their profile, stalk other people completely undetected or message women without any risk of stray notifications alerting anyone else to their activities.

Anyway, the phone number search brings up James's Facebook profile straightaway - that was easy. He has 900 friends. That's quite a lot but I guess not too many for a young guy. He's only twenty-eight and some men in their twenties do still put a lot of stock in popularity; they think the more friends the better. Maybe he's one of those. Most of the profile is private but his friends list is still public, which is also good news for me. I scroll though the rather long list, hovering my mouse over each one; there's a 70:30 imbalance of female to male friends, nothing extraordinary about that either, social media is a massive ego-stroker for men. I click on a few profiles, specifically those with profile pics that are obvious 'sexy selfies'. These are the heavily made up pouty faces with cleavage, the sort that are thought to appeal to all men. Of the first five I click on, I find that James has liked the odd photo here and there but again that's hardly a crime. This sort of reconnaissance can take quite a while and I spend the next hour flicking between profiles trying to build a picture of his FB activity.

Then I move onto his Instagram, tapping his name into the search box. Erin already gave me his usernames for everything, so this is a super quick find. He has 660 followers and is following 1250 - obviously quite an active Instagrammer. It's a right bugger when a target is following so many people; it makes my job a lot harder. I slip on my Kate Spade eyeglasses, my favourite pair of square frames with the contrasting cream inside. Scanning the page I see that of the seventy posts he's made, there are a few photos on there with my client Erin. It's clear, at least from my perspective, that he has a girlfriend. I click on the 'little-used' tagged photos link and see ten posts, two of which are from Erin and the rest from mates on group nights out. I click on one of the photos of him with a bunch of lads and check to see who else is tagged. Then I methodically click on each and view their profile, applying the same strategy: is he featured in anymore of their photos? Maybe in the background of a drunken pub night out?

After establishing nothing of significance, I go back to his 'followers' list and check for young, attractive females, I cross reference to see if he is also following them and again methodically discount or make a note of each one based on what I can see. There are a couple of women that stand out, they are the right look, right age and apparently single, in each case they are following one another. I turn my attention to his profile photo, which isn't a great indicator as it's so small on the site, but I can see from the style how much a man might be on there to attract members of the opposite sex. If he has one of those muscled up and topless photos or the classic 'just woke up' in bed pose, which seems alarmingly de jour these days, then he's looking for single women to notice him. By the way what exactly is up with that? Loads of the guys on my Whatsapp have this look as their profile photo, 'just woke up, give the camera a smouldering look and apply 10 filters to this picture to make it as hazy as fuck'. But James's profile photo is a pretty standard face shot. He's a fairly good-looking lad; he has a nice face and good smile, but just looks like a regular guy really. Now what I really need is access to his feed, so I can easily see what sort of photos he likes and his general activity.

Ah, the Instagram feed: completely invaluable for stalking a person's social media behaviour. The only downside is that you've got to be on it constantly as it updates every second. Being able to see what photos a person likes, and whose photos they like more than once comes in very useful for building a picture of a person's activity. In fact, Instagram provides a PI with a whole lotta information: their location, their followers, who they are following and pictures they've been tagged in, so then a PI can easily cross-reference with who likes those pictures and now your target is cropping up all over the place. If I were training Cas right now, I would tell her to always look for the anomalies: the things that aren't present, but should be.

Take the following scenario, for instance. I was once investigating the habits of my ex-boyfriend Jad, I just knew he'd moved on fast after our break-up and I was hell bent on proving it. From unfortunate prior experience I knew he had a thing for hitting on models and had access to said models as he worked in the fashion industry. It was sad, really. He totally fucked up our relationship, because he was so frickin intimidated by my strong-willed ways that he had to 'chat' online to 'models' (I use the term loosely) to make himself feel more like a man. Anyway, that's beside the point. I already had a few targets in mind, so I stalked one of these: she'd recently started liking all his Insta posts and he'd also added her on Facebook at 4am - info curtesy of the Facebook feed (no man adds a woman on FB at 4am innocently). On her recent Insta was a photo I recognised as being taken in his shared apartment, but oddly no one had been 'tagged'. I mean if you're in someone's apartment and if it's innocent then usually *someone* is tagged in the photo. Red flag! I could then tell from her profile she had a boyfriend so I realised that it might not just be my 'ex' trying to keep things under wraps. From her photos I located her friends and then from their Insta feeds figured out which photos were taken with them present and therefore could be ruled out as irrelevant. Then there were photos of her at places he'd taken me to before: spa's, scenic locations... and I just instinctively knew he was behind the camera, but again she had no tags, just cryptic statuses. *Who did that bitch, think she was fooling? Really!* PI work is often like one of those puzzles where you have 100 wires all tangled together and you have to figure out which wire goes where and which ones are complete red herrings and lead nowhere at all. Sometimes, like with Jad knowing your target personally, helps detangle those wires other times being too emotionally involved is more of a hindrance - you literally can't see the woods for the trees.

Back to Erin's case. I know I'll have to use an old friend to get the access I need, so I log out of my regular Instagram page and log back in as Irina. Irina is a Polish model, who is twenty-five years old, five-foot-nine, and has tanned olive skin, long tawny brown hair with natural tussled look, hazel eyes and a body to die for. She's a curvy size eight and has one of those accents that men just swoon for. Her Instagram photos are a mix of professional modelling shots and cute tourist photos taken on her travels as a model. She currently lives in London, is modelling for the season and is keen to make new friends. She's also purely a figment of my imagination.

I have a nearly endless amount of fake profiles. I have separate ones on Tinder, Plenty of Fish, Facebook, Instagram, Twitter and tons of other dating sites around the world. The first time I ever made a fake profile (and with the advent of shows like Catfish, it's now as common as fuck and fairly easy to do), I realised that to pull it off effectively, it sure takes time - a whole lot of it - and dedication, too. I remember feeling distinctly uneasy that first time: taking pictures of someone else's life and creating a profile to trap someone else entirely felt invasive and immoral - to most, it still does. Yet I have to rationale for it; I'm doing it for a purpose: to trap love rats.

So to make a realistic (and therefore useful) fake profile you need two main things: lots of photos that are natural looking enough and plenty of friends. It's the first thing people check out when you friend request them. So first, I have to find a random person on the internet who has lots of photos. This can be someone's existing FB profile (risky, but it can work as long as I'm in a different country and that person hopefully never notices) or some other distant social networking site - Russia and Eastern Europe have many, for example. Then I need to take enough photos in varying scenarios to make it seem real, and then I need to add in quotes and random holiday destination shots and general scenery. In terms of a name, I never copy someone's actual name. I have to decide which country my new fake profile is from and then I pick something suitable. So I'll Google search the most popular girl's names in say France, for example. Then to the 'friends' part. This is now easy thanks to our friends in India who have set up a million businesses just for this purpose. So I'll go online and start by purchasing 100-200 friends - I usually try and get a deal where they throw in fifty photo likes all for the princely sum of a few dollars. So once I'm off to a good start, it's then time to get the profile some real followers. I have to think strategically for a minute: who is my target? Then I'll request people in the same town or people who went to the same school as him/her, and then when I've gradually gotten some real followers, I'll try adding a friend or two from his/her friend list. No one too close to my target, of course, just the odd person here and there, so that my profile has mutual friends in common - which is another major consideration when deciding whether to accept a friend request or not. Then comes the nitty gritty. Photos and friends is not enough to convince someone your profile is real; so the profile will need likes and comments from legitimate looking profiles and photo tags. There's got to be a certain level of interaction; really, everyone's a detective these days and if there aren't any likes, it looks suspicious. This is the part that takes the time, because after I've slotted in the fake friends, then I have to take the time to request 'real' ones and have them like my stuff.

Irina is the online equivalent of the honey trap. She catches would-be cheaters in the act of trying to cheat; she's also brilliant for catching those serial chatters and ego-boosters, who love a bit of attention from a hot girl. So Irina is the perfect woman for this job. Sometimes a man doesn't want to actually cheat - and by cheat I mean penetrate another woman other than his own - sometimes he just wants a fantasy to jerk off over or someone to massage his poor wounded ego after a good nagging from 'her indoors'.

Now this is when it really comes down to what kind of woman you are and what you consider cheating. For me, the second my man chats 'in a sexual manner' to another woman, I'm done. I can't deal with the betrayal. I'm ridiculously loyal and I expect everyone else in my life to be, which is probably why I've had so many disappointments in my life with lovers and friends alike. Not everyone prioritises loyalty anywhere near as highly or defines loyalty in the same way I do. I know I may just have way too unrealistic ideals…but well. To me, it's just a fickle, fickle world out there.

So I, or rather Irina, follows him after first liking his most recent photo: a picture of him on a mountain bike. Then Irina likes another photo at the gym and another of a scenic countryside view. I tend to find that this prompts a person to either look at your photos or start following you back. Real hard-core Instagrammers are on this shit; it's just a big game. It's quid pro quo at its finest: like my pics and I'll like yours, follow me and I'll follow you back. In this case, I don't actually need him to follow me to get access to his feed because his profile is public. So I just follow him and once that's done I sit back and wait. If he's the player his girlfriend has him pegged as, we'll see results in no time.

Insta isn't exactly the easiest app to get chatting on, though. In fact, few people even know that you can even PM on this platform, but in my research I've found that it's definitely growing in popularity for dating. This could possibly be the case because women are less immediately defensive - hell, we're all used to being hit-on on Facebook. Although that's also why the amount of people now with totally private FB profiles is much higher. Social media means it's never been easier for a person to profess their interest in a total stranger. Better still, as the recipient you can check that person out, look for signs of significant others and pick up on any weird habits and general deal breakers. Then if it doesn't work for you, you can ignore the message with no repercussions. If you're interested, then you've just gotten a sense of your suitor from a good bit of online stalking. Instagram is full these days of couples documenting every step of their relationship. It's insane how much information is available at your fingertips - it great for my job. Personally, I've been burned and refuse to showcase new love online, because when it's all over it gets icky: do you delete the photos or leave them as a permanent reminder of your fuck-up? If you meet someone new do they really want to see your lovey-dovey photos and ready your sickly sweet sentiments from the past? Do you want to be reminded every day of someone you now wouldn't piss on if they were on fire? Personally I leave the photos; I don't care enough to delete them. But I've learnt my lesson. I now keep my business to myself.

I keep myself busy by checking out other online profiles for Erin's boyfriend: Twitter, LinkedIn and so on. Then sure enough, half an hour later I get an Instagram notification. In fact, I get five. He has liked five of Irina's photos. I flick onto my follower feed to see what else he's liking (if I can pin a person down to a specific time when they're active, I gotta milk it). After liking my photos, he's also liked a few quotes, a gym photo of a guy and two photos of another girl. Noting down her name for later inspection, I continue to play the game. I like two more of his photos and wait for the 'new follower' notification. It's like taking candy from a baby, this is 'Instaflirting' at its easiest. And bang! There it is. Now I just have to wait to find out if he's really up for it and whether or not he'll PM me. I'm also expecting him to follow a few other people. I've found that it's common to cover up one 'meaningful' follow with a load of non-meaningful ones - a purely a tactical move to remove suspicion from his girlfriend who might be all over his shit.

I get so immersed in social media and the intricacies of this behaviour that time just passes me by. In real life, I get annoyed when a person lives their life through their phone instead of their eyes and often feel like shouting, 'Look up once in a while, mate! There's a whole world out there'. But when it's for my job, I'm engrossed. Luckily, it *is* just a part of my job I can put away until tomorrow.

I glance at the clock; it's already 6pm. *Wow where did my day go?* I have to get to my kickboxing class. Martial arts entered my life as a basic training requirement for PI's, but soon became an addiction and my favourite way to kick the crap out of a shitty day. I may be small but I'm deadly with a pair of Lonsdale's. I follow this up with a few 'body attack' and 'body combat' classes a week and if I want a really good workout I do a pole fitness class. Boy does that give you one hell of a body. My love for pole dancing inspired me to get a pole in my house, which lay unused for about six months along with all my other at-home exercise equipment, but now I love to have a quick spin in the evenings. It's a bloody brilliant seduction tool as well - because let's face it; all men love a pole dancer. But more importantly, perfecting a hard-core pole fitness move like the Ayesha or the Jade Splits is an accomplishment like no other. The first time I did so I felt so empowered and feminine and fierce.

So I head off to Shoreditch to take part in 'Fighter Fit' a ninety-minute session that always leaves me feeling ripped as fuck and as calm as a Buddha. I still find I'm thinking about this grey area 'soft cheating' issue as I walk the ten minutes it takes to arrive at the Oxford Circus tube.

I once heard an old proverb, something about it not mattering where the kettle gets warm as long as it boils at home. But I can't embrace it, it bothers me that guys are out there flirting with strangers online all day at work and then going home to their loving women like everything is gravy. Is it preferable to my boyfriend physically cheating? I guess they are one and the same to me. I take it very, very personally that I can't keep a guy's attention on me, but I'm not sure my expectations are realistic anymore. The dating landscape has changed significantly in recent years and maybe the availability and accessibility to millions of singletons is just too tempting for far too many of us. When it comes to 'soft cheating' are we all just fighting a losing battle?

I make a face to myself, realising that I've made the half hour tube journey to the gym on autopilot. My job is bloody annoying sometimes. It sends me down the rabbit hole of questions that filter into my life long after I stamp out. I should have been a vet like I always wanted, but then again I was rubbish at chemistry and apparently excel in duplicity. I get changed super-fast and slide into the class just as the instructor, Gary, a very ripped forty-something militant, is telling everyone to drop and give him twenty. I relish the chance to focus on nothing for the next ninety minutes except punishing my body for god knows what - ah, yes I remember now: for being a fond smoker, a sometimes party girl and ever-so slight alcoholic.

"Rita Tinder"

My alarm goes off at 8am and I sit up with a start. *Owwww, oh my god.* My stomach muscles are killing me, and I love it. I feel like I've actually done something productive when they hurt that much. Stepping gingerly out of bed, all I can think about is coffee and a cigarette: I'm nothing if not a dichotomy.

Today I've decided to focus on Tinder. I still need to do more work on Erin's case and get going on a few others, so I intend to spend the morning surfing the net in the comfort of my own home office - otherwise known as my large, comfy, faux suede cream sofa. *I love my flat.* As I look around, coffee in hand, a sense of content settles over me. It's decidedly shabby-chic, a stark contrast to my minimalist work office: white chalk painted floorboards, over-stuffed bookshelves, bursting with psychology textbooks, self-help guides and poetry books (only in my house would Milton's '*Paradise Lost*' sit comfortably next to '*Why Men Love Bitches*'). Duck-egg blue baroque curtains hang from the tall sash windows and vintage furniture is scattered everywhere sourced from flea markets and vintage fairs around the world.

I love to take a weekend trip to Paris every once in a while just to browse the Saturday morning markets on the Left Bank and then spend the afternoon cheese and wine tasting with friends - cheese and wine is officially the best thing ever invented, throw in a bit of bread to the mix and I'm in heaven. Occasionally, I combine it with a date with one of my continental lovers. I do on occasion like to 'go French' although according to popular opinion they do not like to 'go down'. They also seem to have a predilection for the ass - take that as you will. Although I don't think it's just the French who are known for their reticence to give head. I recently did a straw poll of Middle Eastern men while on a business trip (I was bored and they were available), regarding their thoughts on 'eating out'. *God, how many cringe euphemisms for oral sex can one fit into one sentence?* The response was unanimous that they wouldn't go down on a woman the first time they had sex or in fact at all unless they were in a committed relationship with someone and they all cited reasons of hygiene for their reticence! Only one out of five said he enjoyed doing it. I mean, seriously, I can hear the pot ringing to call the kettle black. Interestingly, none of them had a problem with women showing their oral skills; neither did they feel like it was necessary or polite to reciprocate. Feminism has changed many things, but in the bedroom it seems that plenty of archaic traditions still remain.

Anyway, I've totally distracted myself again. But honestly, if you're a single woman who enjoys men and sex you've got to know what you're getting into. Prior research saves a lot of time wasted - act in haste, repent at leisure and all that. Bad sex is the worst; it's worse than no sex at all. Although speaking of no sex at all, there's a strange phenomenon developing these days. The phrase 'All mouth and no trousers' springs to my mind; it's an expression I learnt from an early age from my Irish mother. Although men are often primarily motivated by sex and the pursuit of it, when it comes down to the wire they are the aforementioned 'all mouth and no trousers'. For example, I have a beautiful, totally together, successful girlfriend who has no trouble getting a man. She always has a string of them on the go, but she tells me that on at least ten occasions a guy has failed to perform when she's taken them home, often citing the reason as being that they are just too intimidated to sleep with her. Crazy yet true. I mean, come on guys. Why the fuck are you crazy assholes running around chasing pussy only to back the fuck off when it's offered to you?

It's all about bloody 'fronting' these days, isn't it? As a single woman, I get a fair few messages a week from ex-boyfriends, male friends, old first dates who never made it to the second round and male acquaintances. If it happens and at the time I'm in what I classify as an established relationship, I don't respond or of I do it is only to be polite yet dismissive, so the texter doesn't continue. A man will almost never do that; they will almost always answer a flirty message from a woman with an equally flirty response.

Which brings back to my mind my own woeful Tinder tale. Rita Tinder may just be the reason I became a PI, but I don't want to give her too much credit. A few years back I fell in love - not in an ordinary way, but in a big way. I fell into the kind of love that shakes your soul and makes you believe in castles and fairy tales. When I recall it now, I think I was talked into it by a man too young and naive to really understand what he was talking about. I was older enough to have already learned my lessons through cold hard experience. I should have known better; I should have been the mature one. But truth was that he made me feel like a seventeen-year-old girl in the throes of first love. I was like an addict and I needed my hit daily. I couldn't stop it; like a train with no brakes, my love ran across countries and time. I suppose I couldn't resist the image of myself as reflected in his adoring eyes. Love unexpectedly crept up on an old cynic like me and before I knew what was happening I was a 'goner'.

Now I should mention here that Jad and I were in a long distance relationship we had met in Dubai, meeting place of so many lost souls from across the globe. He lived that way (Bahrain) and I lived the other, Jad was tall and dark with a penchant for wearing V-neck muscle tees, he wasn't classically handsome but he had a strong manly vibe and a brooding demeanour that I found quite irresistible. I remember thinking that whenever we left the hot sands of Dubai that that would be that. But he persisted and soon I was sold on long distance love. Truth be told, it suited my nature, I was free spirited but in need of security, so I got it all. I thought it was a slam-dunk.

The cultural differences were an issue at times, being Middle-Eastern he had ingrained beliefs about the traditional roles of men and women, so dating a tough independent British chick was a learning curve for both of us, but we overcame them all and we did it for 'the love', which was intoxicating and deeply intense. The cracks showed during our longest separation, three months to be exact, but we worked hard at it and I figured that he was 'the one'. I savoured our nightly Skype calls, the morning messages and the goodnight love quotes directly out of Pinterest - just type in 'lovey dovey smaltz' and you'll get the gist. To start with, I was carefree. confident and in control of my shit, so I didn't seem needy or jealous. No, at the time I was dealing the deck and the cards were all falling in my favour. Yet it was too good to be true, because soon the jealously set in and I began to question his frequent nights out. He lived in a country that embraced a twenty-four-seven nightlife and a good night never ended before 3am - and that was him on 'his best behaviour' and 'sacrificing' for me, Jad was a party guy with a heart of gold but my untrusting nature couldn't reconcile the two.

But I had already started the Facebook stalking then, that kind of obsessive checking morning, noon and night that was not remotely helped by something I'd read online: that there was something to that little 'friends' window you see when you open a friend's FB page, showing six of their friends. Well apparently that window may just be a little technical glitch that in fact pops up according to your most frequent interactions. Well this small nugget of information sent me on an absolute destructive mission. I became obsessed with who appeared in the little window on his page and one name kept reappearing; I could see that before we had met he had liked all of her pictures. She had that girl next door look and she was kind of attractive, but I was smart enough to know she wasn't a patch on me. But still, that little voice in my head kept whispering her name and every day I checked and there she was again in that little dreaded box. Little did I know what I do now, that the act of me clicking on her profile every day was most likely contributing to her showing up like a proverbial bad penny.

And did you know that if you use Facebook on a laptop, you open yourself up to a whole world of new stalking info that most of us never knew even existed? It's one of the best things I've ever figured out. On a laptop when viewing Facebook, at the top left corner you can find a continually updating news feed of what all your friends are liking and commentating on. So for my job, if I know when my target is most likely to be online (for men its first thing when they wake up and maybe on their way to work and then again at lunchtime and again at home time) I can check in on them. But the best thing is that unlike Instagram's feed, you can scroll back twenty-four hours or more and see every activity that you missed. This is a useful tool and saves me from meticulously having to go into every contacts page to see if my target has liked something.

But back to the "six" box. I became a woman possessed. At the first available opportunity, I brought up this bloody woman in the conversation - lucky for me, he randomly mentioned her first. So it turned out that Miss X is actually an ex-girlfriend of three of his close friends and from the way he talked it seemed like he had no interest in her romantically. I mean guys are strange like that; they definitely don't like to be incestuous with one another's exes. But he was curious why I'd jumped onto her name so suddenly and I honestly don't recall how I got out of it. I mean, I could hardly say it was all about the 'six box' now, could I? He was a little indignant that I was slightly jealous at all, but he was also totally at my mercy in those early days of heady passion and never wanted to risk losing me. So he placated me by telling me he hadn't seen or spoke to her in years and that in fact she was a point of ridicule amongst his friends and therefore no threat at all. I was suitably placated for the next few weeks, which passed by happily, but yet I was still checking that little FB box - like an addict, I was hooked on the intrigue of it all. Isn't it strange how we are wired to seek pain? Programmed to dig it out at all costs, secretly do we all just want a bit of drama, or is it a subconscious compulsion of the complex human brain that feeds on pain, pain and more pain?

But this all started with Rita Tinder, didn't it? A few weeks before this conversation, Jad attended what he described as a boring dinner party of friends and family. His frequent texts while at said dinner party had me relaxed and unconcerned. I never dropped my obsession with this girl though and weeks later, one drunken Friday night in an ordinary conversation he mentioned that Miss X was at that very dinner party. I remember I took at least a minute to cotton on, but when I finally did, I turned icy cold.

'Whoa. Back up there a second, what did you say?' Ah, those are the words a man always dreads hearing because he inherently knows that now he's fucked it and his tiny little brain is shouting 'Get the fuck outta there!'

In any case, I learned that in fact the girl I had been cyber stalking was at a party that my boyfriend attended just weeks earlier, but yet he'd lied and told me he hadn't seen her in years. Why would he lie? He must have something to hide was the only answer my mind yelled back at me. So I went at him like a cop on his first ever bust.

Now it would be fair to say that my boyfriend and (formerly) one of the best men I'd ever known panicked. He was already wasted and in his car driving home from an evening out when things began to unravel. He frantically starting calling every one of his mates and putting them on conference call to tell me he had never or never would have any interest in Miss X. I only became more enraged and disbelieving of the whole thing, so when he got home he Skyped me. This is where a fair bit of divine intervention comes in, because sometimes when you're digging after one truth an entirely new one surfaces.

He became like a man obsessed and showed me his phone via the laptop camera. He scrolled down his Whatsapp conversation list, completely steadfast in his resolve to prove his absolute commitment to me and general trustworthiness. What happened next almost made me feel sorry for him; he couldn't have seen it coming in his poor drunken state. I saw a contact name that read 'Rita Tinder' and once again uttered those dreaded words: 'Whoa matey, hold up there a second…who the fuck is Rita Tinder?' At this point I should probably mention I was pretty inebriated myself and was chain-smoking like crazy. He paused for a drunken moment and replied, 'She's a friend of my mom's from work'. I guess he hoped I would swallow that and I did for all of ten seconds before coming to my senses, 'No, no that doesn't make sense. Why would she be messaging you?' and at that point the wonder of technology failed me and Skype went dead.

After furiously redialling for a few minutes, I got him back and there he was all composed and prepared. So he shows me the messages he's exchanged with his mom's friend from work: all innocent and something about a second-hand fireplace she was looking to buy. I suppose he believed that I'd be convinced with such evidence (and maybe another woman would have), but somewhere deep down in my subconscious I must've known something was off.

'Hang on. I don't believe you. I've never heard you mention this woman and I know when I first saw that conversation I could swear I saw emoji's'. He did his best to convince me otherwise but he knew he was beat. He even gave me Rita's surname and told me to check her on Facebook. I struck Facebook quick as bloody lightening and as he watched me scrolling, he gave up the jig.

'Ok so, I've just lied. I'm sorry. I panicked. There is nothing to hide, but I knew you'd think there was, so I've just given you the Facebook page of a total stranger. My mom does have a friend at work called Rita but she's not on Facebook. I needed you to believe me and she did message me to ask about the fireplace, but I didn't think you'd believe me about that either'.

I listened to that story half drunk and I probably didn't pay it the attention it deserved; when you're intoxicated, riled up and your adrenaline is going, you just can't see the woods for the trees. I was so hell bent on finding out about Miss X that I had totally bypassed Rita Tinder. That night, I went to bed drunk and confused.

Now I believe there's two types of women in the world, the type that let's things drop and the type that would rather die than let a single thing drop. It's no surprise which one of those I am. At the time I was working at a job I hated and the following day I went to work with a heavy heart and a brain that was working overtime, so it took full day for it all to click into place: 'Tinder. I don't know how I hadn't seen it before, who in the world has a surname 'Tinder'?

So there I was in absolute turmoil, gut twisted, already imaging that my boyfriend, the perfect man, had been a regular little Tinder lothario and none of what we'd meant to each other meant shit. That day I went through a tornado of emotions: total fear to absolute panic about the possibilities of endless deceit. I didn't hear from him all day and eventually after desperate calls to my best girlfriend and sounding board, Sasha, I sent him a message: 'I think we need to talk'.

That night I anxiously dialled Skype and he knew straightaway - he even finished my first sentence for me, 'This is about Rita Tinder, isn't it? I'm so sorry. I was so scared that you'd get mad', and out tumbled a story that really showed the level of deceit he was capable of in a split second of blind panic and madness. At least that's how I saw it. Now that I knew what he was capable of, I couldn't forget it.

Turns out that in the moments where Skype was down, he had gone into his Whatsapp conversation list and renamed his mother's friend, Rita, as 'Rita Tinder' and deleted the guiltier, original chat of with the real 'Rita Tinder'. Rita Tinder was in fact a girl he'd met on Tinder before we'd met and just a few weeks ago by sheer coincidence he'd ended up speaking to her on a random work call to a call centre he'd reached out to a book a parcel pick-up for work. She'd figured out he who was and after he closed the call, she'd sent him a Whatsapp message saying, 'Was that you I just spoke to on the phone?'

'Babe, I only responded just once to be polite and that was the end of that. We exchanged pleasantries and that was 100% it, I promise'. Of course I asked to see the original message, but he couldn't show it to me as he'd deleted it in a panic.

It was as that moment he lost me; neither of us knew it at the time, but I viewed this breach of trust as too calculating - this kind of calculation has no place in true love and I wasn't going to be able to excuse it or trust him again. Some relationships suffer a slow death and such was the case with the man who I once described as the love of my life. But there's another part to this sorry tale and it has a lot to do with the fact I'm a woman who doesn't suffer fools.

You see, even though I was very much in love, I was still one hell of a smart ass and I felt that in the name of love I had likely swallowed one hell of a load of bullshit. It didn't sit well with me, not one bit. Christmas came and went and so did New Year, we were apart but we were together. I knew all along what I was going to do. I felt that I needed the truth - all of it. I needed to redeem him or damn him, but this limbo of trusting him after he'd been so calculating was not going to work for me.

I'd already found the girl in question. It was simply a case of entering her first name, the company she worked for and her location into Google. Once I had her full name, it was easy. I found her Facebook and Instagram and a plan formulated in my mind. At this point, I was just an indignant girlfriend angry at this bitch (as I'd taken to calling her) for hitting on my boyfriend. I mean the bitch had to know he had a girlfriend when she messaged him, right? His Whatsapp profile picture was a beaming photo of me and him on holiday, happy as pigs in mud.

What happened next has become legend as the best case of amateur Private Investigation in history amongst my friends who know the story. Finding out her email address was easy, I emailed her company's 'info' address saying I had received great service from one agent and wanted to deal with her again. I gave them her full name and asked for her company email, so I might thank her in person. The responding agent was only too happy to provide her email address and the fact she was on holiday for two weeks (a fact I was already clear on, I had her Instagram after all). Now I knew I had the power to find out the truth, it was just a waiting game. Then one night I got drunk and it was the final bit of courage I needed. When I'm drunk I write one hell of an email (not for nothing am I considered the meanest 'wordy bitch' out there) and I fired off the email that had been brewing inside of me for the past two weeks, along with all my rage and pain of betrayal at my boyfriend's lies and subterfuge. And yes for the record I knew it was a little extreme and bordering on crazy and yes maybe this girl didn't deserve the full extent of my wrath but contacting her was merely a 'means to an end', it was the only way I could find out just how much of a liar Jad really was.

Hi Rita,

I'm writing to you first before speaking with your manager regarding my complaint about a service issue, as my complaint is about you.

I believe you are familiar with my boyfriend Jad, You spoke with him at the call centre about 4 weeks ago when he called to arrange a delivery, and after you finished the call you thought it appropriate professional behaviour to send him a message on Whatsapp using his customer account contact details, essentially to hit on him. Is this something you do with all male customers who phone your company to book a delivery?

I'm sure you can see the issue, and I'm sure you'll understand how this looked when he told me what happened. I do not find it acceptable that I need to be concerned whenever he calls in the future whether he'll be receiving suggestive messages from the agent after the call. I have waited to draw this to your attention as I was informed when I called that you were on vacation.

If you'd like to add anything before I make this complaint formal, then I would suggest doing so now.

Regards"

There was a moment before I pressed send where I knew that all might not be as it seemed or as I thought it might be, but I sent it anyway. Her response was immediate, as I knew it would be - she feared for her job, after all, implying that she'd used personal data to contact him rather than a number she already had, did the trick. She offered me her number and suggested we talk on the phone - she couldn't risk being further implicated at work.

It took precisely five minutes of exchanged messages for her to send me the screenshots of the conversation. This is what I had wanted. I knew that deleted conversation could only exist in one other place: her phone. And I'd found a way for her to give it to me.

The exchange started just as he had relayed, he was truthful about that. Everything happened exactly as he described with one exception: he carried on the conversation rather than end it. Once I got to the point of reading his comment that her voice was 'hot' and 'I'm so glad I will get to talk to you so much now I know where you work', I felt sick. In that moment my perfect, respectful, loyal boyfriend reduced to just an ordinary man, no one special and not above caving to the temptations of ordinary men. He never forgave me for the actions I'd taken to uncover the truth and I never forgave him for his disloyalty and for breaking my heart. We were together for five months after that unfortunate incident, but it was never the same, a weak man never can love a smart-ass woman and a strong, smart woman can never again respect a weak man.

Men hate to be made to feel stupid in front of the woman they love, they also don't like the feeling that said woman is smarter than them. His anger stemmed not from regret for his actions but from being made to face exactly how foolish he had been. So if you choose to uncover such truths in your own relationships, don't be surprised to be met with arrogance and a complete lack of guilt. On the contrary somehow you will become the guilty party for not trusting him, for not leaving things be. So choose your stance now: blind ignorance and a happy man or smart ass bitch and an indignant one.

He lost his halo that day and I lost my rose tinted specs. But in throwing out the specs, I learned something: never doubt yourself, listen to that voice, don't accept less than the whole truth, never accept less than your worth and don't accept a man who during a normal Saturday afternoon, a period of perfect bliss and for no reason at all chooses to entertain the actions of a basic bitch. It was there that the PI was born - it would take a while before I realized it, but it was the heartbreak that led me to the profession.

I walk over to the IPod and select a random but appropriate track: Robbie Williams's 'Better Man' blasts out of my speakers with its opening line 'Send someone to love me'. Now, it's about time I get back to the task in hand.

Tinder is one of the best and easiest ways to catch a cheating partner, you only need a few basic details the most important one being 'distance' if you can ascertain the proximity of a certain person and then have certain personal details such as age your set; It can take time, if for example you're looking for someone who lives and works in central London where the sheer number of people per square metre is so high but eventually if they are on there you will find them. You don't need to pay a PI for this it's actually easier to do it yourself because if you're sitting next to your boyfriend anywhere you only have to flick onto Tinder set the distance to within 2km of your location and if he's on there he will come up relatively quickly. A quick glance at his phone over the shoulder should tell you if he has the app installed. Tinder is great because it has the time stamp so you can check last log in, so lies about how 'he had the profile from when he was single' become redundant if you can see he was online 10 minutes ago!

I have several fake Tinder profiles and one on Grinder, fake profiles take time and dedication, if you've decided to create one, be it for revenge, general snooping or entrapment you will have to put in the hours building the profile and keeping it up to date. Actually it's a great idea for revenge, say your 'ex' cheated on you and is now in a relationship with the 'cheatee' well with patience you can play a great little game of fishing, try and get your ex into a full on chat with your fake identity and when you've got enough proof slap it all over the internet tagging his new girlfriend - karma sure is a bitch if you're smart enough to act like one.

"Chicks without Dicks"

After a few hours of what is frankly a depressing task, I'm ready for a Starbucks. I mean seriously how depressing is Tinder? And who tells these men what makes a 'good' profile photograph? What's with all the pouting, photos with tigers and the car selfies? Tinder only makes a woman more disheartened about being single; whereas I sense it makes men feel quite the opposite, have you seen them on Tinder gleefully swiping like kids in a candy shop? I reckon by my own reasoning I swipe right on maybe one in every hundred guys whereas men, I'm sure swipe right on at least every other woman abiding by the law of averages.

My phone rings and Beyonce's 'Drunk in Love' blasts out at me. Still laughing, I answer with a 'Zup'. I already know who it is, having assigned certain ringtones for certain people. This incidentally is also a little trick I've learnt is employed by serial cheaters. The logic is that if you assign your wife and your mistress a different ringtone, you know in advance who is calling and whether you should pick up or not. So if your partner suddenly gets different ringtones, you should be suspicious.

Whenever I hear good old Bey ringing, I know the conversation will most likely start with 'Omg I think my boyfriend is having an affair', or 'Omg I left my faux leather jock strap in a guy's car last night'. I kid you not. Harry has been my GBF for the past four years since we both worked part-time in a fashion boutique in the West End. I was trying to get the money together to get the business off the ground and Harry was studying fashion marketing at London College of Fashion. We hit it off right away: we were both non-conformists, mad as a bag of frogs and we both love to grind. Harry is seriously the best down and dirty grinder I know and Beyoncé is his weapon of choice.

'Omg Dyl I need you right now'. He sounds breathless.

'Harry, are you jogging?' Wait - no that can't be right. Harry doesn't really do exercise. He's that kind of lanky six-foot-two, entirely slender man whose metabolism is kind enough to let him eat takeaways all day long and never get remotely fat.

'Jogging, no. I'm not jogging - I'm running at an all-out sprint. I've just woken up next to the barista from Costa Coffee and I've legged it out of there'.

'Whaaat you went to Costa?'

'Dylan, really! Focus! This is not the time to discuss my choice of coffee shop, okay?'

I'm silently laughing. 'Okay, okay, but I don't see what the panic is. You waking up in a strange bed is hardly an unusual occurrence now, is it?'

'Just meet me ASAP, okay?' he pants a bit before continuing, 'It's a level ten emergency situation. I'm jumping on the tube now and am headed your way'.

'Okay, okay. I'm heading to Starbucks anyway - the usual one. Meet me there in half an hour?'

'Oh great! More coffee! Just what I need', he says before the line goes dead.

Charming. But I'm intrigued to hear today's colourful story, albeit also slightly alarmed by the whole 'level ten' comment.

I'm still in my Agent Provocateur pink silk PJ's, so I quickly apply a light make-up base, a slick of Kiko's coral lip pen and my signature black winged eyeliner - done. Making a swift outfit choice, I pare my Margiela black leather skinny trousers and Bella Freud 'Ginsberg is God' cashmere sweater with my treasured 1950s faux leopard fur coat, lightly slung over my shoulders. I grab the Chanel large-quilted Le Boy briefcase in petrol blue to complete the ensemble and I'm ready in less than fifteen minutes. I've always been a quick get-readier. I remember countless nights sitting drinking while my friends did their hair and then their make-up and then their hair again. After the hours had passed and they were finally ready, I was usually totally sloshed and ready for bed.

Walking to the high street I think back on all the times Harry and I have phoned each other over the past four years with tales of hideous one night stands and drunken mishaps. I'd like to think we've got better with age, but I think we're just getting worse. Level ten is our code for 'this is huge news'. Harry has been fairly abusive of this classification as of late though. Last week 'level ten' was evoked because the dry cleaner shrunk his vintage Japanese silk kimono. The week before it was because he accidentally copied his ex-boyfriend in on an email to a guy he was cruising who works in Wholefoods. *'Shoot'* I drop my keys and as I bend down to get them, a woman literally trips over me, blimey love how about a bit of personal space, 'gosh I'm so sorry I wasn't looking where I was going' she exclaims looking embarrassed, she's young with cute eyeglasses and a French braid, she hurries off still apologising half to herself and disappears into the distance. 'Bloody Londoners' I mutter to myself with a just a hint of annoyance.

I see the welcoming and familiar green mermaid sign and I feel instantly happy. Ordering my coffee and Harry's regular brew - java chip mocha - I grab a comfy two-seater in the window and flick through my personal Instagram feed. It's a luxury for me to browse my own social media. I don't post much and definitely nothing personal; it's usually just travel pics, architecture, prolific quotes and the like, but it's nice to see what my friends are up to. Travel is a big part of my life and sometimes my job and I'm lucky to have a ton of lovely friends around the globe, even though I don't get to see them as often as I'd like. Happily, they are the kind of friends you can pick up with exactly as you left off, as if no time has passed at all. Everyone seems well and super successful; they are a good bunch, not to mention incredibly talented. I love seeing that they are grabbing life with both hands. I'm a proud friend today and I close my profile feeling good.

Harry struts into view, looking somewhat dishevelled, which is unusual. He's a groomed sort of character and your typical former fashion student. He's one of the most stylish people I know. But this morning, he's clearly wearing last night's clothes and he looks crumpled and decidedly grey in the face. He slides into the chair opposite me, grabs the java gratefully and he stares at me for the longest time before he finally says, 'I have no words'.

'Well you better bloody find some doll face, because I haven't come here to stare at your mug for an hour', I laugh affectionately. 'So come on, spill it'.

'Ahhh,I can't believe I did it. Ugh. I was insanely hammered... naturally...and...oh god...when I woke up this morning and full on flashbacks smacked me in the face, I just panicked and well, I ran!'

'Hang on. Am I missing something here? You woke up next to a strange guy...that's not too odd, right? Why did you run?'

'Well, ummm, that's the thing. The barista from Costa...ah...isn't a guy'. He blurts out the last bit in a rush so that it all blurs together into one word 'isn't-a-guy' and then covers his face with two hands, sinking lower in the chair.

Oh lord. I can't stop the look of shock from crossing my face. 'You slept with a WOMAN?!' *Shit. That came out loud.* I can be quite loud at the most inappropriate times.

'For fuck's sake, tell the whole shop, why dontcha?' A strangled moan escapes from my formerly gay now possibly straight/possibly grey area bi best friend.

'You weren't kidding this time with the whole level ten business, were you?' This is the biggest news since Harry slept with the father of one of his uni mates circa 2012. Tentatively, I ask, 'Soooo, how was it?'

'Well', he says with just a hint of his usual good humour returning, 'remember that time you slept with the guy with the one-inch mushroom penis? It was worse'.

'Well thanks for bringing that highlight back up', I retort, 'Nothing like dragging me into the mire to swim with ya'. We both look at each other before bursting out into fits of giggles. I'm laughing so hard at the combination of the thought of Harry in bed with the Costa barista who rather unfortunately had a vagina and at the memory of the Arabic guy I slept with and his mushroom penis that I can barely get control of myself. Sometimes all you can do is laugh.

'Kalas, kalas', I say with resolve (I've been given to burst out into spontaneous Arabic from time to time: remnants from a series of relationships with Arab men). Harry is having a hysterical meltdown right there in Starbucks and people are looking at us strangely. I'm supposed to be covert at all times for my job, so I have to pull this shit together.

'H', I say firmly, 'This really was more of a "my living room with a bottle of wine conversation" rather than an 11.30am in the Kensington Starbucks sort of convo, don't you think?'

'How the bloody hell did this even happen?' And with that, the while story tumbles out. He'd gone out for happy hour in Soho, which had turned into post drinks at the Victoria in Dalston, and then back to some random person's house party, which was where he happened across Sam, who serves him his daily morning coffee on the way to work. He was hammered and she was rocking a kind-of masculine vibe and somewhere between there and 4am, he had ended up back at her flat share in Camden. 'I think I made the first move, she was talking about how much she loved the new fall line from Saint Laurent and then she said she had a thing for sexually ambiguous men, and after ten shots of tequila I wasn't exactly sure what that meant and so I kissed her - well the drunk-me kissed her. I dunno I suppose I felt compelled to try something new', he says dramatically. To be fair, Harry hasn't been having that much luck in the love department either and has also been suffering from a run of bad sex and horrendous Grinder blind dates, so I can't blame him for trying to change his luck by dabbling in the unknown.

'Babe was it really that bad? Is she at least cute?'

'Actually', he conceded, 'she's pretty hot and you know how much I'm crushing on Ruby Rose right now'.

'Ain't we all, brother', I reply, pausing for a moment to appreciate the total mix of beauty, androgyny, coolness and raging sex appeal the rather intoxicating Aussie actress has. 'Chalk it up to experience; you had to go there at some point. Surely it's a rite of passage?' I'm trying to be sympathetic but likely failing miserably as this is one sexual misadventure that I can't really relate to.

'I need some cock', Harry announces suddenly, sitting bolt upright.

'Amen, you do'.

'Will you come cruise guys at the Harrod's beauty hall with me?' he pleads.

'Oh sure, like I have nothing better to do. You might want to think about getting to work at some point today, too, kiddo. I gotta split - too much to do and too little time', I say, kissing him on the cheek affectionately. 'Go raise hell and call me later. Oh and no more pussy for you'. I give him a wink and I'm gone. What drama and its only midday.

I get maybe a block down the street before my phone rings again. It's my friend Jay.

'Hey doll how you doin?'

'Arghh, Dylan. I'm so confused, this fucking guy!' It would be fair to say that Jay hasn't had it easy in the game of love, but she's come out stronger from the adversity and finally healed from the last saga that dragged on for over two years. She just started seeing a new guy and everything was going so well before it suddenly imploded. He seems to have massive control and insecurity issues.

'Shoot, what's happened now?'

'I've been watching his Whatsapp for hours and he hasn't come online once. I think he thinks I'm spying and is doing it to wind me up or else he has a new love interest and is off shagging her somewhere! He's making me crazy. What do you reckon?'

Arghh Whatsapp both a blessing - how many of us are guilty of that unhealthy Whatsapp stalking? watching when that guy is online and how often and then getting all wound up creating a story that suits our insecurities, he must be chatting to other women, then we get really mad and when he finally messages we are hostile because we told ourselves a story based on few facts and made it real, its downhill from there on in, he gets the hostile vibe so doesn't want to message again and you get more and more annoyed.

'Well, hon, there could be many reasons he's not online that don't include another woman. But on the other hand, he could be winding you up. Who the hell knows with these bastards?'

'These men...they ain't never met bitches like us, because they are so bloody average, you dig?' I laugh at Jay's ghetto fabulousness.

'It's all about games, hon. We just never seem to win them'.

'We need a real man - that's the problem'.

'There aren't any, babe, only little boys and all of them are fronting'.

'True dat, true dat, I'm gonna change my status and my profile photo just to really fuck with him though'.

'Oh lord. Try not to do anything at all, Jay. Don't let him know you're bothered'.

'How the fuck ain't he online still? He's with a bitch. I know it'.

I can tell she's scoping out Whatsapp, because she's put me on speaker. 'They say a watched pot never boils, you know? Step away from the Whatsapp and go and find something to distract yourself. He'll come back when he's ready and if not then onto the next!'

'I just want to know where I stand. Is that too much to ask?'

No, it's not, I think to myself. I'm actually in a similar situation with a guy I call my 'New Yorker' at the moment. I can't figure him out and it's driving me a little crazy, too. 'Jay, you know what they say: if you don't know where you stand with someone, it might be time to stop standing and start walking'.

'I know, D, I know. Have you heard from your guy?'

'Yeah, on and off, but nothing like his level of persistence before that weekend we spent together. I don't get it either. He came on so strong and it was amazing, but since we got back from the weekend, it's just been very different'.

'I feel ya, he's just retreated - too much intimacy all at once and he's pulling back on the rubber band. He'll be back, 'circular dating' remember'.

'Hope so - really thought that it might be something. Guess I'll take my own advice and get on with my life. And yeah 'circular' date other men and what not and just leave him on the back burner until he decides to step up'.

'I'm already messaging another guy', she giggles and I can actually hear her typing.

'That's the best way, doll. And seriously try not to stalk Whatsapp, learn my lessons, it never leads to anything good. It just winds you up, cos really we have no idea what these people are doing. We can't just make up a story, convince ourselves its true and then get mad about it. You know?'

'Nah, I hear ya, I'll leave you to it and call you later, love ya'.

'Peace out, weirdo' I laugh, 'Talk to you later'.

When will it all stop being so confusing I wonder. Is any relationship ever straightforward and smooth sailing? Have we all just become a nation of online stalkers?

"Now I ain't sayin she's a Gold Digga"

I happily find myself with a bit of quiet time this evening to wrap up a few cases and generally chill out. With all the liars and cheats to deal with and my own personal quest for love and hot sex, I'm pretty much exhausted. There's always several cases going on consecutively and sometimes it gets very confusing, so it's nice to be at home wearing my cashmere sweats and just relaxing. At times like this I indulge in a bit of 'secret single behaviour' otherwise known as stalking my exes and checking out their new girlfriends. Sometimes when I stalk people's or my own exes, I find myself really liking the girls and kind-of wishing we were friends. One guy's ex-girlfriend seems so cool from her profile - she posts the best quotes and links to random songs that I love - that sometimes I have to stop myself from hitting the 'like' button.

So after a pleasant few hours spent with no particular agenda, it's 2am and I'm sitting with a glass of Pinot listening to old school American rock when my phone beeps with a message. *Somebody's up late.* It's not unusual to me to get late text messages anymore - it's when all the men are most drunk or horny. I open the text and a small smile washes over my face: it's Jacob,

"Dylan sorry for the late text but I'm in Monte Carlo at some boring ass work conference and thinking of the time we were here…"

Sentimental old fool, I think affectionately. I once broke the unwritten rule of dating a client; and that client was Jacob. Jacob is the sort of man that makes otherwise sensible women weak at the knees. Six-foot-two with the brooding good looks of an Italian lothario and with the same salt and pepper hair originally made famous by George Clooney, Jacob is forty-five and completely drool-worthy.

Now I suspect you're wondering what brings a man like that to hire my services. Well, Jacob had got himself tangled up with a particularly nasty creature: Natalya, a budding actress from Ukraine who he met when she came to audition for a movie that he was producing with his business partner. He hadn't exactly been impressed with her acting skills but he was rather taken with her unusual, striking looks - not to mention her super long legs. He, like most men I know, was a sucker for an accent and that combined with the subservient air prevalent in many Eastern European women had an intoxicating effect on him for the first few months.

Jacob is wealthy and successful and his dabbling in the movie business guarantees he is always surrounded by a bevy of young, attractive women. He travels extensively for work and has never married - a fact that bothers him greatly as he feels it is the one area of life in which he has failed to be successful. As such, when he hit forty, he decided to grow up and find a wife. It proved more challenging that it first sounded. Sure, he met a ton of women just gagging for the opportunity to be called Mrs Jacob Shaw - but for all the wrong reason. He realised, to his chagrin, that this would not be an easy job. I believe in almost desperation to stop the rounds of dating, disappointment and dent to his bank balance, that he chose the next half-decent woman who came along.

And so he entered into a relationship with the ambitious Natalya and all was well, at least for a while. So eventually he popped the question at sunset on a balcony in St Tropez that overlooked the azure ocean. The cracks started to show once she had the ring on her finger (1.2 carat princess-cut diamond on an encrusted platinum band to be exact). Suddenly, her petulant pouting face became a regular occurrence and her blatant ambition and hounding for a part in his latest project was hardly attractive, plus she had started to enjoy making him jealous with a series of male friends, all much younger than him, which did nothing for his machismo. He was starting the get the distinct feeling he may have made a big mistake.

And so he came to me on a referral from one of my corporate espionage cases. Oh, how I remember that first meeting well. It's not every day such a fine specimen of a man walks into my office flashing his killer smile, smelling of Tom Ford's Neroli Portofino and wearing a fine-cut Italian suit by the same master of couture. I distinctly recall wishing I had applied my make-up better that morning, but was grateful for the spray tan I'd gotten two days earlier and for the fitted Wolford fatal dress I had worn underneath a floor length cashmere camel cardigan, paired with my nude Louboutin patent peep-toes.

As we talked over a coffee, brewed on the Nespresso machine that never stops on the side table in my office, I started actually flirting *'Yes totally unprofessional I know'*. I rarely spark with guys and when I do I become all girlish and goofy. I knew I had to keep it together; I had to be professional. At least that's what I silently repeated over and over again to myself.

He asked me to simply do a thorough background check on his fiancé and do a complete a profile of her activities, he just wanted something - a concrete reason to walk away. I don't think I've ever been more motivated to give someone one. In that first session we ran over by half an hour, because we were both totally engaged in the conversation and neither of us wanted it to stop. It was a mutual, instant attraction. Little explosions of brain cells and nerve endings fired off inside my body, telling me that no matter what else happened I had to have this man. And so I did, because what Dylan wants is pretty much what Dylan gets, no matter how much it's against my own personal rules.

I kept everything totally professional for two weeks. I knew I had to get the job done first, otherwise I'd really be compromising my integrity and pushing my concentration to its absolute limits. I also needed a bit of time to assess him in the way only a private detective can. We spoke on the phone quite a bit. I always found some new piece of information I needed from him and he would phone with little updates and more titbits he thought might help me. But really we both just wanted an excuse to talk more. As it turned out, the case was fairly cut and dry. I did the relevant background checks with the help from a friend in Immigration and for the more practical aspects I tailed his fiancé enough times to know that she wasn't actually cheating on him, but she was certainly doing a very good job of making it look like she was. She was playing a very old game that's been around since the dawn of time: 'treat em mean, keep em keen'.

I really believe that she knew he was too good of a thing to lose for a quick fumble with some gym-obsessed twenty-something - if anything, she was looking for someone as a backup. I myself witnessed her clever targeting of the private member's clubs in Mayfair and Chelsea and the way she collected business cards as she lived the life of a socialite. I envisioned her sitting at home at night, long limbs crossed, surrounded by a pile of cards, studying the job titles, Googling the company names then tossing those of no interest and filing the rest for future reference. These kinds of women are what pop culture has come to know as 'Gold diggers'. These women are a different breed altogether. They have been raised with one goal in mind: find a rich man with a good job, stability and sometimes - Green Card status. They are coldly composed characters and so will put up with a fair deal from the right man - they'll turn a blind eye to the odd indiscretion and continue to play the perfect wife and homemaker while smiling sweetly. They were often raised on the mantra: 'be a wife in the kitchen and a whore in the bedroom' and they live this to the letter. They often have cleverly drafted agendas that they will happily take years to put into place; in my business, we'd call them lifelong honey-trappers. They will trap a man for a lifetime if they can swing it. And you've really got to hand it to these women, boy, do they do a good job. They make a man feel like a king, attend to his every whim, feed him a hundred kinds of bullshit, which he swallows like a good little boy, and makes him adore her for the fact that she makes his life so damm easy and so damm sweet. This is ignoring the fact that she'd likely slit his throat while he slept if someone told her it would be for her gain. If you've ever lost a man to one of these women then you have my sympathies, because you're in for the long haul if you want him back. These bitches will sink their cheap acrylic claws into him so deep that nothing short of a bullet to the head will make them leave until they are ready.

I was so bloody excited knowing I was going to see Jacob again in order to present my findings that I was undeniably a ball of nervous energy all day. We met at my office at 5pm and when he walked in I got those butterflies and a girlish urge to twiddle with my hair, 'Dylan, looking beautiful as always'.

I should hope so, I think while glancing down at the Victoria Beckham form-fitting midi dress that I'd spent a fortune on yesterday; I couldn't resist it, it makes me look teeny tiny and totally ladylike. 'Lovely to see you again, Jacob'. I smile as he leans in and kisses me on both cheeks. I could smell his heady manly musk and the hairs on my arms stood up involuntarily. Then he touched my arm, right in the crease, which only served to give me more tingles.

'Listen Dylan, I'm not sure if this is appropriate client behaviour but would you like to do this meeting over a glass of wine? It's been a very long day and all this Natalya talk is tiresome at the best of times. I'd feel a lot more relaxed with a glass of Merlot in hand while we do this - assuming, of course, that I'm your last meeting of the day?'

For anyone else, I'd have immediately made the excuse that no, he wasn't my last appointment and that my schedule was hectic to say the least, but hell I *wanted* to go and sit with this charming, mature man a while longer. Not to mention that deep down, I was easily led then when it came to men, it's something I'm still working on; I always have been I'm a little devil at heart wearing the outfit of an angel who's perfected her poker face. Some men have an innate ability to thaw out the edges of even the iciest of queens.

'You know what, Jacob? I think that sounds like a great idea. A wine right now sounds perfect'.

His face lights up and for a second I can see that this confident self-assured man has a vulnerable side. 'Great! I know just the place'.

As I grab my coat, he actually takes it off me and drapes it around my shoulders and ushers me towards the door with his hand rested gently on the small of my back. *God, this guy has the moves.* He's a man's man and I allow myself just a second to imagine what life would be like as his woman. *Cut it out, Dylan,* my more sensible side screams, *he's a client nothing more.*

'I should ask. Is Soho House okay with you, ma'am?'

'Perfect. Let me fill you in on the case as we walk'.

I present a fairly uneventful case file with some leads for possible corporate guys she was targeting and some names of younger guys she'd been spending time with. *Damn it.* I really wanted to have something juicy to show him, but I am nothing if not a true professional and I had to tell it like it was.

'So in your professional opinion, Dylan, do you think my fiancée is a manipulative bitch?' He laughs deeply, but I can tell this situation doesn't sit well with him at all. I glance at his handsome face and try to read his thoughts. I suspect he's approaching a shut down - that point when a man is really and truly done with a woman and there's nothing anyone can say to change his mind.

'Oh Jacob, you know my job isn't to give relationship advice, but from an outsiders' perspective, in the long run I think she's invested in the situation 100% but I don't know if she's actually invested in you'. His face jolts towards me and I see him take a deep breath and digest this piece of information slowly.

'A refreshing bit of honesty, Ms Sheriden, and much appreciated'.

'Sorry Jacob. I don't want to mislead you and really I can't speak for her intentions, I can only call it like I see it'.

'Let's go get that drink, Dylan. Now, I really need it'.

We arrive at the Soho House, a private members club, and we head straight to the lounge upstairs.

'So wine?' he asks.

'White would be perfect - something dry'.

He orders a bottle of Sancerre, an excellent all round choice of wine for wine neophytes, and he specifically asks the waiter for it to be served extra cold in Riedel wine glasses. If this was a first date I'd literally be wet with excitement - a man who knows about wine, and glasses and the finer things in life. For some reason, I usually get the guys who don't know their white wine from red and always order a 'small' glass on a date, never a bottle. Oh if only these dumbasses knew how quickly I wrote them off for such a seemingly small error. I always felt that if you're going to be a cheapskate on a first date then you're gonna be a cheapskate in life and I don't want to wake up to that every morning. I feel that cheap men are like cheap wine, they taste okay for the first sip but you've had enough by the second and you wouldn't want to drink it for the rest of your days.

Jacob and I don't even get around to finishing our discussion of the case. In fact, he hardly mentions Natalya again, apart from the four times I observe him silence his vibrating phone. But I don't want to think about his high-maintenance fiancée or the fact that he has a fiancée at all, and as this is still a work meeting and absolutely not a date I manage to convince myself that there's 'no harm no foul' in enjoying his company a while longer. One bottle of wine is followed by another and another and then we decide to start on 'Black Label' on the rocks. The conversation is easy and he's utterly charming.

'So a woman like you must have plenty of men beating down her door for a date, right?'

'Ha you'd think so, wouldn't you? But it's not all that easy, this dating lark'. He perks up at the idea that I might have a tough time of it, too.

'I think it's pretty fortuitous that we met, you know; I'd never normally get to meet such an extraordinary woman'.

'Darling I think you should know that I respond rather well to flattery'. I'm horribly drunk but buzzing as we get the check and again feel his breath on my neck as he slips my Max Mara camel coat around my shoulders. We make it downstairs to the doorway where he presses me up against the original Georgian entrance and pushing his hand into my hair, he kisses me with a desire and a force that damm near takes my breath away. The kiss lasts long enough for me to realise that I'm fucked both professionally and otherwise, because ultimately I intend to have this man and it's most likely going to bring a whole shitstorm down on my head. But the heart wants what it wants and who am I to argue with that? *I know, I know* - I'm being a hypocrite, but god the controlled, meticulous nature of my work dictates I keep such composure at all times that sometimes the risk taker, the thrill seeker in me, just surfaces and takes over completely.

Common sense did prevail the next morning, when I woke with a thundering headache and my mouth tasting as if someone had slept in it. I realised I've seen too many affairs and too much complexity on a daily basis to become entwined in someone else's mess. So, I called Jacob. It would have been easier to have text, but I know better than to ever put anything down in writing that can be later used against me. He answered immediately, sounding worse for wear himself.

'Dylan, I'm glad you called, I wanted to apologise. I was out of line last night and I'm sorry if I've put you in a difficult position. I just couldn't help myself...' his voice tails off and I'm reminded of a naughty school boy who is both reckless and charming. I smile to myself at the thought of his soft lips and stubble and the smell of his skin, and I silently give an involuntarily shudder of pleasure at the memory of his kiss. I must have paused a little too long because I'm snapped out of my reverie by 'Dylan, are you there?'

'Yes, yes, sorry, of course. Don't worry, I'm not remotely offended. I mean, we were drunk, please let's just forget it'.

He doesn't sound relived and I don't think I sound convincing, but we both know at that point that we are snookered and for a while, at least, things just have to be the way they are. I bid him a good day and go back to work, all the while wishing that I'd have said this or he'd have said that. At 5.30pm that same day, I'm smoking at my desk and getting ready for drinks with an old friend when the buzzer rings downstairs. 'Dylan' It's him. I buzz the intercom and calmly finish putting on my lipstick and open the door just as he reaches the top step.

'I broke it off with Natalya this afternoon', he pauses, seemingly wanting to continue but perhaps lacking the right words. I look at him for a very long moment and he looks back at me. Then without another word, he strides purposefully toward me, cups my face in his hand and kisses me - gently at first but then more insistent, hotter and wetter as he uses his tongue. His other hand slips inside my jacket and around my waist and I am like a puppet in his hand, totally mesmerised and once again totally fucked.

We dated for two months after that, taking weekends away and enjoying each other as often as we could. But Jacob, like most powerful men, was damaged goods with an inherent 'player' mentality and plus he knew what I do for a living. His insecurities over being with someone real after being with a professional gold digger proved too much for him to handle and things got too bloody hard. Besides, I got sick of being rubber banded. *Every woman needs a copy of* Men Are From Mars, Women Are From Venus *on their bedside table*, I think for what is likely the millionth time. So essentially, I got really tired of the power plays and the tug-of-war between feeling or acting aloof and then feeling or acting desperate. I really, really liked Jacob, but I was just over it.

I'm so sick of the rubber band. Why can't we all just be honest? If you're into me, why not you just tell me? Game playing isn't attractive on anyone. Who really wants to sit at home wondering why the person they're crazy about isn't calling?

Ah the rubber band. Supposedly in any new relationship you and your significant other live at opposite ends of a rubber band, battling for control. Boy likes girl and she knows it; she enjoys the attention and is flirty, but the entire time is really just trying to keep the control. She plays it cool and boy starts to think she's the perfect woman - you know the really cool type of gal who won't get too attached and turn into a crazy obsessive bitch. He's thinking about getting laid, she probably is too, but the difference is that that's *all* he's thinking about.

She's playing the game; she's holding her position. When he's with her, he's like putty in her hands and she can feel it and relishes in it. Yet when they're apart, he doesn't send any messages - he doesn't want to show his cards, because she's making him feel feelings that don't sit so well with his machismo. He feels like he needs to keep her in line, make her chase him. Then if he can get her on the hop, he'll feel in control again. If he can get her to instigate the messages, then he's winning. Once he's winning, he pulls back even more...hence, the rubber band. Ultimately, the girl, who is now fully hooked to the relationship, feels the band go tight and panics. She pings right back towards him. He pulls away more, needing his autonomy, and she feels more and more tension on the band. It's palpable:, he's pulling away. So cue lots of calls to her girlfriends about what it all means. They will most likely tell her to keep it cool and go back to being aloof, but try as she might, now she can't. She's all invested in the future of this would-be relationship and the more he pulls back the more she runs right to him. Eventually, her friends will tell her in the words of Monica Geller: 'We said be aloof not a doof'. Now if she can get the self-control to once again be cool and distant, then she'll be the one stretching the band and right on cue he'll run right back towards her - this time with way more intensity than before.

Rubber-banding is relevant to online dating, too. Girl meets boy, they exchange a bunch of messages and after a week of hour-long chats and the exchange of deep thoughts and information, he suddenly doesn't message for one day…and another day and another. She's sitting there thinking: 'Eh? What did I say?' Now here's the problem: she can't really know why the rubber band suddenly became so taunt. She doesn't know where he went. And this might have been avoided if she *met* the guy rather than chatted for so long. Think about it: How many would-be relationships fail in the early stages of 'chatting' because a person says something that is taken entirely wrong? Humour is subjective and, perhaps apart from a varied use of emoji's, very hard to define or interpret via texting, emailing, or any other kind of typed messaging. Personally I prefer to imagine these guys simply died - I mean they just disappear, if you don't message them hence slackening the band again chances are you'd never hear from them again, at least not in the foreseeable future.

The dating habits of people are intriguing and inexplicable. One of the best things I ever read by the spiritual luminary Eckhart Tolle is that 'nothing is personal'; circumstances change and someone's words or actions usually have nothing to do with you. This idea is wonderfully encapsulated by the quote: 'People will love you, people will hate you and none of it will have anything to do with you'. If you can learn this lesson, then navigating dating becomes much easier. Of course that's easier said than done and no one in throes of a new relationship manages to ever stop taking things quite so personally.

And I guess this is the answer: sometimes through no fault of your own, circumstances change at the other end of the band. Maybe his ex-girlfriend wants him back, maybe he decides he can't really be bothered with a new relationship, maybe a cute girl hit on him in a bar last night and he's moved on to the next, maybe you said something you thought was hilarious and witty but he just thought you were a wise cracking bitch. Without actually petitioning these guys with a post chat questionnaire and actually asking them what the fuck, I think we'll never know what's going on in their heads, so sometimes it's just better to brush it off or, if you're like me, I think it's far better to assume they died.

Now, Jacob and I always seem be at opposite ends of the rubber band. I don't hear from him for a few weeks then he pops up again. He wouldn't want me forgetting about him now would he? They keep you there, these men. They want you just waiting for the message or the call. I say fuck the call. Let them play their stupid games, I refuse to participate in this particular little dance. If he wants me, he'll catch up. If not, oh well. I want a bloody man who is secure enough in his shit to go for what he wants and fuck the games.

I leave Jacob's message till tomorrow, I'm not a woman who sits at home waiting for a message from a guy who's suddenly got all sentimental. I crawl into bed and program in the last song I always play at night: Dido and Citizen Cope's 'Burnin' Love'. Damn, that woman has one of the most soothing yet heart-breaking voices ever. *'I've found no peace in the lies that I've told, I'm only hurt by the blows that get withheld... without you I've been burning love'*. Usually I think of the men who broke my heart when I play this song, but tonight I just play it out of a soothing kind of habit.

"The Myth of the Nice Guy: 'If he seems too good to be true he probably is"

The sun is shining through the window so I rise uncharacteristically early the next morning and decide to make the most of seeing what pre-9am looks like - plus it looks like a crisp spring morning that's just perfect for a run. Opening the doors to my amply stocked walk-in wardrobe, which is actually a spare bedroom lovingly converted into a huge closet, I head for the workout section. Yes, I have a workout section. I believe a person should always be stylish - no matter what the occasion and since Stella McCartney capsules for Adidas, I have a perfect excuse.

I pull out a turquoise crop top with added support, both God and my mother blessed me with an ample chest that looks great in a bikini but rather in need of support elsewhere and a pair of plain back cropped leggings with a turquoise trim, looking longingly at my array of high tops - Adidas Originals, Yeezy, Converse and Nike - and select my per functionary Asics running shoes. After a nasty case of shin splints when I was eighteen from running in DKNY fashion trainers, I am super anal about wearing the correct trainers to run in. iPod Nano strapped onto my arm, I program in Akon (I love that gravelly voiced ladies' man) scrape my long blonde hair into a high pony and I'm good to go.

High Street Kensington really is a lovely place to live; it has the village-in-the-city sort of vibe going on. I run past the Italian café turned grocery store where I buy my freshly baked bread on a Sunday morning and the little designer resale turned vintage shop where I always manage to find some treasure. Running helps me to think and today I divert my mind from my own set of neuroses to those of my clients. Today's topic: the 'nice guys'.

I'm currently working on a few cases involving supposed 'nice guys' which means I've been asked to investigate a man whose partner feels almost guilty to be doubting them - the 'after all, he's such as nice guy, joe average, really the salt of the earth' sort of thing, I suppose Erin's guy James would fall into this category (but I'm hoping he will turn out to truly be 'a nice guy'). Yet here is a woman spending her hard earned cash on certain hunch. And herein lays the myth of the 'normal' guy.

There was a time when the hot guys were the bad lads - the ones women love to hate and can't trust but have endless drama trying. There's an altogether deadlier male in town these days: the nice, normal, average-looking chap. A woman thinks, 'Hey, why don't I give the nice guy a chance for a while? Bet he won't be shady'. So you give the nice guy a go and at the start everything goes to plan. Then just as your thinking you've cracked it, the relationship conundrum happens and everything flips.

Turning, I'm heading towards Hyde Park at a steady pace and start thinking about my own 'nice guy'. My nice guy - Carl, was a short fellow, a little too short, really, but just a tad taller than me when I was wearing flats, which I hardly ever wear, but that's beside the point. So I decided this wasn't a deal breaker and plus I felt better about 'dating down'. Surely as I was so much hotter, I would ensure his continued worship. He had a nice face - I'll give him that - and a really great northern accent (what is it with us women and accents?)

He was soft spoken, gentle, a great cook and half-Italian to boot. He was twenty-nine, but had been married pretty young and was now divorced he also had some emotional 'mommy issues' and was clearly, fragile and more than a little insecure, a fact he covered up nicely in the beginning.

He was the guy that all my friends would say *'oh he's soooo nice, so down to earth and normal! - we've got a really good feeling about this one'*. I was unfortunately at a real low point emotionally after a recent failed relationship and it's got to have been my abject vulnerability that opened me up to the possibility of a relationship with this clearly damaged man. He wasn't the most exciting guy, absolutely no banter but he sure could kiss well and was so soft, gentle and different to other guys that I started thinking he could be a contender. Now here comes the rub: he was absolutely crap in bed - literally the worst lay of my life and very, very poorly endowed. Now it's always the worst kind of shocker when you're really excited to go sleep with a guy you really like for the first time and then the pants come down and, well…there really are no words to accurately describe the crushing disappointment when 'it' isn't as you hoped. Okay, size isn't everything; it's what you do with it that counts, right? That was where things really took a tumble, because he didn't have the first idea about ANYTHING and I mean anything. No foreplay and a helluva lot of jack rabbiting going on: 3 hours' worth to be precise. I like a man with a bit of stamina as much as the next woman. It's nice if it's at least enough for me to achieve a moderate level of pleasure. But I do not appreciate jack-rabbiting by any means. I mean one position with a relentless steam train of fast, monotonous sex? I swear I was starting to chafe and it was not pleasant.

I actually cried the next day at work over it. But I continued to date this man because at the time I thought that the bad sexual technique was almost endearing as it clearly showed inexperience, right? And who doesn't love a guy who they think hasn't bedded half the population? So I carried on with the bad sex, which never really got any better. He even took me to Rome for a romantic break during which he didn't make the first move even once. I'm in the city of romance and passion and I've got nothing, zilch, nada. Strangely, nothing about this guy made me suspicious. In fact, his ineptitude utterly threw me entirely off the scent.

So here's where it got weird: I was offered a job in Qatar and because of some other shit going on at the time involving my stalker (we'll get to him later), I took it. Cue lots of teary conversations with the boyfriend, but I was absolutely committed to making this shit work. I told him we'd get him a job so he could come join me eventually. So the day I left, I presented him with an expensive watch engraved for his preeminent thirtieth birthday and I dropped him home. He didn't know how to drive - another red flag in hindsight as what man worth his salt hasn't learnt to drive by the age of thirty? In any case, I clearly remember him walking through the front door of his new flat that he'd only moved into a few weeks earlier and which I'd never even seen inside - pay attention: this is a crucial fact for later reference - and waving goodbye before tearfully driving off.

There were some seriously soppy phone conversations at the airport and I know the word 'love' was bandied around quite a bit. I got on that plane massively sad, but convinced I was in a relationship with a great guy who was going to move abroad to be with me, he had no personal career ambitions so was happy to follow me with mine. Imagine my surprise forty-eight hours later when I hadn't heard a bloody word from him and had received no reply to my birthday messages or calls. Imagine devastation and confusion only made worse by the fact that I was in a strange country all alone. Two days later, I still hadn't heard a word from him.

Things went downhill rapidly for me. I hated my new life. I was living in a hotel and insanely homesick. Then what transpired over the next few weeks was one of the truest relationship shocks I've ever had. When I finally I got him on the phone, he announced that his ex-wife had been in touch and wanted to give it another go. And BAM: he isn't actually divorced. BAM: they were merely separated. BAM: Since I'd decided to move abroad, he'd decided to give it another try with her.

So I'm four thousand miles away from home and completely distraught. The homesickness was taking its toll, making me distracted and unable to settle. I wasn't even giving it my all at the new and seriously high-powered job and then I decided on a whim to fly home to try and sort it all out with him. In the process I blotted my copybook with my new job for good. I mean I suppose they had just flown me over not even three weeks earlier and set up a new life for me, which I promptly turned my back on to sort out matters of the heart. That's never gonna endear you to your new boss, is it?

Carl was suitably shocked when I made my announcement that I was home...and not that keen to see me. Finally, we met at a local pub and it was then that I started to get a feeling of real unease. I started to fear that I'd been made a fool. He seemed distant, evasive and totally immune to my charms, but still played his well-worn nice guy routine. After a long and inconclusive talk, I walked him back to his nearby house and I went back to the pub to meet a bunch of friends who were all eager to see the little jetsetter they had only just packed off. I drank...a lot and when I got home I had the ingenious idea of tracking his wife/ex-wife/who the fuck knew on Facebook.

I found her fairly easily as I now knew to search using her married name, her profile photo was a candid shot of her and my boyfriend/ex-boyfriend/who the fuck knew. This was long before I started my PI life and so my detective skills back then were part instinct and part luck. These days I could tell you how to find someone on Facebook in about five seconds. Anyway, I did what many drunk, scorned women tend to do and fired her off an angry little message about how she should back off my man, she had her chance and she blew it and blah blah blah and went to bed drunk and victorious.

Victory was short lived. I woke up with a cracking hangover and 'the fear' - that unidentified feeling you get the morning after drinking a lot when you know you've done something bad but you haven't yet recalled exactly what it is you did. I very tentatively reached for my phone and of course there was a message and of course it was from her.

"Hi Dylan, I think we need to have a talk, here's my number if you want to discuss this further. It seems there's a lot that you don't know"

There's a lot of moments in dating life that fill you with that little knot at the pit of your stomach but none more than the phrase 'there's a lot you don't know'. What you pretty much know at that moment is that you're not gonna like the next bit. After a very terse phone call, I arranged to meet her at a coffee shop in town. I carefully applied my make-up and made myself look utterly fabulous. It really helped that at that point I more or less weighed practically nothing - stress, a million cigarettes and not eating for a month will do that to the best of us.

But before coffee was a whole serving of drama: In the course of the next hour, several phone conversations were exchanged between me, her and the guy. He must have been shaking in his tiny size seven shoes. He asked to meet me first to explain a few things like: the fact that he was never divorced and it had only been a trial separation all along, the fact that he'd been in constant contact with the wife the entire time - including physical contact as he was still sleeping with her and staying over a few evenings a week - and the fact that his recent 'move' was a move back into their marital home.

DISCOVER THE GIFT

IT'S WHY WE'RE HERE

SHAJEN JOY AZIZ

DEMIAN LICHTENSTEIN
CO-CREATOR

BALBOA.
PRESS

A DIVISION OF HAY HOUSE

Balboa Press books may be ordered through booksellers or by contacting:

Balboa Press
A Division of Hay House
1663 Liberty Drive
Bloomington, IN 47403
www.balboapress.com
1 (877) 407-4847

Print information available on the last page.

ISBN: 978-1-5043-6443-0 (sc)
ISBN: 978-1-5043-6444-7 (hc)
ISBN: 978-1-5043-6451-5 (e)

Library of Congress Control Number: 2016913172

Balboa Press rev. date: 09/01/2016

I still didn't get the full truth until I met her and that was two hours of my life I'll never get back. Sitting completely shell shocked opposite his insipid, drab and frankly ground down wife, I listened to her woeful tale about his previous affairs and callous behaviour, but she also informed me that they'd been *fully* reunited ever since he'd first known I was moving abroad months earlier. I think the worse thing was the realisation that she had known about me all along and put up with it. I shuddered when she described the nightly phone calls I'd had with him. She'd been listening in and even recited things back to me to prove her story.

Finally, we decided to tag team him at work and have him face the two of us together. Have you ever felt like an awkward spectator at others people's domestics? Because if so, it will pale in comparison to what it felt like to sit opposite the man I thought was my boyfriend and his wife of 10 years and watch them implode. It's shocking how fucked up two people can be. Carl was a pathological liar, his wife was a complicit victim and I was a complete mug taken along for the twisted little ride.

I boarded a flight back to Qatar at 8am the next morning. I remember when the shock that he'd been living a double life gave way to anger and that's when I started with the abusive text messages about what a crap lay he was. I believe the wife took him back after protesting for all of twenty-four hours, after he 'apparently' slept in a shop doorway and I can only presume that this pair of sad bastards are still together now weaving their very sad little web of deceit.

What was really weird was how his wife thought I was her new best friend. She proceeded to message me regularly with updates and copies of pleading text messages he was sending her, declaring his undying love. Oh and the real cracker that always stuck with me was the house that I walked back with him to and originally dropped him off outside of was never his house. He never actually lived there;

73

he had walked himself to the front porch of a house he didn't live in, waved me off and then walked back down the road to get the bus home to this wife.

With the benefit of years of self-study, reflection and dealing with a ton of other 'Carl's' with my clients, I now know he was what you might call a 'covert narcissist' a person who flaunts their vulnerability, their shyness, their damage as way of reeling in victims, who naturally want to nurture or help them. They mould themselves into a version of themselves that matches up with your values and ideals, they disarm you with niceness, they prey on perceived weakness. But it's a mask and what lies beneath is sinister, cold and damaging. Carl had all the signs of covert narcissism in hindsight: failed ambition, insecurity, a victim mentality, whining about being misunderstood by the world, overly self-deprecating and the list goes on.

There's a lesson in this story and it is as follows: never presume you know anyone, never convince yourself that you're holding all the cards and never ever think you've bagged yourself a 'nice guy' and slowly allow your obvious fabulousness to be diminished, otherwise you may find yourself one day sitting in a coffee shop across from your boyfriend and his wife thinking how the hell did I get brought down to this. Learn my lesson; don't ever lower your standards to a point in which you fight tooth and nail for something that was beneath you in the first place. *Gosh Dylan could you sound any more like the proverbial woman scorned?*

But as for 'the nice guy' there's a great film starring the rather gorgeous Tom Hardy in which he plays a hapless nice guy who in the end turns out to be a hired assassin and right in the very last scene the cop who couldn't quite nail him says 'I bet they never see you coming' and that just about sums up this guy and his brethren, that's how they get you, and that's the kicker...you absolutely never see him coming...

"The Flip"

Gosh, I was thinking so much about that asshole that I didn't even notice I'd been running for over an hour and had already lapped the lower part of Hyde Park twice. I turn in the direction of home feeling very smug indeed; it's only 8.30am and not only am I awake and in the land of the living, but I've actually exercised and still have the rest of the day to fill. I run past the florists and the bakery and see a face that registers in my mind for some reason. She looks familiar, but I have no idea why. This happens all the time to me; I deal with a lot of people in my line of work and faces become familiar. Anyway it's not ringing any particular bells right now, so I filter it as irrelevant. The whole 'nice guy' story irritates me, partly because it also makes me think about 'the flip' as in 'that guy really flipped it on me' he chased me, I eventually invested and he screwed me over, and we know I bloody hate to feel stupid.

Now this little or rather a large relationship phenomenon is what I like to call 'the flip'. If you can wrap your head around it and anticipate or altogether avoid its arrival, you will be on your way to cracking the secret of a lasting healthy relationship. So what is 'the flip'? By my definition it is:

'The key moment in a relationship when the balance of power flips unexpectedly from one to the other'

I must talk about this to at least ten people a week, especially clients who sit in my office tearing their hair out after a break-up and they all say the same phrase or words to this effect *'I don't get it he/she was so into me in the beginning, they chased me like crazy, what happened how did I end up feeling so out of control, now I'm chasing him/her'*. Everybody who ever met anybody romantically will know exactly what I'm talking about. 'The flip is something that keeps catching us women out, because we're the ones that usually start off being chased.

Let's say for example a hot desirable woman, meets a less hot but nice enough man, who worships the ground she walks on. She basks in the reflection of herself that she sees when she looks in his eyes and she secretly can't believe that finally she's met a man who's so entranced by her very presence that he'll never stray. She enjoys wielding her considerable power for the first few weeks and months, throwing the odd tantrum and threatening to break it off every time there's a hint of a dispute, he is clearly terrified at the prospect of losing his queen and so he placates and complies. This little dance continues sometimes for months, but then before she knows it, the queen becomes quite addicted to wielding her power and starts to do so more frequently. She starts throwing little hissy fits just to check the status quo is all the same. Besides, it feels so good to be so desired and in control, doesn't it? Trouble is, she's losing her crown with every strop but she is so fixated on her own position that she doesn't realise it.

Then one day - and she can never quite put her finger on exactly when it happened - the phone doesn't beep with her usual goodnight text message on its standard cue. Then when she creates a little drama, he withdraws from the conversation and doesn't call her back till the next day or worse he tells her to pack it in and stop being a child. The woman finds that she's the one suddenly initiating the daily calls and texts; she starts to get a little clingy and starts paying more attention to what he's doing. Some evenings he doesn't call at all and is entirely nonchalant when questioned about it.

Gradually and almost unknowingly, the woman gives over her power little by little. The man who once told every day that he couldn't believe someone so beautiful had chosen him and waxed on about how lucky he was to have got her, doesn't seem to feel particularly lucky anymore. In fact, he now wields all the power and payback is a bitch. He's the desired one now. The next time they get into a fight; he makes no attempt to contact her. She finds that it's her that has to do the running, the apologising and the grovelling, regardless who might have been at fault. And 'the flip' is complete.

Once the flip has happened it rarely flips back. The woman will never be quite so adored and he will never bend over backwards again not to lose her. She will find herself lamenting to her friends with 'how did this happen?', 'I wasn't even that in to him at the beginning', 'he did all the running', 'I mean he practically talked me into it', but there she is chin deep in love and totally out of control. The flip has got some of the best women I know, including me.

The worst thing about the flip is the sudden unexpected arrival of a complete stranger into your relationship. He used to be called your boyfriend, but now you barely recognise him. Once you lose your power and your man has flipped to a galaxy far far away, you will always be in the wrong and they will always be right. This often signals the beginning of the end. Because even they *are* wrong and you are not being unreasonable, now they won't apologise. Whatever has flipped or switched in their brain has reprogrammed them entirely to know that they don't have to be sorry, because you'll be still chasing after them no matter what.

You see, what usually precedes 'the flip' is a set of not-so-desirable behaviours, he/she does something a bit too 'cray cray' imagine you're on a huge power trip and you feel like you got this 'in the bag' so you stop understanding or considering the boundaries of what the other person deems acceptable. When you push those boundaries you might get away with it once or twice, but when it becomes a sustained pattern, your partner will eventually start to lose the blinkers and question if the highs really justify the lows. Of course the flip doesn't always have to involve a high maintenance woman or a quiet unassuming man, there doesn't have to be undesirable behaviour for it to happen either that's just one example. The most important facet of my flip theory is that it's about power, so whoever starts out with it (and let's face it there's always one who's a bit more into the other) will eventually lose that power to the other and that's why it gets us women every time - because traditionally the man chases the woman then somewhere down the track she finds she's become the one chasing him.

I speak totally from harsh experience; the flip has happened to me in just about every relationship I've ever had. You see I'm a force of nature, a bloody strong independent creature and a bit of a firecracker and I seem to have gone through this life collecting men who are shall we say.... calmer, simpler beings. Whether it be it looks, brains, or general chutzpah, they shine less. I'm drawn to them for their niceness and their humility and they are drawn to me for my fire. I seem to attract men who have a desire for adventure, who want to dip their toes in unknown exotic waters and feel passion and spontaneity but not necessarily men who've ever dated anyone with oodles of that before. This has ultimately been my downfall.

Because all the men I have ever loved have had to talk me into loving them. They've had to chase me, to declare undying love and to coax me slowly and surely into it. But when a passionate woman finally falls in love, she falls hard and that's when everything changes. It's almost as if I have a little sign on top of my head that says 'Okay, I'm in it now, please screw me over freely' and screw me over they have.

My life has been a 'flip' over and over again. In every relationship, I've been pursued relentlessly, charmed the pants off and generally hoodwinked and then the minute I've committed to the guy 100% and decided to give him a fair shot, and dare I say it - actually fallen in love, he's stepped back, to a palpable enough extent and I've found myself wildly out of control and freaking the fuck out.

Jad told me he loved me the day after our drunken one-night-stand. This, on reflection, was a red flag. But he seemed like the perfect man. He loved and adored me with a magnetising power that bowled me over; we travelled and we loved across countries and boundaries. But one day when he got tired of being the chaser he flipped it on me, and nothing that he did including being caught 'chatting' online with a series of highly masculine looking models and a barely-ever-talked-about slap to my right jaw, ever made him admit he was in the wrong. That's right, a slap! The one and only time in my life that a man has ever laid hands on me, and it's something that my brain dismissed almost as soon as it happened, the brain decided in its infinite wisdom I should forget the magnitude of this action and instead do the 'monkey dance' of sifting over the evidence, the detritus and the bones of everything that had brought us here. Worse still, I took responsibility for the slap because I had provoked him, it became secondary to his cheating. Domestic abuse is an awful thing and not one to ever be glossed over or forgotten lightly, thankfully this was an isolated incident and not necessarily indicative of his character or the relationship but I removed myself from the situation and I choose not to dwell on it for the sake of my sanity.

So I stopped fighting for a person who wasn't worth it and never really had been, what a truth to have to accept that the person you loved and respected wasn't who you thought they were at all. These days he can be seen flaunting his latest conquest - a fairly odd looking Russian wannabe model that cheated on her boyfriend to be with him, because he had more money and better prospects. Yes, Instagram stalking certainly provided me with a whole heap of information about that one.

The best part of being a PI is the power to see what a mug your ex-boyfriends are being. Nothing can make a woman scorned feel better than seeing said ex-boyfriend delete all their photos in a bid to prove to his new fleeting love how serious he is and then tag her in a series of lovey-dovey pics only to observe said woman then un-tag the photos. Those little nuggets of information make you smile briefly if nothing else. The universe provides us nothing if not balance in all things. It gives and it takes away.

There's a guy I've started seeing recently who's ticking all the boxes - my New Yorker: he makes me smile every day when I get a message from him; he's great on paper; has the best job; and has it all going on. I'm might be in real trouble with this one. We met for the first time face-to-face just two weeks ago, he flew in from New York to see me for forty-eight hours: a grand gesture that's for sure and it was nothing short of amazing; I've never had a first date be that incredible. We completely connected, the chemistry was insane and I didn't tell a soul - not a single one of my friends. For those forty-eight hours, I was in heaven and completely happy. But it may just have been a good bit of fantasy he acted out for me and possibly a classic case of pillow talk. He spoke of what our kids would look like, he asked me what I thought about moving to New York and living with him there and he went over and over how he was so confused by his feelings for someone he'd just met. He sucked me in and before I knew it this cynic was confessing feelings and opening up her soul to the extent that I even told him I thought he was a 'gift' sent from 'up above'. He may have played me, big time, I haven't decided yet. He's back in New York and the attentiveness isn't quite the same level, sure he's still in touch, playing the charmer but it doesn't feel like before, his pursuance is nowhere near as intense. My best mate Jay keeps telling me it's the 'Waterwheel' effect, he's filled up on me and intimacy for a while and I've got to wait for his desire to fill up again and then he'll 'pour' all his love and affection over me again. Only time will tell I guess.

So the lesson is this: 'the flip' will most likely occur no matter which side it starts in favour of. So just be aware of it and it won't be such a shock when you end up on the other side of the fence from where you started.

But it's made me think… Are we all just massive egotists in the end who need who need our egos massaged before we contemplate giving away a piece of our hearts? Perhaps think before you leap. Yes, it all feels so nice and cosy; yes, it's a little like heaven for your ego (at the start at least). But at what cost? Wouldn't it be far better to enter into a union as equals, who are both equally invested and both certain of what they want? Wouldn't it be better if no one pushed the boundary of the balance of power? Wouldn't it be better if neither of your held any cards? Wouldn't it be wonderful if it wasn't a game at all? I wonder.

I mentally tick off what needs to be done for the day, but the main thing that springs to mind is getting laid - I firmly believe that regular sex is a healthy and relevant part of every successful woman's week. Tonight I'm seeing Brogan, a man I've been casually dating for a month or two now.

Turning into my quiet residential street, I stop outside the grandiose front porch and catch my breath. Using the wall, I stretch my legs out; my muscles are burning, but in a good kind of a way. The three flights of stairs I climb up to my door are still a struggle though. When I enter, the sun is shining through the flat making everything look shiny and bright.

Stripping, I step into the shower and stay there for the longest time enjoying the feeling of the hot water on my skin, I do some of my best thinking in the shower, I've cracked so many cases in these quiet times of contemplation without even realising it. Grabbing my bathrobe and a fluffy white towel, I wrap up my long hair in a turban and sit down at the vanity and carefully apply my make-up.

I'm already thinking about my rendezvous this evening with Brogan. I want to look 'deshabille' sexy like my all-time muse Brigitte Bardot. Lingerie is key, and also one of my favourite pastimes - part of me suspects that the location of my office in Soho possibly had something to do with the proximity of the Broadwick Street Agent Provocateur store. I've long been obsessed with AP underwear and I've secretly always wanted to be an AP girl - those hot Betty Paige lookalikes with the 1950s hair, tattoos and tiny pink Westwood designed dresses that button down to show a flash of the latest lingerie collection and are cut super short with suspenders and fishnet pencil-back stockings. I really need to procure me one of those uniforms; you'd think with the amount of money I spend in there they'd make me an honorary staff member.

For my 'dinner date' - really my hook up I want my underwear to be banging. I know just what to pair with the nude, cashmere and sleeveless roll neck midi dress I'll be wearing. It'll go with the Jimmy Choo nude Agnes pointy-toe pumps I've already picked out, too. I open the vintage Louis IV wardrobe that houses my lingerie and pull out my newest purchase; it's still wrapped in the decadent black tissue and in the signature pink box. The 'Cate' set is comprised of nude, barely-there pearlescent French embroidered net, and the bra has amazing crossover straps that meet just below the neck perfect for the halter cut of my dress. I slip on the teeny matching thong and instantly feel like a million dollars - beautiful underwear has the power to do that to a woman.

Completing the look with my Max Mara camel full length coat and a flash of Rose Gold Michael Kors on my wrist - I do love a masculine oversized timepiece to complete an otherwise femme ensemble. I've put on just a bit too much Lauder Perfectionist make-up base, knowing that over the next eight hours it will fade a bit and look just natural enough for my date. I'm all about the lips and the eyeliner, so I'll do those later.

So, Brogan. I met him online on a new, fairly high-end dating app called Beautifulpeople.com. It's been called a tad materialistic, because you have to be voted in by other members based on your looks, which is actually quite funny when you're watch the little bar chart ticking off the votes that fall into four categories ranging from 'no way' to 'beautiful'. I imagine it's less fun for the people that don't get accepted. But anyway, I've met quite a few interesting men on it so far and frankly I don't care about the whole voting on appearance part. Isn't all online dating based purely on appearance? Brogan is thirty-four and a city-living private tutor who sometimes moonlights as fitness model. I love a good body on a man and this guy has the best one I've seen in years. His shoulders! I have a serious thing for big, defined shoulders.

On the downside though, he's possibly a bit too clean living for me. He doesn't smoke and he only drinks low-carb beer, which frankly is not beer in my book. I guess all that modelling does involve quite a bit of self-sacrifice. But he's easy on the eye and kind of fun. We've been doing the dating dance for about a month now. Because I'm keen to keep this one ticking over for as long as possible, it has certain benefits.

I'm really getting tired of trying to meet decent guys who look good and aren't intimated by a strong woman, so I'm being super cool and nonchalant and blatantly using him for the hot sex, but at the same time I actually kind of like him and think he could be more than just a hook up, and that puts me firmly into the danger zone, I'm putting a vibe out there that I'm not looking for anything serious but at the back of my head I'm quietly considering him - potential 'flip' alert! So I had better be careful.

"Forget about the guy who forgot about you"

This morning is my meeting with Karen, scheduled at 11am. I arrive early and order my customary drink: a soy vanilla latte in a takeout cup. My usual Barista hands it to me with a 'Have a nice day Dylan'. I love how they do that; Starbucks knows their regulars and they make you feel just like one of the family. It's quiet now since the rush hour has quieted down, so I select a comfy armchair seat by the window and mentally go over what I know about my new client and her missing boyfriend.

I recognise her immediately when she walks in a few minutes later. She has that look of fragile apprehensiveness mixed together with a vaguely misplaced excitement. I estimate that she is in early thirties. She's attractive, slim, has long brown hair, and is dressed neatly. She's very 'normal girl-next-door'. I wave and gesture her over and she looks relieved not to have to search for me.

'Dylan?' I extend my hand for a shake and give her a warm smile.

The most successful female PI's are empathetic whilst maintaining an air of control (or so it says in the manual), the client has to feel comfortable enough sharing their most personal emotions, yet feel confident enough that you are going to take absolute control from here on out. Up close, she looks tired and a little gaunt.

'Sorry', she says, as if reading my mind, 'I haven't been sleeping so well recently'.

'Perfectly understandable under the circumstances. Let's see if I can help you with that. Would you like something to drink?'

'No, no, I'm fine. I'd rather just get on with it. I don't want to take up too much of your time. I know you must be busy'.

'Okay, then. Please tell me what's brought you to me and exactly how I can help you?'

Her story tumbles forth and as she talks, I shudder silently. It's not a new story to me on any level: the fear that a person feels after a break up and the total lack of control you feel over that person who was once your whole world. She details fairly concisely the relationship, the break up and what's happened since - I sense that she probably rehearsed what she wanted to convey beforehand.

'We had a big row. It's not unusual. We live together and we fight like any couple fights. It was over nothing really, just a bill he forgot to pay. He blew it all out of proportion - I'd never seen him like that before, so I told him to go stay with his mate for the night to cool down. Except he never came back. He cut off all contact, blocked my calls, deleted me off Facebook and cleared out his stuff while I was at work. Then posted the house key back through the letterbox three days later', she pauses and takes a deep inhale, 'He's literally disappeared. That was five weeks ago and I haven't seen or heard a thing from him'.

I understand her distress only too well. She spent the last few years being happy and making plans for the future. Then one day, almost out of the blue, he's gone. It's the shock that always gets a person and then your mind begins with the relentless questions that it asks you over and over again, making you crazy. No one with a broken heart can ever be objective and see things clearly and they have to be careful not to allow their mind's worry to convince them that a possibility or a fear is an actual truth.

'So Karen, did you try and contact him, track him down?'

'Yes of course. I didn't do anything for the first few days; I just figured he was throwing his toys out the cot and I left him to cool down. How wrong I was on that front. Then I started to get a bad feeling, so I called him - no answer. I tried a Whatsapp call and that's how I realised he'd blocked me. I checked Facebook and my heart went cold when I realised he'd blocked me on there, as well.'

'Okay, so then what happened?'

'Well I called his office, they kept stonewalling me, saying he was in meetings, or "not in the office". His direct line went straight to voicemail every time. I tried waiting outside his office at lunchtime and after work, but he never appeared.'

'What about parents or friends? Did you try and contact them?'

'He's not close to his parents and I've never met them. I tried his closest friends - the ones I know anyway - and none answered. You know what, Dylan? We've been together for almost two years and I only just realised how little I really know about his family'.

That's not unusual, I think to myself. Loads of men in their thirties don't do the whole family thing, especially city-dwellers who are far from home.

'I think there must be another woman', she blurts out. 'I want so badly for that not to be the case, but I can't make sense of it otherwise. Why else would he just not get in contact at all?'

She looks deflated or defeated or both and I ponder the question for a beat before I answer.

'The truth is that it would be the most plausible explanation and would explain the silence and the strange behaviour, but then on the other hand, you guys broke up, right? Men can be very black and white. He's taken it as red you are over and he's operating under that assumption'.

'Oh', she looks taken off guard at that. She just saw an argument, but he could've seen a break up. Men do that. I've realised they see things as they appear, they don't see all the other layers that women see. 'He's thrown me away, hasn't he? I've been forgotten?'

I've learnt from bitter experience that there is a kind of pattern that a lot of men can fall under. It's not every man, but enough of them that's its one of the staples in my philosophy. Once a man has been truly in love and it didn't work out, he will most likely marry or move in with the next woman he meets. Not because of love, but quite the opposite. It's something about a broken heart for a man that sends them quite loopy, many become desperate to fill the emptiness and replace the person as fast as they can. In my experience a broken-hearted woman will do the opposite: she'll run for the hills at the possibility of another big commitment, last thing she wants is her heart broken again.

Women, including me, my clients and my friends, are endlessly disappointed at the speed at which their man moves on after a horrible breakup - it feels disrespectful. We question if they ever cared about us at all. But sometimes I think about what a big compliment it is, too. His heart is really broken and maybe now he wants yours to be, too. It's fucked up, but just remember you wanted more, you deserved more, you *are* more. It's his loss.

But being forgotten - whether you're a man or a woman - is something one never quite gets used to. It's an uneasy, unpleasant feeling, even if we've been guilty of forgetting others ourselves. But in my book, people aren't supposed to fall in love with someone straight after loving someone else - it's not how we do things.

I was born with a pretty heightened sense of intuition. Some may even call it psychic ability. I'm also a realist. I've always been able to see things that haven't happened yet and sometimes I just know shit. But during the most difficult breakups of my life I haven't been able to discern my intuition from my own mind playing tricks on me. So sitting across from Karen, a woman who just looks plain broken at the moment, I totally get it and I want to help. But first I need to be sure that it's actually the truth she's after.

'So to clarify, you'd like me to track what your ex is doing and has been doing since he left? Are you prepared for me to unearth certain uncomfortable truths, things you might not want to hear or see? Are you absolutely sure you feel strong enough to face whatever it is I find out?'

She falters long enough for me to know that she's not actually sure whether she can handle it or not, but I know she'll say yes. Most people strive for the truth - even if we reject it as nonsense when we get it. 'Yes, I just want to know now. It can't be any worse than I'm already thinking'.

'Okay then, well let's get started. I'm going to need as much information as possible about Richard. Let's start with the basics. I need all his social media usernames that you know of, I need a phone number, email addresses, his workplace and his home address, and then as much as you can tell me about his habits, which pubs he likes to go to, who his best friends are, does he have family? Sisters?'

It's always a good idea to first check if your target has a sibling of the opposite gender. I made this mistake once right when I was a newbie. I was convinced I had cracked a case of a cheating boyfriend and spent a week tailing some woman around, watching him meeting her on a regular basis. But when I triumphantly presented my client with the case file, she looked at me incredulously and simply said 'That's his sister'. Epic fail - and the last time I was ever willing to look that stupid in front of a client.

I write furiously for the next half an hour. Funny what with all this technology at my fingertips I still favour a notebook and pen for these interviews; maybe I'm just an old fashion gal at heart. I like Karen. She's just a regular girl, going through a really shit time and dealing with the shock that she didn't know this person as well as she thought. It's pretty difficult when a partner leaves you, whether it's for someone else or not, as you're not just dealing with the loss of the person but also the loss of the life you dreamed about and planned. Not having the benefit of knowing the inner workings of a straight male brain, I often wonder if they do the same thing we do - with the planning, I mean. I literally only have to have a few dates with a guy that I like and my mind is already seeing trips and afternoons in bed. It's really crazy because it's my subconscious mind that does it, my conscious totally rational mind tells me to shut the fuck up and stop being so ridiculous and so it goes the constant battle for balance. I wonder whether guys think anything like that.

'Okay, Karen, so here's what's going to happen next. I'm going to start preliminary research, which will mostly be done from the office. Once I have a picture of what's going on and once I've located his whereabouts, I'll then actively follow Richard at a number of different times over the week. Honestly I can't tell you what I'll find or what to expect until I do a bit of digging, but what I will say is that try and leave it in my hands now. Giving the control over to me may allow you to relax a little and stop worrying so much, too'.

I think she does look relieved and a little less fearful than she did half an hour ago. 'Thank you', she says, 'You've been really kind. I guess you've been through this, too?'

'Unfortunately yes and more than once. I know that a broken heart feels like the worst of all pains, but know that it does get better and you do survive'. I know as I'm saying the words that they mean nothing to someone who's world has been turned upside down without notice. In fact, I'm sure it's pretty annoying to hear that 'it takes time', but the thing is, it really does. Sometimes time is the only healer for all wounds.

'Thanks again, Dylan. I'm really going to try to put this to the back of my mind for the next few days at least, maybe with the help of one or two bottles of wine', she smiles wryly.

'Atta girl! You know', I venture, 'I'm not sure it's my place, but if you want the benefit of my experience, the only way to get over a man is to get under another'. It's such a cliché that one, but I know myself you've got to put as many distractions as possible between you and the person that broke your heart and eventually it won't sting as much. 'I'm not suggesting you start dating or anything like that, but maybe get yourself online. Talk to a few guys. It will give you an ego boost. Then when you're ready, you can start to get out there again. There's a million eligible men in this city. Try not to let the one who couldn't see your worth stop you from finding one who will'.

'My friends have told me that, too, but the thing is', she hesitates and I know what she's going to say before she does, 'I don't want to move on yet in case Richard comes back. I mean I don't even know what the situation is yet; he might just need some breathing space or something'.

My heart sinks a little for her, because what I know is that most men only run if they have someone to run to. I'm reasonably sure her boyfriend of 2 years has met another woman and I'm reasonably sure that he'll be happily ensconced in a brand new relationship when I find him.

I'll be sorry to be right though, and if he is the jerk I assume him to be. I truly feel for Karen, I once had an 'ex' marry someone else three weeks after we split up. He literally turned to his father and just asked for an arranged marriage (as is often done in Arab cultures). Duly, a bride was shipped in from the Yemen. The marriage put a perfect little patch over his wounded pride and broken heart. I mean it was more than a bit extreme that he needed to marry another woman to get over me, but I'll take that compliment. Who knew I was such a hard woman to forget eh. The greatest compliment Jad 'the cunt' ever paid me was deleting me from his life, every social media photo, every mention, until not a trace of me or the relationship was left - if someone has to try that hard to delete you from his life it only proves you are still very much in his heart.

I love to conduct break-up focus group research whenever I'm in the company of a bunch of men. You can glean so much information from them and break-ups are my favourite topic. I was recently on a night out with a bunch of young twenty-something guys and we were all drinking, so I brought up the subject. They all agreed that it can take up to a year to finally move on after a big break-up (not physically - they all admitted to sleeping with women pretty much straight away - but emotionally). They described major lows and depression and one guy in the group who was affectionately known as 'dead man walking' had been permanently changed by a breakup and had never been the same since. They told me they did stalk their ex's social media - not obsessively, but they looked - and what drove them most crazy was thinking of their girl with another man. But no matter how sad they were or mentally fucked up they were; they wouldn't call or show a weakness. One pretty tuned-in guy actually echoed what I've always personally believed. He said that men are still hung up on their exes long after the girl has moved on, even though guys are often the first to meet someone else. It's so bloody fascinating to get a man's perspective on stuff like this.

Another one of my favourite break-up research tools is reality TV; it provides me with a great study of human behaviour. Those reality dating shows where contestants live together for a set amount of time and have to find their perfect match are absolutely class for observing how men and women think about the same situation. If you ever wanted to watch what happens when you're not around, what he/she says to his/her mates and how differently they both react to a given set of circumstances just tune in to one of the plethora of actual reality shows. Especially the episodes featuring a couple breaking up or arguing for the first time, it certainly makes you look on your own 'crazy' behaviour more favourably when you watch those pyscho's in action.

'Look Karen, I don't want to scare or alarm you unnecessarily, but I have to warn you of the likelihood that Richard has met someone else. It's a possibility that you have to prepare yourself for. I hope that in a week's time, I'm going to be telling you the exact opposite. I hope that there is some other explanation for his behaviour. But either way, you should be prepared to accept that in his eyes the relationship might be over for good. His actions to date aren't showing the best track record for reconciliation and I just want to make sure you're really prepared for whatever I might find. I wouldn't be doing my job properly if I didn't pre-warn you about all the possibilities'.

I watch her visibly draw herself upright, straightening her spine as if telling herself to quit being a baby and face this head on, 'I'll be fine. I just need the facts and then I can start to move on', she says.

Checking her watch, she continues, 'I really should be at work, but please if you need any further info or clarification, just call me on my mobile'. She gets up puts on her Aquascutum mac and belts it into a knot. I can tell she's lost significant weight because the belt loops are now way too big - ah, the heartbreak diet. She leans and touches my hand, 'Thanks again for everything. You've been really great'.

After she leaves, I go outside, sit on the bench and light up a cigarette; the smoking ban is seemingly everywhere now. I really hate being exiled to corners and roped-off shelters for a smoke; it's probably why I spend so much time in the Middle East, that and they fact that the cigarettes cost like £1 a packet. But on the plus side, you do meet the most interesting people huddled together in restaurant doorways sheltering from the rain. We're kind of like a bunch of social misfits seeking solace with our kind. Seriously, this smoking thing and dating gets me riled up, especially in the UK. What's up with all these men who won't date a smoker? I'd love to meet a man who actually likes a woman who enjoys a smoke once in a while; I mean not a twenty-a-dayer or anything, but someone who understands the simple pleasure of sitting on a balcony somewhere warm with a glass of wine and a Marlboro light - that's my paradise personified.

Karen's case has really got me thinking about break-ups again. So many people who come to me are in serious distress after a break-up; they come either totally lost and confused or mad as hell. All things considered, I'd rather take the time to heal, work through the pain and the emotional hurricane than jump into another relationship just to cover up/distract from the real problem. Because if you've taken the time to heal, then when you're ready, save for maybe a few slip ups, you move on and rarely ever look back.

A great quote I saw posted on Instagram was: 'I closed my mind to you... and then the dust settled'. When the dust finally settles, I wonder if the people who rushed into another person's arms finally let the pain seep in through all the little cracks that never had time to heal, or do they just keep papering over the cracks with relationship after relationship until they finally forget all about the person who stole their heart so long ago?

There are a million books that have been written about the differences between men and women. Yet the theory that we might as well have originated from different planets just about sums up everything I've learnt in my adventures, too. How men and women are wired is just plain different. The old adage that 'men internalise and women verbalise' is really true.

I don't know how is it possible that we can spend our lives with a person, wake up next to them, sleep next to them, and then one day a few years later not even remember the sound of their voice. I think this is the part of dating life I've never quite gotten used to: how can two people become nothing more than strangers who once knew each other so well?

It's funny though isn't it, that no matter your coping mechanism, you always think with absolute certainty that you'll never fall in love again after suffering a broken heart. Yet somehow you always do. But there's a question that worries me. What if we only have a finite capacity for romantic love? And what if when we reach our capacity, we simply have no more left to give? I think some people are just broken, after that. And I think maybe I am one of those people.

"A girl's gotta eat, right?"

The day passes quickly after meeting Karen and the afternoon brings a phone call that I'm still preoccupied with thinking about. It was from the personal secretary of some frightfully wealthy Sheikh in the Middle East who wants to put me on retainer to work on numerous 'unspecified' projects. *Hmm not sure I'm overly excited about the term 'unspecified'.* He's been fairly persistent with the calls since I met him at a charity benefit in London last month and now he's upping the ante by offering to fund the set-up of a new branch of Lipstick. Inc. anywhere I want in the world if I take on the contract! I believe that's known as 'greasing the wheels' and it's working because my dream has always been LA. He wants to fly me out to meet with him but I'm slightly balking at the thought of the destination - Bahrain, because it's going to cause me to face some rather deep-seated demons. I've been burned more times than a person should have to be in love, but there are a few times that stick in my throat and are so painful to recall I try my best not to think of them at all. However, with this particular one, it seems fate has decided that I am to face a ghost head on.

I spent a lot of time in Bahrain during the long distance nightmare with the asshole known as Jad. That place will forever hold some of my best and worst memories in life. After a year spent immersed in that culture, I now find myself with lifelong friends and a deep-rooted connection to this beautiful archipelago. I haven't been back in quite some time but I knew that at some point I'd have to take the plunge; you can't allow someone or someplace to scare you.

It seems that if I choose to take this assignment, I'll be once again back in the city that is my emotional nemesis. Doing the one thing that scares you the most might just be the very thing that sets you free, right?

For me, taking a trip back to a country I had first come to know with a previous love is a big deal; it scares me on so many levels. How would I feel being back there now that the love had moved on? Would I feel the same about the place that I loved? Would it bring back my very hard-to-cover heartache or would I arrive and realise that I too had moved on?

I'm feeling like a bundle of nervous energy just thinking about it when my mate Sasha's voice rings in my head saying: 'you live for this shit'. I really do, though. I'm always heading off somewhere having new adventures - it keeps my brain occupied. I've heard that it takes half the time you were with someone to get over them. So if this grandiose statement is in fact true then I should be completely over my ex by now. And you know what? I think I am - well at least as much as anyone ever really gets over a great love.

Sometimes though, you leave a place and you know that you'll never go back: it's a chapter closed and a lesson learned and no good can come from being reminded of the past. So I'm pondering as to whether this a is contract I really want to be considering. I'm already inundated with work here but the prospect of opening a new U.S. office is really too tempting. I decide to stop thinking about old loves and focus on new ones, and before I know it, it's 6pm and I have a date to get ready for.

Brogan has already been in touch to confirm that we're still on; I like a man who does that. How annoying is it when you have a date at 7pm and its 6pm you haven't heard a word from them all day? You start feeling like you're about to get stood up.

I pick up my phone and scroll my personal messages, looking for one in particular. Ah, there is he is, my New Yorker. I literally can't stop the smile from spreading across my face as I read his text: 'Hey Kiddo, at work and thinking of you naked on top, under, next to me. Miss you". I involuntarily get a little shiver of excitement and what can only be described as a 'clenching' down south when I remember the incredible sex I had with this guy. Dammit, he has such an effect on me; I literally feel like a little girl around him. He's just so manly and commanding and tall, very *very* tall. *Stop It Dylan!* I can't think about this guy for too long - he's too perfect and I have a funny feeling he might just be *the* one…and that's a thought that scares the bejeezus out of me. Weird, I'm going to meet one guy while clearly obsessing over another. But hey, I got to play the field and 'circular' date until someone puts a ring on it, right? Ah, circular dating, which literally means date (not sleep with!) a circle of people even when you're in a new relationship just to keep you from obsessing over one person and throwing all your eggs in one basket. In principal I like circular dating it keeps my brain from fixating and you know its gonna go one way or the other: you'll either be totally convinced your guy is the right one or you'll get enough perspective to keep your options open.

I'm meeting Brogan straight from work at Beach Blanket Babylon - otherwise known as BBB - in Notting Hill. I love this place; it's opulent, boho and glam all mixed in one. Friday nights it's chock-full of Notting Hill hipsters and I love the laidback vibe and the sumptuous décor. It's all decadent French-Chateau feel and lit by candlelight. I'm looking hot, I decide. With a quick application of M.A.C.'s Chatterbox pink lipstick, a slick of YSL's liquid eyeliner and some serious contouring courtesy of the Anastasia Beverly Hills contour palette, I'm all set. I'm getting a cab - something I rarely do - because I don't feel like battling the Friday night tube, especially while dressed up to the nines in skin-tight neutral tones. Hell, I earn enough money to stretch for a cab when I want, even for a London black cab, which for the price it charges you, should throw in a free foot rub with the ride. The cab pulls over right outside, so a quick spritz of Chanel No. 5, a slick of lip-gloss and a smoothing down of my skirt, I slide what I hope is gracefully out of the car.

He's rather cutely waiting for me inside, having grabbed a good spot and already ordered a bottle of wine on ice - a ten-pointer right there. I bloody hate it when a guy sits and waits for you to arrive before ordering the drinks or worse still just orders one for himself. He stands up to greet me and I watch his eyes sweep me from head to toe before taking my coat from behind, very old-school gent style.

'Dylan, you look amazing. I hope I did okay with the wine. I know you're a bit of a connoisseur'.

'Brogan, are you drinking too or just trying to get me drunk?' I ask eyeing the bottle.

'Well, I thought I'd have a glass with you. I've got the weekend off'.

He hasn't taken his eyes off me and I can feel the chemistry buzzing in the air. BBB is starting to get busy and I'm glad to be out. I spot a few women eyeing up Brogan. He does look pretty fine tonight; he's wearing a slim-cut petrol blue suit with a matching blue shirt - one of my favourite looks on a man. He's not super tall, about 5'11", but the suit seems to give him a few extra inches. And boy, do his shoulders look banging: wide and defined, tapering down to his trim waist and very peachy ass. One of the things I remember from our last liaison is his exceptionally toned rear. *Mmmm, I'm getting distracted. Get your head back in the game, Dylan, you're trying to keep this one ticking over, remember?*

His cell phone rings. He covers the receiver before saying, 'Just a work call, give me sec', and as he talks, I find myself feeling a tad guilty that I'm not seriously considering this man. Brogan's a good guy, no doubt about that, but I make myself feel better by concluding that he may just be in it for the sex, too. There's no judgement here; it's why I get myself into half of these situations. But I'm thinking of a conversation I had with a very cool girlfriend of mine, who is coincidentally happily engaged to a younger guy. The younger guy doesn't have a problem with the age gap - quite the opposite - he sees it as the huge compliment. Anyway, I digress. Point is, she once told me that apparently she has a 'look'. She had enquired about said look with one of her mate's husbands and he told her not to be offended but essentially she had a look: there was something naughty about her and guys just basically wanted to fuck her. I totally get it. I don't think this 'look' business is something you can cultivate, because it's not about the way you dress and it's not the way you act, it's just a certain *je ne sais quoi* that some women possess.

There are women men want to marry and there are women men want to fuck, and they are often mutually exclusive. This situation kind of sucks if you are a woman blessed with the 'look'. Trouble is I'm thinking the same about Brogan; he also has a look and I'm suspecting that he might be a bit of a player on the quiet. I've done my due diligence. He's not big into the social media; he's very work orientated; and he's very much 'all about him'. He just has the right package that makes him perfect for the game: he is good looking, not a kid, and has a body to die for. His personality is friendly and engaging, but I always get the distinct feeling when I'm with him that he's holding back - or maybe that's just me projecting. I am known for my twelve-foot high walls and it takes a very determined man to traverse them. Turns out I'm not exactly an easy woman to love.

The world is full of easy women and I don't mean in the sack. I mean women who don't ask questions, don't throw jealous fits, dumb it down or turn a blind eye. These are the women successfully ensconced. They don't give their partners an ounce of hassle; they don't question them or threaten their pride - and they play their part dutifully. But dutiful becomes boring and those men, although perfectly content, find themselves gravitating towards the dangerous women, the volatile and the unpredictable. They don't want to *be* with that woman; they just want a temporary distraction. The wilder women amongst us, well, we have our own set of problems. A savvy, switched-on woman is never easy. She is a ticking time-bomb waiting to explode; she gives little warning signs of her wile in the early days and a man prone to deception will hear little alarms going off in his head; they inherently know they aren't going to get away with much, men naturally employ the 'flight' response with us. Often they get more than they bargained for: we're the ones after the break up that get labelled 'crazy' - though I prefer to label us passionate.

Anyway, fuck it. I need to get out of my own head and enjoy it for whatever it is. He's coming back inside.

'Sorry babe, that was a booking for Sunday - a fitness shoot for a major protein supplier - and I can't afford to turn it down. It's more than I earn in a month tutoring'.

'Well at least you still have tomorrow off'. I lean forward and touch his arm right inside the elbow and give him a little smile. The combination of the touch and the eye contact makes him reach out and cup my face with his large hand, he plants a kiss on the side of my neck. I get a little shiver of pleasure in response.

'You know; I've been thinking about the last time I saw you a lot. That was a hot afternoon, Dylan'.

'I remember it well'. I smile coquettishly, recalling how we got it on in my office when a mid-afternoon coffee turned into late afternoon nibbles.

Who are we kidding? We both know why we're here and it isn't for the atmosphere. We've been exchanging pretty suggestive messages since our last hook up and he hasn't managed to give me the 'ick' yet.

Hot men can sometimes seriously give me the 'ick' factor with their pathetic attempts at flirtation. It can happen in the split-second press of the send button. I can be turned off instantly if a guy says the wrong thing in a message - something cheesy and overtly dirty will usually do it. Dirty talk should be done face to face and in the right context. It just feels plain wrong to be having *that* kind of conversation in the cold light of day at 11am on a Monday morning when you don't feel remotely horny. But god, we've all been there - in that place where you're trying to simulate something hot and steamy when in fact you're actually doing the washing up. I remember watching a documentary about phone-sex girls and most of them were captured on camera in their sweatpants mopping the floor while they told some guy how much they would enjoy sucking their huge throbbing cocks. Amusing thought, right?

I'm still battling with the notion that I don't really know if I'm considering Brogan as a prospective boyfriend. Because, if so, am I doing the right thing by making it so obvious that I'm up for it? *Well, you dope, you probably should have thought about that before the afternoon office sex, shouldn't ya?* Right. I'm going to try my best to actually find out something about this guy. Then at least he can't get the idea that I'm only after one thing. That's happened to me a few times lately. I've had to deal with frankly 'hurt' men who have said they aren't just around for booty calls and are looking for something more meaningful. Oh boo-fucking-hoo. I'm so sorry I hurt your feelings...not. Gosh, if we act like we think they want us to, they don't like it and if we act too full-on they don't like that either. Seriously what the fuck has happened to the dating world as we know it?

I realise I haven't said anything in maybe two minutes and probably should.

'So Brogan, how was your week? How's the tutoring going? Busy?' I grab my wine and take rather a large mouthful.

'Not bad, got a few new clients this week and a possible full-time teaching job at a college in Kent'.

'Oh that's good!'

'And you? How's the consulting? What big project are you working on right now?'

Oh lord, that's a question with many possible answers. This week I have to trail three different men, try and get one to suggest that he wants to sleep with me, and then I have to masquerade as a Burlesque dancer and then a lesbian to try and snare my rich client's cheating and now gay wife. But I can't exactly say that, can I?

'Oh, just some branding work for a new health food brand'. *Dammit, Dylan! Why did you have to say health food? He's a bloody health food nut.* After ten minutes of health food small talk, my mind has wandered again...and so has half the bottle. I resolve to stop drinking now; I hate drunk sex, it's absolutely impossible to come.

It's been two hours of blatant flirting and we know this is only going one place. 'Shall we take this back to mine?' he asks, giving me a grin that suggests that he clearly knows the answer. 'Mine's closer' I say ever the control freak.

One quick cab ride later - with some serious PDA action going on in the back seat - and I'm totally horny and a little drunk as we barely make it through the door of the building before beginning to undress. We're in the communal hallway of my building and I'm already slipping off his shirt and dispensing with my dress. There's no way we're waiting to get into my apartment, so he lifts me up carries me to the staircase, leans me up against the wall and in one practiced move grabs a condom from his back pocket and tears the packet with his teeth. Moving my thong to the side he enters me - no foreplay, no lovey-dovey shit, just full on hot, gotta-have-you sex served straight up. The illicit thrill of someone coming through the door any second is only more of a turn on. I making so much noise that he has to put his hand over my mouth, which only turns me on more.

'Fuck Dylan, you're so fucking hot', he pants as he lifts me up and achieves the almost impossible feat of carrying me upstairs while still inside me. We make it to the first landing and stop. With my back against the wall, I grab his muscled, round, hot ass and draw him deeper inside, moaning involuntarily. He's kissing my neck, my nipples, all the while holding my bodyweight entirely in his arms - one excellent reason for dating a fitness model. I can be a bit of a guy when it comes to sex and I find myself admiring his body, his ass, his juts - those gorgeous bits on a ripped man just inside the hip bone. I definitely need something pretty to look at to get me off. It's urgent, hot and impatient sex and he comes right there on the stairs. *Well that's what I pay a property maintenance charge for, I suppose,* I think wryly. I have one shoe on and one off and my Wolford dress is around my neck. Giggling, I pull it down hastily and we scoot up the stairs and into the flat. I swear I heard next door open - bet they had a front row seat on that one.

It's dark inside the flat, so I light a few candles while he flicks his Spotify on and Damien Rice's 'Canonball' starts. Oh, he's so got his moves down, this one. He comes up behind me, nuzzling my neck - that's something I like about Brogan: he's always ready to go straight away, He's got the stamina of a twenty-year-old with the moves of a much more experienced guy. He bends me forward, holding the back of my neck with one hand and slipping my dress up with the other, a total act of dominance I love. I might be a ball breaker in the boardroom, but in the bedroom I just want to be controlled. He enters me hard and I gasp. Slipping his hand across my hip bone, he finds me already welcoming and wet; I moan and draw him closer to me. Grabbing the wall in front of me, I can feel myself coming hard and for those next few minutes I don't have another thought in the world. It's gonna be a long night and I can't wait.

"Entrapment"

I wake up the next morning in my own bed feeling lazy but satisfied. It's Saturday, but as they say there's no rest for the wicked and I have to work tonight - well kind-of work anyway. It's what we in the business call 'Honey Trapping'. But I currently have a man in my bed and he's hot and ripped and I do kind-of like him, so I'm torn between a Saturday morning love-in and preparing for work later. When you're single, I think the one thing you miss most about being part of a couple is the affection - you know, that cute time spent lying in bed cuddling, kissing and being all 'coupley'. Personally, I can live without half the things that come with relationships, but that is the one thing I still crave. It's so hard to meet guys who you can keep around to have sex with when you feel like it but who also give you that much-craved affection. It's bloody hard work keeping these guys' period; they are so temperamental. I decide I'm just gonna enjoy another hour curled up in Brogan's big strong arms and maybe another quickie before I pack him on his way and get on with my day at the office.

I'm currently being bombarded with requests to take on entrapment cases, all of them from women who are convinced their boyfriend is a cheat and cannot find any proof. They are usually at their wit's end and believe that the only way to get absolute proof is to hire a woman to try and seduce their man. I blame a recent TV show that aired on Sky, a sort of expose show about female escorts and the sorts of jobs they get hired to do. One of said jobs was entrapment. Whenever anything is featured in the magazines or on TV about cheaters, I'm suddenly inundated with enquiries. Now entrapment, or honey traps as we call them, are a tricky business and not one I indulge in often or willingly. Apart from having no place in a court of law, entrapment often results in nasty outcomes for both the client and me. Women are almost always the requesters of this kind of service yet they don't really think through the repercussions of such a request. I have found through hard-won experience that it is possible to trap any man, but women are not as easy. If someone is laid out on a plate for a man he will take the offer and consider the repercussions later - and that is exactly why I always advise my clients against such action. Countless times I have warned an emotionally distraught woman that every man can be caught if you try hard enough, so it isn't smart to tempt him. It's just in their nature and honestly isn't even a sign of their deceit as much as their stupidity; they simply can't turn it down. But when a client has her mind set on something, it's not my place to judge; I'm running a business, after all. These days, I mostly outsource these types of jobs to one of my freelancers, which includes a roster of delectable and cunning men and women. Now: I do not run a high-class whore house. None of my people ever do anything with the target other than the bare minimum needed to prove likely infidelity or at least the indisputable intent.

One of the more straightforward entrapment jobs I personally undertook was for a rich divorcee who had become engaged to a male model from Croatia, who was a rather beautiful specimen of a man some fifteen years her junior. They had met on a cruise around the British Virgin Islands six months earlier, where her now betrothed, Peter, had been moonlighting as a waiter (male models have it hard these days and this sort of employ is common for a model out of season). Their eyes had met across a lunchtime buffet. Sara is an entirely glamorous and well-put-together woman, the kind that is groomed to perfection from 8am to 2am and that I imagine has swans drifting around her penthouse apartment in Mayfair while wearing a silk robe and smoking slim, Vogue cigarettes through an antique cigarette holder. But this is of course purely conjecture and just one of my daily musings meant to keep me entertained for hours after first meeting a client.

Sara came to me one crisp winter day after a brief and equally crisp phone enquiry. She arrived ten minutes early wearing head-to-toe Chanel. At 5'8", she was slim and athletic and made quite an impression. She seemed neither nervous nor embarrassed and was entirely business-like for the half an hour we spent together. She described her relationship her fiancé and her goal in detail - and it was simple. She had only one request: to find out if Peter was legitimate and if, in fact, it was true love and not merely the age-old tale of a rich older woman is being taken for a fool by hot young chancer. I remember feeling slightly unnerved by her direct and cool manner that neither denoted shame or concern. Of course, I knew deep down that like all strong women, she had a carefully constructed wall that surrounded her heart and a manner that deemed strong shows of emotion in public to be inappropriate.

During our meetings and calls I like to think that we developed a relationship. Certainly, the moment that I handed her the manila folder containing photos and transcripts of calls and messages from her man to me and various other women, I saw enough of a crack of the armour to know that she was hoping for the best but expecting the worse. Sara never did marry Peter. In fact, as she relayed to me several weeks later, she had returned to her apartment and packed up his belongings with a note asking him to never call her again. She had never answered a single call or message from him. Some people are like that, and I remember her voice as she told me, 'Honey, when I'm done with them, I'm done'. I guess for some people some things in life are that cut and dry.

I reckon the only time entrapment is a valid tool is when someone wants out of a marriage and needs an excuse - though obviously not one that would be admissible in court. Once I've ascertained that they have fundamentally emotionally detached from the person in question, then these are the easier cases. Of course, the fact cannot be used as actual evidence, given that entrapment is and will always be an illegal practice, but if done carefully and smartly the target never knows he was entrapped until it's too late and will feel like an absolute fool. They generally turn out to be guilty of something anyway - everyone always is - and the proof we provide just lays it out in black and white. These situations usually involve a lot of money and people who have assets to protect. When it comes to money; people can be surprisingly cutthroat.

I personally screen every entrapment enquiry I receive. Nine out of ten aren't serious about it once you outline the reality, but some women won't be dissuaded once they get an idea in their heads. So I somewhat reluctantly agreed to help one woman, a young newly-wed called Megan, because boy has she got herself in a pickle. Megan is twenty-four and is married to Mark, a thirty-five-year-old alpha male she met online last year. After a whirlwind romance, he moved into her Islington two-bedroom flat (a house she owned outright - bought with an inheritance from a wealthy and much loved relative) and all seemed well. But her intuition was telling her something was off. She was happy to not be single anymore and to have found a man she was in love with, so she ignored it and continued to move forward. They made plans for the future and over the next six months everything ran smoothly, but still Megan couldn't quiet the gnawing at the back of her head. She caught him a couple of times on his phone and he'd jumped guiltily, but he was pretty clever at keeping his phone within range at all times. In the absence of any real proof, she ignored her instincts and decided not to be a 'typical' paranoid woman. Here's where the story gets really interesting.

Megan had a weekly routine of playing the lottery and buying the odd scratch card once a week. Just like everyone I know, she dreamed of wealth, holidays, a house on the beach and a nice car. So dutifully she would take her chance and buy a card from her local shop every week. One notable Friday evening, after a drink out with the girls, she bought a £5 scratch card. 'How extravagant of me' she had thought to herself, blaming the wine she'd drunk earlier. It was only later while sitting at home that she remembered the scratch card sitting in her purse. So grabbing a penny, she dug it out and sat scratching off the silver panels. As the symbols underneath began to take shape, she got a very funny feeling. I like to imagine everyone who's about to win a lot of money gets this feeling right before it happens. So she's sitting there in her small flat in North London, slightly tipsy, and shaking her head violently trying to clear the fuzziness, because she was sure she was seeing things. But no, after composing herself for a few minutes and checking and rechecking she realised that she had won - not £1 or £10 but £1 million! It still hadn't seemed real, so she had immediately run into the bedroom to wake her sleeping boyfriend. Shaking him and finally jumping up and down on the bed chanting, 'We won! We won!', she managed to wake him up. Mark was pretty annoyed at first as most people are about being woken up in the middle of the night, but after he fully digested the news, he too found himself jumping on the bed.

Imagine that split second where your life changes - I imagine life is very exciting for a while there and apparently it was. Megan told me how they'd gone a bit crazy the first few months - taking trips away, buying new clothes, buying a new car for Mark and then, in the spirit of spontaneity, Mark had proposed to her under the Eiffel Tower on a weekend trip to Paris. The ring was a beautiful one-carat solitaire on a platinum band, paid for out of the winnings, which were in a joint account he'd opened for them. He insisted they get married as soon as possible as he was sure she was the one he wanted to spend the rest of his life with. Within a month, Mark had made all the arrangements - in fact, he had become a proper little bridezilla. Megan was swept away with it all (and to be honest, who at 24, wouldn't be?). So less than four months after the big lottery win, she found herself in a church in Hertfordshire in a white silk satin Vera Wang dress with a princess-cut neckline and huge meringue skirt feeling very much like a fairy-tale princess, but strangely not at all like herself. She told me that she knew at that very moment that it was a mistake, but she felt like she was in too deep to get out and went along with it hoping against hope that things would work out just fine.

Of course they didn't. After a two week Barbados honeymoon, they returned home to their flat in North London and then it started. Mark's behaviour turned somewhat questionable; he was going out a lot, coming home drunk at all hours and calling in sick to his job in IT most days. Megan, on the other hand, was still working at a West End hair salon five days a week - sensible enough to know even at the tender age of twenty-four that a million pounds doesn't last a lifetime, especially at the rate her new husband was spending it. Mark bought watches, private memberships to health clubs, all manner of gadgets, a new IPhone, designer suits and more. And sure, he usually came back from such shopping trips with a gift for her, but it wasn't enough to stop her seeing what was clear as day: with the cost of the wedding and all the vacations, in addition to his shopping habits, Mark had spent over £200,000 of the winnings within six months. By the time Megan came home for the fifth day in a row to find him on the sofa playing video games on the 40-inch TV he had bought last week, she had just about had enough. She had finally confided in her close girlfriends and they had stated out loud what she already knew deep down: that he was using her for the money and had probably married her for the same reason. There was other stuff, too; between the late nights and the days off work, she could never be sure of exactly where he was and she had become more and more sure that he was cheating on her. So when she found a second phone in the glove box of his new BMW, she was convinced.

And so she found me through a Google search. She told me she had chosen me over all the other websites because I was woman and she really liked the logo (that made me laugh), so we met a week later at my office where she told me the whole sorry tale. I must admit I felt pretty sorry for the naive young woman who sat opposite me. Petite with masses of honey blonde hair made fuller with extensions, French manicured acrylic nails and a bit too much make-up - the standard for a twenty-something glamour puss totally influenced by today's reality TV stars - she was sweet and had that typical chatty hairdresser vibe and a strong northern accent, from Bolton to be exact. She'd been living in London for four years since taking a transfer to the London branch of a well-known central Manchester salon. She'd purchased the flat in Islington two years ago, wanting to invest her inheritance wisely, and it was currently valued at around £450,000.

Straight away I told her she was also going to need a lawyer, a very good one who could advise her about her assets and how to keep them in the event of divorce. I gave her the card of a good friend of mine and the best lawyer I know - he was totally ruthless and very charming. I made a mental note to call him in advance and tell him not to hit on her, because she was just his type. In a case like this, Megan needed a lawyer more than a PI, but often a PI can provide the necessary evidence needed to prove infidelity. The fact that Megan and Mark were married was also a big plus as it gave me the required permission to tap his phone line: 'a spouse retains the right to obtain any and all information from family computers, smart phones and other devices'. Megan also really wanted to go down the entrapment route, even after I explained it wouldn't be admissible in legal proceedings, I guess because she just needed to see in practice how much of a dick her husband actually was.

So two weeks into this case, I had already installed Keylogger on his laptop and phone via Megan, who turned out to be not quite as ditsy as I first thought. Next was the honey trap. I had decided in this instance to do the deed myself and was just after establishing the perfect opportunity: Mark's work party happening that night at a local wine bar in Central London.

So now here I am on a Saturday, getting dolled up in my office once again. This part is kind of fun because I'm playing a role: I need to look hot - I mean sexy-hot. So out goes the usual uniform of black and tailored and in comes a maroon Herve Leger bandage dress with keyhole neckline paired with Louboutin butterfly heels in cream and a lot of make-up. I take out my Foxylocks hair extensions in 'honey spice ombre' shade, and give them a quick brush. They are easily the best clip-in's with the ability to make you look Kardashian perfect. I apply M.A.C.'s false eyelashes and I stand back and survey the final look in the full-length mirror. Woah, I actually like being overtly sexy for the night. My curves are looking banging and the Queen Bee aesthetic I was going for is complete.

I've roped in my dear friend Kristina who's always up for a night out and can be relied upon to be the perfect wing woman. She rings to let me know she's downstairs and I buzz her up.

'Hey darling', I say in greeting to my tall, slender Swiss friend as she appears at the door.

Kristina lives between Zurich and London working for an international bank. We met three years ago whilst both trying to buy the same pair of shoes in Harvey Nichols - turquoise silk Nicholas Kirkwood heels. We both needed a size 38 and, after chatting on the beige sofas, decided on a compromise. I let her take the only size 38 and I took a 37.5 - that's the thing about friendship, it's all about compromise - and we've been firm friends ever since. She's also close enough to me to know the finer details of my job and I could absolutely trust her with my life and my secrets.

Whenever she's in London, we spend many happy nights drinking wine and talking about or more often slating men. At age thirty-six and as high-powered businesswoman, Kristina is a formidable female and a fairly happy singleton. She dates a lot and between the both of us we always have plenty of war stories to share. She's beautiful and also smart as fuck. I'm not actually surprised that she's single; it's a rare male who is man enough to tame such a woman. From what we know about men from personal experience, it seems that they like to sleep with alpha females, but they don't often care to marry one. Tonight Kristina is looking hot in a masculine Tom Ford suit worn without a shirt and, by the looks of it, without a bra. She has that slight lipstick-lesbian vibe with her short cropped blonde hair and she always reminds me a bit of a young Isabella Rossellini.

'Damn girl, you look hot!' she exclaims warmly as she plants a kiss on both my cheeks - so European that one.

'Let's have pre drinks', I suggest, already opening my well-stocked mini bar, 'Whiskey?' I pull out a bottle of single malt, knowing we both like the finer things in life.

'Of course, darling. Make mine a large one; I've had such a bitch of day'. I pour and listen to her chatter about her colleagues and a meeting she had earlier with what she describes as a fat sexist arsehole who she promptly put in his place with the ice-cold demeanour that only she can pull off. I light a cigarette and take a sip of the Jura over ice; the liquid is smooth and warm as it slips down my throat. Smoking a cigarette with a drink is one of life's great pleasures for me; doing it with good company is even better.

I could easily have stayed there in my warm cozy office chatting all night, but I knew I had a job to do. So we grab our coats and make our way out onto the bustling London street. Linking arms, we make quite the statement duo as we stroll through Soho.

'So how are we getting into this private party then D?'

'Oh don't worry about that. I booked us a table in the restaurant'.

'Oh a free dinner, too?' she laughs, 'You know how to treat a lady'.

I figured out a long time ago that to get into any venue, you can usually charm your way in, but if they have a restaurant, then diners will always take precedence over those at the door.

'Apparently the party is in the bar area. So after we've eaten, we'll drift in there and catch ourselves a love rat', I say sardonically.

A short while later we reach the venue, which is just off the bright lights of Piccadilly Circus. I love to walk in London whenever I can, soaking up the atmosphere of the hustle and bustle. It's not as easy to do so in four-inch heels, but that's an art we women perfect from childhood, practicing ever since parading around in our moms shoes at nursery school. As we are ushered into the dark interior lit by a hundred tiny candles, I immediately scope out the venue. I see the sign for the private party; it looks pretty quiet so far, just a few people huddled around tables. *Perfect*. We can eat and should be able to get in there just as the party is in full swing. I notice the toilets are just inside the party area - even better. Now I can do a few fly-bys during dinner and check out the vibe.

We are seated by one of the large sash windows and the restaurant is pretty busy. That's the great thing about London; like any major city, venues are always busy, no matter what time of day or night it is. I glance around at our fellow diners and spot a couple on a first date - so easy to see as first dates are the worst and so awkward. I can tell the guy is way more into the woman; she looks casually disinterested with a permanent fake smile plastered on her face as she keeps nodding. She's pretending to listen intently, but she's also draining her wine glass at a rate of knots - man, I've been there. I turn my attention to the lone diner. He's a businessman who's reading the Independent newspaper and nursing a glass of Merlot while furtively looking over the top of his paper at a table of women - most likely figuring out which one he'd most like to fuck. The group haven't noticed - groups of women tend to do that - and are instead all talking excitedly at one another. No one's really listening - that's the thing with people, we listen to respond not to listen. While the person we're with talks, we are really just thinking about a story of our own we want to tell, just waiting for them to take a breath so we can dive in. We all do it and it's a hard habit to break.

'Darling, I thought I was your date for the evening', Kristina pouts playfully.

'Sorry, sorry, you know me, always on the job. Okay, I'm all yours. Tell me about the boy' I respond, remembering that Kristina had a date with an old fling a few nights back.

'Well he remains beautiful and funny but an international playboy who wishes for nothing but fun, so fun we had...and that is about that', she replies in her clipped ladylike tones. I envy her ability to dismiss men and never get emotionally 'checked in'. Seriously, in all these years I've never known her to once show even a hint of crazy over a man. 'So I'm onto the next', she continues, 'I'm prospecting a rather young stud who works for the Credit Suisse. We've been messaging so I might throw him a bone and let him take me out next week', she smiles broadly.

'Kris, you are an absolute legend. The way you toy with these men is bloody awe inspiring. You should totally write a book you know'.

'Well yes, my darling, I suppose I could but I can hardly say I have had success now, can I? My longest relationship has been under a year, hardly an accomplishment'.

'I'm not so sure, you know. Maybe you have the best idea out of all of us - no mind fucks and no heartbreak. Want to trade with me?' I ask, half-sincerely.

'Speaking of mind fucks, how is your dear ex-boyfriend?' She finishes the last word with a snarl. 'Is he still trying to make the whole world believe he's happy with that gold-digging ho?'

'Yes I believe he is', I smile in response, because recently I've been making headway with the whole moving on. I haven't been stalking much, hardly at all actually, and plus I've filled my life with a barrage of men since that unfortunate incident. Him and his games are now beginning to thankfully seem like a distant memory.

'I do not like that one. What an absolute nightmare that whole business was'. She's right; it was a nightmare and I totally lost myself trying to figure it all out.

'Yes, quite right. I can't imagine now what I was even thinking back then. Anyway, enough about that douche'.

'Right! Let's order. I'm famished'.

I opt for the melanzane to start, followed by a broccoli and asparagus egg pasta. Good thing this dress has all the sucking-in qualities of a pair of Spanx. Kris opts for the steak, naturally. As we enjoy our fine Italian meal, I keep a check on the party in the area opposite - watching who's coming and going. It's starting to fill up now and I'm trying to locate my target. A group of men have just arrived all suited and booted, and I place a mental picture of Mark in my mind - his height, hair colour, weight, facial hair - and scan through the group until my gaze lands on him. He's handsome in a kind of normal way; he has dirty blonde floppy hair and dimples when he smiles. The dimples help. Women do love a man with a good smile. I imagine when he was younger he had boyish good looks that are now a little more rugged. His physique is also consistent with a man who used to work out but now goes to the gym to exercise his jaw with his mates more than his pecs. He's laughing and greeting people as he makes his way through to the bar. He seems awfully cocky as he greets groups of females. That's another thing about men who are actively cheating: they become naturally flirty with members of the opposite sex, definitely more cocksure and convinced they can get anyone they want. In any case, now that he's here, I can get started.

'Kris, I'm just going to the bathroom', and giving her a wink, I saunter off in the direction of my prey.

Nailing the first look is key. Mark is standing, leaning on the circular bar and chatting to another man. Fortunately for me, he has his back to me so I bypass the toilets and walk straight into the party, circumvent the bar, appearing at the other end so he now faces me head on. I keep my gaze on him as I strut down past the bar, as I get closer, I'm willing him to connect. Men are pre-programmed to check out every piece of ass that walks by, I mean *every* piece, so he sees me coming and I watch as his eyes travel from my face down to my more than ample cleavage and back up again. Our eyes lock and I hold his gaze for at least ten seconds, before giving him what I know is a seductive smile and then I'm gone. Flyby complete. I guarantee that if he's as much of a player as I assume, he'll be thinking about me for the next half hour at least. So when I return. he'll be ripe for the plucking.

'Ick', I say out loud to Kristina on my return to the table. Even now, it still gives me the major ick when I see what people's husbands/boyfriends/wives/girlfriends are up to behind their backs. Unfortunately, a look isn't enough to prove a guy is a cheater; no, honey trapping has to extract more nectar than that.

'I don't know how you do it, darling', Kristina says for the millionth time since I've known her. 'How do you still believe in love?'

'I'm not sure that I do, doll, if I'm honest'. I then fill her in on the various men in my life currently giving me a run for my money. 'I'm thinking it may not happen for me. We may have to stick to our original plan and marry each other if we both hit forty and are still single'.

'Fine by me, darling', she nods amenably, 'As long as I can still cruise hot guys, I'll happily come home to you on a Saturday night'.

That might just be the answer, I think, going all Sex and the City for a moment. I'm thinking of Charlotte's classic line: 'Maybe we can be each other's soul mates. Then we could let men just be these great, nice guys to have fun with'. She was really onto something there, but I can't dismiss the nagging feeling that having a successful, lasting relationship with a man is the Holy Grail. I want so much to find it, but not quite yet perhaps, as my job hardly makes it practical, now does it? Here I am on a Saturday night in a bar about to try and pull a man just to prove he's a love rat. I can't think of a guy I know being happy about that. It's why I try and keep my work largely a secret; most guys I date think I'm some sort of creative consultant for the fashion industry and that works for me, I do love fashion and one day when I have to leave the world of private investigation I'd definitely think of going into luxury brand consulting, in the meantime I'll settle for just shopping it.

That's the other major thing Kristina and I have in common; she is another fashion fiend. We spend all week sending press releases and screen grabs of Net-a-Porter to one another with our new must-haves. *Women often bond over either men, fashion or wine, and they also fall out over the exact same things*, I think playfully. I'm really enjoying my melanzane, which is essentially aubergine and tons of cheese in tomato sauce. Kris is tucking into her medium rare steak; she can eat and eat and still be as long and lean as ever. We polish off a bottle of Pinot Noir - it's one of my favourite reds, 'Garnet' by Saintsbury, a 2009 bottle and one of the best with its medium-bodied velvet of a grape that slides down nicely. I resist the temptation to order another bottle. I can't forget that I'm technically on the job, so we skip dessert and make our way into the private party, which is now looking a lot fuller. There must be over a 100 people crammed inside. The atmosphere is typical of a work party in full swing: lots of already drunk-looking people and there's a couple getting it on outside the toilets. I hate how incestuous work get-togethers are, all that hooking up with each other and flirting away their days for want of anything better to do.

I want to observe Mark for a while in his natural habitat, so we press into the background. Kris is looking around for eligible men, but I know there's no one here who will take her fancy, she's a bit of a 'modeliser' and she likes her men young and athletic. Mark is definitely enjoying the attentions of quite a few women. I watch as one - a typical office chick all dolled up in a cheap dress and cheaper shoes - playfully smacks his ass as a greeting. They appear deep in flirtation for a few minutes. I get Kristina to take a photo of me with her clearly in the background. I want to remember her face in order to check her out online later and see if maybe there is something going on there. After she tootles off, I observe another female two-some approach his group. He seems quite cosy with the blonde; there's a fair bit of touching going on and I watch as she whispers in his ear. He looks smug. In fact, he's irritating the hell out of me. God knows how I'm going to feign interest in this creep. I snap a quick picture of the blonde and decide it's about time I broke up this party, 'Drink, Kris?'

'Bourbon, darling, on the rocks'.

'I'll make that two, be right back'.

I saunter towards the bar. It's pretty busy, which works well in my favour. I almost walk straight up to Mark, locking eyes I brush past him and squeeze alongside at the bar, then proceed to stick my ass out and lean onto the bar, so that we are just about touching. I shout my order to the bar tender and turn to look at Mark.

'Hi, sorry there's just no room in here'.

'Don't apologise. It's not often I get this close to such a beautiful woman'. *Urghh.* He's verging on sleazy. I glance at his left hand and the empty ring finger - there's only one reason I know of that married men do that.

'I haven't seen you before. You don't work for Octopus, right?'

'No. I just did some remote consulting work for your boss a while ago. We finally had a meeting today as I'm only in town for a few days'. He seems to like this piece of information; I'm not immediate threat to him being found out cheating. I don't live here and he won't have to bump into me at work in the future.

'I'm Mark and you are?'

'I'm Dylan and I'll be right back'.

As I head back to Kris, I can see she's being hit on from all angles. She can handle herself and I know how much she likes to play the game. I think she's a bit like me in that sense; she also uses men for a bit of research and practice. I walk over and hand her the Bourbon.

'How is it going, my little kitten?' she asks.

'All to plan, my lovely. Listen, he's definitely up for something, I just need to nail it down. Don't feel like you need to stick around, okay?'

'Of course, dear. These boys are not my cup of tea, but I'll toy with them a bit longer - just for fun, you know. Are you gonna be alright?'

'Yep, you know me. All in a day's work. I just need you to do two things for me. Before you leave; can you snap as many covert photos of us together as you can? Preferably when he's touching me or something. And then, a little later I'm going to send you a text. When you receive it, can you just call me? I'll need a diversion'.

'Of course, I'm at your service, darling', she kisses me on both cheeks, 'Talk later and be safe'.

I walk back to the bar, Mark watching me all the way. 'So Dylan, I love that dress on you'. I reckon he fancies himself as a bit of a playboy this one; you just get a feeling about guys like that, low down dirty cheaters with tickets on their shoulders that they're something fancy. There's a ton of desperate women out there who fall for their rather dubious charms. I'm not one of them, but I'm gonna have to act the shit out of this one. Sometimes it can be fun to play a part, act out a little fantasy and pretend to be someone else for a while - aren't we all just looking for a little escapism? But I just don't get a kick out of buttering up some asshole. Although buttering him up and then ditching him is going to be fun; I'd like to take that giant-sized ego down a notch.

'So you're here alone?'

'Yes, I came with a friend, but she's just left. I thought I'd stay a while longer and see if there's some fun to be had'. He perks up at this obvious come on.

'Really, so you're after some fun? Maybe I can help you with that'.

'I'm sure you could. You certainly seem like the life and soul of the party. So is one of these your girlfriend?' I gesture around at the women.

'Oh god, no. They're just work colleagues, but I think a few might have a little crush on me, you know?'

He actually has the gall to feign modesty. 'So single then I take it?'

'Absolutely, Dylan. Just waiting for the right woman, you know', he replies as he winks lasciviously. Now I really want to punch this guy in the face. He has a gorgeous young wife at home and he's dismissed her out of hand and for what? A quick lay with a stranger? Oh, but what am I saying, that's got male fantasy written all over it.

For the next ten minutes, I stand listening to this overly cocky asshole droning on about how amazing he think he is. I drain my glass and order another; anyone would have to be slightly drunk to listen to this bullshit. His come on is basic and too-cheesy innuendo. I finally decide he's a bit drunk, at least enough to push it.

'So Mark, you're obviously the big guy around here. You must have had a few office romances?'

'Well', he grins stupidly, 'Maybe one or two, but they don't really hold my interest as much as you do right now'.

'What a lucky girl I am'. Somehow, I manage to say this without even a hint of sarcasm.

'I love your tattoo, as well', he says, trailing his finger over the small inking on my forearm, 'Very sexy. Do you have anymore? Maybe hidden ones I can check out?'

'Actually I do, but I really can't show you those here'. I need to wrap this up; he's literally irritating the fuck out of me. He takes the obvious green light, thank god.

'Listen, this might be a bit forward, but there's a hotel around the corner. How do you fancy taking this somewhere more private?'

Jeez, he works quick.

'Well', I lick my lips seductively, 'I am only in town for the evening. Why not make the most of it?' He looks like the cat that got the proverbial cream.

'I'll get my coat', he says, pausing. He seems a little intoxicated but is holding it well. 'And I just need to make a quick phone call'.

I bet you do. My guess is Megan is about to receive a call from her husband saying he's going to be late. He comes back looking slightly harassed. 'Ready Dylan?'

We walk down the street towards the Premier Inn - *classy, eh?* He snakes his arm inside my coat and around my waist, nuzzling on my neck and making an annoying *mmhmm* sound as he does so. I hear my phone beep with a message, and surreptitiously I sneak a look. It's from Megan: 'Mark has just called to tell me he's staying out late'. I won't reply now, but soon enough, I'll have plenty to tell her. At check-in he provides a false surname, but he does pay by card, which I'm very happy about - it's the perfect evidence for Megan; she can legitimately use that later on to prove infidelity. While he's paying, I fire off a quick text to Kristina: 'Call me in 5'.

We step into the elevator and he leans in to kiss me. Now I draw the line at actual physical contact; I'm not here to sleep with someone's husband just to prove he's a cheater. I've already got all the proof I need to nail him. I playfully push him away.

'All good things come to those who wait', I say huskily.

I bloody hope Kristina hasn't fallen asleep, otherwise I'll need a back-up plan. Just as we get through the doorway, my phone rings. *Perfect timing. Thank god.*

'Dylan speaking...okay, yes, one second, please', then covering the mouthpiece I say to Mark, 'Sorry, Hun. I need to take this; it's work'. Before he can object, I slip out of the door, but turn back to face him and whisper, 'Why don't you get yourself ready for me?'

I can see him excitedly taking off his trousers before the door shuts. *Poor bastard will be waiting a while*, I think as hot foot it down the corridor, choosing the stairs for a quicker exit. When I'm outside, I breathe a sigh of relief and hail a passing cab. I can't wait to get home and take a shower. Other people's deception always makes me feel dirty, and sometimes I find that I can't just wash it off.

"Never let a wound ruin me"

Monday whistles around and I need a plan to find Richard, Karen's missing boyfriend. So much of her case resonates with me from my own experience with a disappearing ex-boyfriend, also known as the stalker.

It can be pretty distressing when someone you've been so close to and shared a life with just totally disappears. I mean completely un-findable, gone-off-the-radar kind of disappear. If I were to go on past experience, I'd take a guess and say he's either gone out of the country to get over the break-up or he's shacked up with some other woman, or maybe a man - I've had that one happen to a client of mine, too.

Anyway, I need a plan and things are a bit hectic, so I'm tempted to farm this one out to one of the members of my 'technical support' team, otherwise known as a hacker, who could just go straight in there and retrieve the information I need. Of course, that's costly, and I usually prefer to do the legwork myself. But in this case, there's no point in me trawling around all the hotspots he may frequent hoping to see him - especially when I get the sense that Karen has probably already done that. I decide to make a few calls to his workplace and see what info I can get, and then I'll make a judgement call. I know I'll end up having to follow him at some point; Karen's definitely going to need photo evidence and a detailed report, because currently she's somewhere up a river called 'denial'. Sometimes people just have to see it in black and white to really believe it.

He works at a large utilities company whose head office is here in the city, doing some desk job where he plans marketing strategies. So I come up with a plausible reason for calling and dial the switchboard. Karen already gave me his direct line, but if he's screening - and he must be it - it will just ring out and I won't get any of the information I need. The receptionist greets me and I ask for him by name.

'Yes, can I speak to, hmmm let me see, oh yes, here it is, a Mr Blanding, a Richard Blanding, please?' I deliberately make out like I'm reading his name of a letter I've received.

'What's it concerning?'

'He wrote to me recently and asked me to contact him'.

'Your name, please?'

'Yes, it's Ms White'.

'Okay, please hold and I'll try his direct line for you'. Rubbish background music plays out for the following two minutes and I'm beginning to feel suspicious when finally, she comes back on the line. 'I'm afraid he's not answering, so I've called the next desk and they told me he's not in the office right now. Would you be able to call back another time?'

'Hmm okay', I say and replace the receiver.

It's been my experience that when something fishy is going on, a person's work colleagues often collude together to protect the guilty. I open my laptop and check all the social media profiles using the information I got from Karen. I start by entering his mobile and email address to see if I get any hits. He comes up on Facebook, but the profile is totally private. I can only see a profile picture and absolutely no activity, other than a change of profile picture six months ago. I flick onto my Whatsapp on my phone and add his number to my phonebook. It's another dead end. He must have his profile set to private there, as well - I can't see a photo or a status, and I could sit and wait to see if he appears online, but I also know this to be a fruitless task. I learned the hard way that some clever men have figured out is how to use Whatsapp and never appear online. It took me bloody ages to figure this one out and I only finally did when I was literally tearing my hair out about an ex. It's so simple, as well. All you do is when you receive a Whatsapp message you first switch your mobile data off, then open your inbox and read the message and respond, then exit Whatsapp and switch your mobile data back on. The reply is sent and you never have to appear online. That clever bastard I used to date - sorry, let me rephrase, that, sneaky, sneaky calculating little bastard I used to date.

I have Richard's work and private email and I decide to give an old friend a call. Lane lives in LA and he's a frickin awesome hacker. I'd never use a hacker for matrimonial or legal cases as its clearly illegal, but in a situation like this, where as there is no need for this information to ever come to light, I can halve my workload with one dial to Lane. I'm hoping he's still awake; it's 3am yesterday there but I know he's a night owl like me. He answers on the second ring.

'Dylan Sheriden, you gorgeous human, where have you been all my life?'

'Laney, it's so good to hear your voice. It's been too long!'

'Baby cakes, you've been MIA recently', he drawls sarcastically but affectionately.

'I know I know, I've been putting in the hours on the laptop myself, but man I need a break and now I need your help. Can you hack some email addresses for me? Just get me through the door at least, please. I need to crack this case as quickly as possible and the sonofabitch isn't showing up anywhere'.

'You got it kiddo; gimme twenty-four hours, tops', he says affably. 'I'll have it by tonight okay?'

'You're a star Lane, you know that!'

'I do indeed', he agrees, 'So when you coming to LA?'

'Oh! Sooner than you might think, but I've gotta run, so I'll fill you in next time. I'll wire you the money today, okay? Call me if you hit any roadblocks', and then I put the phone down because Lane can really be a talker when he gets going. He also has a tiny little crush on me and I'm not about to fuel his fires when I need him to crack that email ASAP.

Less than a day later, I've tried the office number again twice and been told directly by the operator that Richard's not at work; she doesn't even try and connect me, I'm guessing she's been filled in about the 'craic' with this one. Doesn't matter anyway, because Lane was good to his word and got me access to Richard's inbox early this morning. Once I log in, I have to be really careful when I access it so that it's not red-flagged to the owner. I decide to log into the work one straight away - as long as I'm quick and don't open any unread emails I should be fine. Of course there's always the 'last log in' time at the bottom of the screen. There's a chance he could notice that, but most people don't and I'm banking on this fact. Quickly I enter his companies Intranet service provider with the log in details and scan the inbox. First thing I realise is that he's out of the office and has been for a while; there are a ton of unanswered emails, over a 100 in fact and a quick check tells me his out of office is on and set for his return to work in 4 days' time. I can see there is nothing pertinent here right now; at least I know he's not at work and most likely not even in the city.

I have to be more careful with the personal email inbox as he might be checking that one regularly and I cannot alert him to anything till I get the full picture. I know I should exercise patience, but I can't resist checking quickly. I'll wait till late tonight to have a proper look. Yes, he's definitely checking this on: there are only two unread messages, both received within the last hour. I quickly scan down the recent messages looking for something, anything, and I see it. Three weeks ago there is an email about a flight booking confirmation for a trip to...I scroll down: Bali. Bloody Bali! He left on a flight to Bali from Heathrow over two weeks ago with somebody named Alison Green and the return flight lands tomorrow at 3:45pm at Heathrow. I log out quickly. I'll log back in tonight. I check the time distance - 8 hours ahead - and the flight duration, and plan to do it while he's flying. I can have a really good dig around then, so any time after midnight tonight, I'll be able to fly under the radar.

In the meantime, I have plenty of time to get the lowdown on Ms Green. I have a sneaking suspicion that she works at the same company - it's usually how it goes with these things. I tap Alison Green into Google along with the company name and I get a LinkedIn profile straightaway. My LinkedIn settings are set to private, so no one can see I've viewed their profile. This search crucially gives me a photo, though it's not a great one; it's a candid sort of shot. I can see she has (or had) long dark hair and too many teeth - and that she looks young, twenty-five or so, I'd say. She's worked there for about five months from what I can see and she's a PA to the Marketing Director. *Ah, it's all starting to make sense.* Suddenly the pieces of the puzzle slot into place. No wonder poor old Karen didn't get anywhere with calling his office, clearly all of Allison's little cronies had her back, blocking Karen's attempts.

I flick over to Instagram and search for Allison's account; she comes up third down on the list with the username '@Ali-Pally'. *Pfft, what the fuck is that all about?* Unfortunately, her profile is set to private. Yes, I suppose that would be a given, seeing as she's off on holiday in Bali with one of her colleagues who just last month was living with another woman! Her Facebook is a bit more illuminating. It's still largely private but there is a new profile photo of her set just a few days earlier. She's sitting on what must be a Balinese beach in the surf. The photo has been taken over her shoulder and she's smiling, all tanned and happy. I'm so glad right now that it's me seeing this photo and not his poor heartbroken girlfriend. These things leave such an unpleasant taste in my mouth. There are also a couple of cryptic statuses that have been made public, one is dated eight weeks ago and reads: 'Love is in the air'. I always find with these kinds of bitches they want the ex-girlfriend to eventually see their victory. Women are nothing if not calculating and bloody vindictive. They parade it around like a bloody trophy, 'Look at me! I got him', all the while forgetting that they really haven't won anything at all. At best they won a man who cheated on his girlfriend and callously left her without explanation and at worse a man who probably still loves his ex and is massively rebounding. Either way, it's all fucked up. Relationships that start from affairs don't end well: they usually end in another affair in what I like to call agreeable symmetry.

At least Lane has saved me endless hours of trailing this douche bag around London. Tomorrow afternoon I'll be at the arrivals gate at Heathrow Airport armed with my SLR. The airport is the most valid place I can think of to take photos without anyone getting suspicious. This has panned out pretty well, time and convenience-wise at least. So wine and Bob Dylan is how I choose to spend the hours until midnight. I check the flight departures for Ngurah Rai

International Airport, the flight's still scheduled on time, so I relax and open a bottle of Turkey Flat, my absolute favourite rosé. I have to buy it online in bulk, which is no problem except that twelve bottles on my wine rack is sometimes just too much of a temptation. 'If You See Her Say Hello' is playing and I close my eyes and listen to the magic of Dylan and am whisked away, if only for a few moments.

I'm sitting on the floor on the new rug I had shipped in from a Moroccan souk I visited a few months ago. It's super soft and vibrant with deep reds and oranges and a thick pile that I just sink into. There are ethnic cushions all over the floor that I picked up in the same souk. There are purples, pinks, lime greens and royal blues, many decorated with tiny gold moons and stars. I've always loved sitting on the floor in here, my back against the large cream couch, a glass of wine on the low oak vintage table that I procured in France, a stack of Vogues nearby and lots of candles lit throughout the den.

At quarter past midnight, I check that the flight has left Bali and immediately flick onto his email account., Good thing I waited; I can see he was replying to emails not more than half an hour ago. I have ages to search now - including connections the flight duration is around sixteen hours. So I go back to the start, I'm banking on this all starting somewhere between five months and three weeks ago. It's fascinating to scan a person's email inbox, see what stupid circulars their mates send and what online shopping they do, but I'm more interested in personal emails - something that will give me a timeline for this budding relationship. I scroll for a while then decide to quicken up the search.

I tap Alison Green into the search bar and the little clock ticks around while it thinks about it. Five results slide into view. The first one was sent almost three months ago and was simply titled 'hello'. It was sent from her work email address and the body of the message reads: 'just connecting, really enjoyed lunch today A x'. The second was sent two weeks later in the evening and came from her personal email, as I'm going through this, I'm furiously scribbling on my notepad whilst simultaneously sending the documents to the printer (scribbling is part of my creative process). I'm thinking she was on a night out. I check the date on the calendar to confirm and see it was a Saturday evening. 'Out with the girls, but thinking about you. Monday can't come round fast enough' and there's a little 'in love' emoji face that signs off the email. Then there was a little gap of about two weeks with nothing. I check the deleted mail and can't find anything relevant there either. The next email would have been about a month into this little affair and the true woman starts to appear: 'Listen, I know we said we wouldn't talk this weekend but I haven't heard from you in three days and I really miss you, are you with her? Please just drop me a message, okay babes?' I make a highlighted note on my pad to check with Karen if they went away that weekend. Interestingly, even though he wasn't smart enough to delete this from his inbox, he was smart enough not to reply to any of the first three. The following two were more recent, dated four weeks ago, and both were responses to emails sent by Richard, giving her the travel details for the trip. He hadn't actually written anything in the forwarded mails just a sign off that read: 'R x'.

I switch over to my laptop and log into his work emails. Now I have a timeline; it's a lot easier. I have to be careful not to open anything or change anything at all. So I scroll down to when the email exchange started and sure enough about a week before the she fired off her first email to his personal account, they'd been exchanging a little flirtation on the work's Intranet. It was just the usual goofy idiosyncratic nonsense people do at work, one such reads: 'you look tense, do you want a shoulder rub?'. So now I'm armed with plenty of info; I know when this all started and, unfortunately for Karen, it was when they were still together. I also know that they've just spent almost three weeks together in Indonesia. I find the actions of some people incomprehensible and with this prick - cowardly.

God, I'm not going to enjoy the conversation I need to have with Karen tomorrow. I've already called her and asked her to meet me at my office in the evening; I was careful not to tell her anything about what I've discovered, because I can't chance she might flip the fuck out and blow the whole thing. I finish up for the night by building a bigger picture of this Alison character and everything else I've gleaned about Richard from his email accounts. He's been up to something for a while and not just with this girl. I retire to bed with a heavy heart that night and question for the hundredth time if I still believe in love.

The alarm goes off at 9am but I think fuck it and hit snooze for another hour. Today will be a long day and a longer evening and there's no harm in a little lie-in is there? I laze around the house, call Cassie and tell her I'm sending a load of raw data to be typed into a case file for Karen. I decide to take the tube to Heathrow, forty minutes or so with no cell service is heaven when you have a phone (or, in my case, phones plural) that ring as much as mine. It's bloody freeing to not be reachable. Instead I take a book: Paolo Coelho's *By the River Piedra I Sat Down and Wept*. I love a book with a good title and it's small enough that I've got a good chance of finishing it on the journey there and back. I miss the days I used to curl up at night with a good book instead of a case file about someone's cheating partner. Today I've selected an outfit fit for a PI, black cashmere jumper, skinny black jeans and Sergio Rossi grey suede ankle boots, all pulled together with a classic Burberry trench coat. I throw everything I need into my Vuitton 'Neverful' bag (which coincidentally is always full) and throw on a pair large sunglasses - Tom Ford to be exact. Then I go through my checklist: SLR with spare battery and remote charger with leads for my phones, camera and iPad, check; tablet and two phones, check; a bottle of Evian, check; and Picnic bar and a bag of Jelly Babies, check. I love to snack and stalk. On my way down to the tube, I stop at the florists and buy a small bunch of red roses - it's an airport, right? Actually why do people take flowers to airports? I never really thought about it before but it's kind of an odd tradition.

The tube is quiet. It's only 2pm and I'm able to grab a seat straight away. I immediately open my book, though I'm tempted to put on my sunglasses and observe my fellow passengers. I love to 'people watch' - bloody good job I guess, given my profession. If you've never visited London or been on the tube, you're in for a treat. The whole of life happens on a tube train on any given day. There is guaranteed to be at least one crazy person, one wannabe musician, some form of a drunk person, a fashionista, a lot of Chinese tourists, someone who is lost, someone who has got on the wrong tube and at least one hot- model-looking man, who I love to create a little fantasy eye-flirtation with, knowing it will never come to anything but is endlessly distracting. *Never fails*, I smile smugly to myself and sink into the seat and program in a few appropriate tracks on my Spotify. There's an unbelievable healing power in music and in lyrics. What bestselling song did you ever listen to that wasn't about love? And what a strange coincidence that so many were written by men. Obviously the words men find so hard to say in real life can be written on paper and transformed into wonderful lyrics that can lift your soul. I'm on a theme at the moment: Lupe Fiasco/Guy Sebastian's 'Battle Scars' and James Bay's 'Scars' are on repeat. Battle scars - boy, do I have plenty of those. That's my last thought before I turn to my book and sink in.

I pull into the Terminal 4 station at around 3pm, so I have time to grab a coffee. The flight is landing a tad early, which is good, so at 3:15pm I make my way to the arrivals hall to get a good spot. I scroll through my IPhone and find the photos of both Richard and Alison and study them; I don't want to miss them after all this. Richard is forty and clearly plummeting straight into a mid-life crisis; he's not conventionally handsome all being told, but he's got a good head of dark tousled hair and deep brown eyes. He's tall, which is always a plus, though he's too skinny for me, more of a string bean than a ripped Adonis. Apparently he's a squash player. Frankly I don't get squash or the men who play it. He looks a bit like a guy who never really grew up, you know the type - they still wear their hair all floppy and they have kind of a goofy childish look on their faces, belying their years.

He must feel pretty smug right about now. I've located Alison's age through her LinkedIn and Facebook school and college dates, and she's around 28, if I'm correct. She's nothing special, though she has a general look like she's up for it. She has long dark hair and wears clothes I think are bought largely in Primark - no judgement there though, even I once in a while pop into the Tottenham Court Road branch for a mooch. Well, that's not strictly true; the few times I've ended up in there I was tailing a target and somehow got engrossed in the plethora of wares they sell and came out with a bag full of stuff I've never even worn.

I check my watch, it's 3:25pm. The TV screens tell me the flight has landed, so it's just a waiting game now. People are filtering through the doors in dribs and drabs, some being greeted by loved ones, others peering around looking for a sign with their name on it. I hate that moment when I go through those doors to a sea of people and signs and have to look for my name. I've been known to skip the town car altogether in favour of a cab rather than have the humiliation of standing there, being observed by a hundred pairs of eyes, while I look in vain for my sign. Yes, yes, I know it's not all about me, but we're all allowed our quirks.

I get the camera out of my bag and shove the roses in one end. Leaning on the rail, I angle the camera at the middle of the sliding doors - you never know if people will go left or right. More and more people are coming through now. They all look tanned. I guess the weather is good in Bali this time of year - plus there's another two flights that landed at the same time from Sardinia and Mexico, so I figure at least 800 plus tanned bods are going to be emerging soon. Five minutes pass, then ten and then fifteen, and I'm getting bored - and that's when I see them. I'll have to watch the rest of this through the lens. I snap some still shots then switch to video camera; they look like a proper pair of tourists. Richard is wearing shorts and not cool nautical ones either - no, these are some kind of print and are baggy. He's wearing a polo shirt and a naf souvenir hat, while Alison is wearing a maxi dress that swamps her figure and makes her large breasts look even bigger. Why do women insist on drowning their figures in fabric and looking like giant tents? And she's has one of those white, knitted, bolero-type cardigans on (a totally pointless garment) and large sunglasses. They are pushing the baggage trolley together, which piled high with cases and duty free bags, and are laughing and joking and being very much a couple. I snap plenty more pics on the camera and then follow them as they head towards the exit. Oh shoot, I will have to do something I really hate doing: I slide behind them in the taxi queue. They start making out right there in front of me and I resist the urge to take a photo of it - there are things that a jilted ex-lover never needs to see. Instead, I slide my phone onto record.

'Baby, thanks so much for this amazing holiday. You're the best man I've ever met and you're also the best lover'. Allison says as she proceeds to full on grope him on the butt, right there in the taxi queue. She has a grating London accent and is talking in one of those baby-like voices that I can't understand why men enjoy. She has got her claws well and truly into this one and, worse still, it sounds like he's funded the whole trip. I'm relieved to see two taxis pull into view. They get into the first and I slide into the second and refrain from uttering those immortal words, 'follow that cab' and instead I go for: 'Hi, you need to follow the cab in front. My friends have the address and I'm not from round here'. The cabbie raises his eyebrows; I'm sure he doesn't buy it but who cares, a fare's a fare.

Following a stranger in a cab is a weird experience because you have no idea where you're heading. I pull up the GPS on the phone, so I can track the journey. They've got to be headed to her place, because I doubt he's heading back to the flat he shares with Karen. The taxi heads towards central and then diverts off towards Putney and ten minutes later takes a left down a residential road. I've got to be so careful now; I can hardly pull up right behind them. But luckily, there's two cars between their cab and mine, so when I see their Black Cab's indicator go on, I ask my driver to pull over straight away. I get out just a few buildings away, pay the cab and dawdle on the pavement, watching as they disembark and unload the entire luggage from the trunk. They go inside and I casually walk past, taking a note of the address. Then I take an Uber back to the office, using the twenty-five-minute drive in the busy London traffic to put everything together on my iPad and check the electoral role for the address. Let's see who's registered as living there.

I get back to the office, download the photos to my laptop and format everything into a coherent order, making sense of everything I know for sure. I have about forty-five minutes before Karen is due to arrive, so I fix myself a stiff drink and think about the best way to approach it. She arrives fifteen minutes early, ashen-faced and visibly shaking. It is never easy to break this kind of news to a woman; maybe a male PI would be more disconnected and cold and just hand over the facts, but that's not the way I work. I want to help the people I work with to act and deal with it the right way.

'Karen, please sit down and make yourself comfortable. I have a lot to tell you and none of it will be easy to hear'. Her face falls as the last little bit of hope she'd been holding inside falls away. 'I want you to listen to everything first, take it all in and then we'll have a chat, does that sound okay?'

And so I outline without embellishment or exaggeration the fact that not only is her boyfriend with another woman, but he has been for longer than she and him have been apart. It's hard to tell precisely what emotions are going through her mind: anger or relief to know the truth? After I finish the whole sorry tale, I ask her if she would like to see the photos. Not everyone needs to, some people take it on face value and choose not have their hearts ripped out by seeing visual proof.

'Yes, I want to see them. None of this can get any worse, can it? My boyfriend of two years is apparently living with another woman and has just taken her to Bali for three weeks'. Her face is devoid of colour and I recognise something familiar coming over her: it's the absolute numbness. I know because I've been there.

'Let me fix you a stiff drink, I think it will help'. I walk over to the cabinet and pour her a Brandy - the strongest I have. 'Here you go, sip this and I'll show you the photos'.

She grabs it gratefully and holds on to the glass for dear life as I turn the laptop around. I start with the photos from the airport, then the social media accounts for Alison and then the screen grabs of the emails-I won't be providing the screenshots as part of the file though; they were obtained illegally and I'd never put myself or my freelancers in a position of handing evidence over that could be used against them. As I flash on the Facebook profile photo, Karen clasps her hand to her mouth. 'Oh god, I know her, I mean I've met her'. Realisation dawns on her tired face. 'I met her at one of Richard's work functions maybe three months ago. Do you think she was sleeping with my boyfriend back then?'

'It's impossible to say. All I could confirm for sure is that their relationship became more than just colleagues around that time - it was probably in the early stages of flirtation then, but I can't give you absolute answers'.

'I don't know what to say. It's just such a shock to have my worst fears confirmed. Actually this is even worse than I thought: the holiday, the deceit, oh god, I feel such a fool...' she trails off in silence.

'Karen, right now you are in shock, which is your right. You need time to process everything. But talking to you as a woman who's been betrayed and hurt in the past, it's likely that soon you will get angry and after that the blind rage will set in, but I need you to hear this and really understand it: there is so much value in remaining the wronged party. Never give him reason to dismiss you as a crazy woman or make you seem like the one who's wrong. Trust me, if you ever want that day of validation to come, that day when he begs you to take him back, then you can never tell him the lengths you went to in order to find out this information. Let him always remember you fondly. Don't give him an excuse to hate you. Men will always find a way to make you accountable for a situation. If you ever tell him about this, about me, then the timeline will change in his brain and you will become the one who made the mistake and ruined the relationship. Take this from my own bitter experience'.

So many times in my own life and the love lives of my friends I've seen what I just described to Karen happen. Because when I get mad, really mad, an icy rage comes over me and I'm absolutely deadly. In the past, I've ended up doing something so crazy that somehow I put myself in the wrong - at least in the eyes of my ex-boyfriends. An ex-boyfriend once told me I scared him, said he never knew what I would do next, and we know men really hate unpredictable women. Us women get a bad rap - yeah we can be crazy bitches, but it's usually not without severe provocation.

'So what do I do?' Karen asks in an almost childlike despair.

'First, let's break it down. Let's go through everything again and we can exhaust any questions you have'.

It's always the questions that get you in the aftermath of a big shock, the million things you forgot to ask and I'd rather she asked them of me than him.

'Okay, but would you mind if I go outside first? I need a cigarette. I just started smoking again after two years of quitting - something I did for Richard', she manages a small smile.

'No need, please smoke in here. In fact, I'll join you'. I'm secretly pleased because I make it a habit never to smoke in front of clients, but hell, its 7pm and the client is the one who's asking, so I don't need any encouragement. We sit, smoke and talk. I help as much as I can and order the timeline in her head to make the story as un-sensational as possible. By the time 8pm comes around, I think Karen has got to a better place. Women talk - it's how we process. We talk and talk until we are sick of talking about it and one day we decide we never want to hear another word about it - and that's the goal. But she's got a long way to go and I feel for her.

However, I need to finish the session by reminding her of the non-disclosure agreement she signed and that the details of how all this information came to light can never, well, come to light. I suggest a cover story for the time when she gets him face-to-face and, knowing he'll be back at work and where he's living, I know that she'll make that happen. A woman always needs the last word; it's a fact. I ask her not to share the photos with him and if necessary to say it was her following him after one of his friends let slip what he was up to.

'Oh, that reminds me Karen…I suspect the people at his workplace are all aware of what's going on, if not entirely complicit, so I would suggest not bothering trying to see him there'. I hate the thought of a good woman being made to look desperate and foolish by a bunch of office assholes enjoying their fix of water cooler gossip. 'I'm so sorry that I didn't have better news for you. I really am and I know that right now the following statement won't make you feel any better, but I'll say it anyway: this guy is not a person you want to spend your life with. He's a coward and a cheat and he's shown you no respect or loyalty. So cry, scream, break things, do whatever you need to do, but promise me you'll wake up one day soon and decide to never to think of him again, okay?'

'Okay', she says resolutely, 'Thank you so much Dylan. I wish we had met under better circumstances but you've been amazing. I hope one day I can be just as strong and together as you'.

I smile and think: *honey, if only you knew.*

"Stupid Guys on my phone..."

No rest for the wicked, eh? I next need to hand out more bad news, this time to Megan. I give her a quick call just to say I have news and would have a full report by the end of the week. I didn't want to fill her in over the phone, knowing that her anger could blow the case before she had all the facts. She told me Mark had been in a foul mood all day Sunday. I'm not surprised. Thinking you're about to get laid and then having the woman leg it from the hotel room is always gonna hit a man where it hurts - his pride!

Tonight I have an internet date, which means I have to miss my body combat class. *Uff!* Dates have become the bane of my life and I rarely entertain them. I dip in and out of the world of online dating. Every time I have a bad date, I stop for a while, then get bored and try again. The only benefit is it provides me with excellent research on the habits of men. In fact, on many dates when I immediately see no future, I use the experience to glean as much information as I can from them and it's easy to do. Why waste those couple of hours when I can come away at least having learned something new? Men, it turns out, just want to be listened to and if they get the sense they can open up, they'll spill the beans on their ex-girlfriend and thus lay bare the emotions and feelings we women rarely get to see. Men, just like us women are all messed up to varying degrees, essentially because some woman long ago broke their heart and they never fully recovered; they just kept moving forward, trying to cover up the hurt, all the while totally confused.

The last blind internet date I went on two weeks ago is really biting me in the ass. He was a nice guy, seemed normal and I didn't have a bad time, he just didn't do it for me on any level and he kept invading my personal space. I'm not down with that, and to put bluntly, I just don't like complete strangers touching me - I think it's an OCD thing. Anyway, right from the start he sat too close and kept touching my leg in a manner far too forward for a first date, but I'm a nice person and I don't, as a habit, like to upset people or hurt their feelings, so I went along being friendly but not giving off any signals. But he took it and ran with it, making plans for the future. Little did he know that he only had until I'd drained my wine glass (never let a good wine go to waste) and that was about as much future as he was going to get. He even tried to swoop in for a kiss as we said goodbye, an action I was expecting and swerved it like a pro. But since that date, this absolute fucktard has been messaging me constantly. Mainly, it's been stupid inappropriate comments about imagining how amazing I'll look in a pair of panties and now I'm officially annoyed. There's a scene in the best TV show of all time - *Friends*, obviously - where Joey picks up the phone and Rachel's dad is shouting away, not realising Rachel has long since left the apartment. Joey listens for a few seconds, shouts back and walks off muttering to himself the immortal words: 'Stupid guy on my phone'. It kills me every time I see it and is why I can be often seen muttering these words to my phone at least a few times a day: 'STUPID GUYS ON MY PHONE'.

Some men just don't get the message. Ignoring just fuels them to keep going and the messages get worse and worse as they try to get a reaction, not realising that with every press of a button the woman is getting 'the ick' big time. With this annoyance in mind, I'm hardly feeling confident in or remotely excited about my upcoming date with one of the three guys I've been chatting to. The first one was the fucktard, the second was a decent-looking man who I had great banter with but when I scoped him out online found out that he has a wife and two kids at home (he went straight out the window along with the 'panties' fucktard) and that just leaves Jean-Benoit.

Internet dating, now no longer seen as desperate, is a legitimate way for single people and unfortunately also non-single people to meet. However - deep breath and long pause - my experience of it has not been positive. Now, I understand that everything I feel can be swivelled right back at me but…people never look even remotely like their photos! I guess it's mannerisms and facial movements, but somehow it's so unexpected that they never look how you expect - I mean never! Even the best looking man I've ever met online preceded our date by telling me he looked better 'in real life' and he in fact did not. Yes, he was still hot, but somehow smaller and a lot more compact than I was expecting, not to mention older. Let's face it. Everyone looks better in photos; we all do - given the best angle, good lighting and a plethora of filters, even the plainest of folk can look 'selfie' perfect. It's more than a little misleading; I've even started to pre-warn these guys by gently introducing into the conversation that I'm not half as groomed in real life. Doesn't matter though, they still expect you to turn up looking like you've just walked straight off the Victoria's Secret runway. I'm convinced I have a 'Chandler' complex, myself - you know, the episode where he tells the guys that he thinks he's too judgemental about looks and every little fault with a woman is magnified in his brain? Well on dates, my internal chatter amuses itself with the classic line 'big head, big head, big head'. That's me. I guess a total 'Friends' fan forever as well as a judgemental bitch.

And then you've got the bloody age factor to consider! Now I honestly believe this only affects those of us without cocks - as if women don't have it tough enough already. Age can be so destructive in a relationship or at least in the finding of one. It gets harder and harder the older a woman gets and all men, no matter what their age, want a nubile twenty-two-year-old - even though the frickin reality is that older women are way better in bed and much less likely to turn crazy-bitch on your ass. Even if you don't look your age, eventually it will catch up with you. Men, seem to have very ingrained beliefs about how they want their lives to run - for example, one standard formula suggests they're to be married at thirty, have kids at thirty-five to forty, but if they meet an incredible woman who's already thirty-five when they are twenty-five, then the maths just don't add up. Once in my life, I made a huge mistake turning a blind eye to a largish age gap with a younger guy who on face value appeared very mature; I was thirty-one, he was twenty-four. Not a huge gap as it goes, but twenty-something guys and thirty-something women really are on different pages when you take sex and romance out of the equation. After chasing me relentlessly and commandeering my heart, decided all on his own that I'd obviously be wanting kids soon and as he didn't for a least a decade it was '*bye bye Dylan - thanks for the memories*'. It was a costly mistake, the implications of which still affect me now (I refuse to discuss my age with men. Period.) You can't be discounted by someone simply because of your age without it seriously fucking with your self-confidence.

This dating lark can be fun but most often it's an absolute mind fuck. It's even more of a pain in the ass when you meet a guy you actually like. It's a scary thing to be a woman; something happens to our brains when we meet a man, or maybe not even 'meet' in person, just chat to one online, and we begin to create a story in our heads, and this story takes on a life of its own and suddenly we are looking at photos of wedding dresses online and imagining the Instagram posts we will be make together. We have imaginary conversations in our minds and picture endless scenarios. This can happen all before we've even had a first date and then when we do have a first date we realise the guy is a complete douche or not cute or not interested and suddenly we are totally crushed not because we lost a guy but because we lost the possibility of the guy. Expectations, it's all about managing them. Even when you're in serious relationship, expectations can cause major trouble. Think how many times you got an idea in your head and convinced yourself it would happen and then you propose said idea to your boyfriend/husband and he dismisses it off hand, you then kick off big time and he has no idea what's happened, not realising that it wasn't just an off the cuff remark but that you'd invested hours of your day creating this idea into a story. I don't think women will ever be able to manage expectations properly; we either expect too much or expect nothing all - and the problem is that either way you're disappointed.

In fairness, we're all a bit guilty of creating our own reality; we've all told ourselves stories, both good and bad, and then convinced ourselves they're true: whenever I catch myself creating a false narrative in my head I immediately remember the acronym for FEAR - 'False Evidence Appearing Real'. On top of all that, though, what is also a major problem for woman is that fact the second you turn your attention to a man is the very second they stop attending to you. What the hell are you supposed to do? If you don't pay a man any attention and don't ever consider him seriously as an option, then you'll never start anything. But if you do decide to give them a shot, this is interpreted as a sign of weakness, a crack in the armour and they'll write you off as desperate. Are we all fitted with some kind of bloody invisible radar that shines red or green? That's a worrying thought, I mull it over for a minute - I'm a bit of a conspiracy theorist on the quiet and I consider nothing to be entirely impossible. There is certainly *some* imperceptible signal that transmits between a woman and a man that seems to let him know when you're invested and equally when you've lost interest.

Gosh, juggling all these men is getting tricky; it's like a fulltime bloody job. And at the end of the day don't we all just want chemistry? That perfect connection with an imperfect person. I know it's why I take a punt on all these blind dates. It's on that off chance that one day I'll be pleasantly surprised. It hasn't happened yet though. Actually, that's not entirely true, I'm forgetting the New Yorker; there sure was some heavy-ass chemistry there, but that's another confusing situation that I can't think about right now. True chemistry isn't anything to do with looks; it's a physical, uncontrollable reaction. I can count on one hand the times in my life I've been struck by true chemistry, the 'thunderbolt' if you will, and interestingly, I never got to date any of the people it happened with: there was the policeman who came to my house to take a statement about my stalker ex-boyfriend, (I couldn't exactly ask him out under the circumstances, being a copper on the job and all); the gorgeous man who hired me to pretend to be an Air Stewardess (whole other story) (he turned out to be married so no go there); and then a rugged guy I worked with on a project in Lebanon over a period of a few years (he always gave be the tingles, too, but nada, zip, zilch ever happened).

So, back to the date in question. I'm meeting Jean-Benoit at the Duck & Waffle at the Heron Tower Liverpool Street. I'm quite impressed with his choice of venue, plus I love the 'Sushi Samba' bar underneath so if the date goes badly I'll escape and enjoy a sushi platter alone. Dining alone has never bothered me, in fact I find it most refreshing: you get to enjoy your food and learn to appreciate your own company. *Tut tut.* I haven't even got on the date yet and I'm already thinking of what I'll do when it doesn't work out. I think I may need to read the 'Law of Attraction' again because this is definitely not in keeping with the principals.

I am looking forward to meeting Jean Benoit, though. We've been chatting for a few weeks, longer than I would normally permit, because as we know I'm not one for all the chatting (plus I think it's a massive waste of time to spend months talking to someone to then meet them and realise you've got no spark). Jean is obviously French and he's been living in London for five years. He works for an architecture firm, and designs fabulous buildings like The Shard, London's iconic landmark. He's thirty-nine, single and never married, so he's good on paper.

He's waiting outside the building looking characteristically French in a linen jacket, blue formal shirt and jeans with loafers. I'm kind of casual as it is only Tuesday evening. I felt like being a little Parisian myself and selected a pair of high-waisted nautical jeans with gold buttons and a stripy Bardot top, off the shoulder. I love to show a glimpse of décolletage and I also believe that shoulders are the sexiest part of a woman - and a man, too, if they're well defined. I'm wearing my Louboutin espadrilles, which are super high, so I'm rocking a good 5'9" instead of my usual 5'6". I wave as I walk towards him, trying to look sexy but nonchalant, which isn't easy in such high wedges.

'*Bonsoir* Jean Benoit, *ca va?*'

'*Bonsoir* Dylan,' he replies, kissing me on both cheeks.

'*Je suis très heureux de vous rencontrer enfin'* I'm hoping that I've just said '*I'm very happy to meet you at last'* but really, I have no idea. I've been trying to improve my French skills and this is a good chance to flex the muscles.

On first inspection, I'm not turned off - so this is not a bad start. Typically, I take one look and think 'not a chance'. Like the time when a guy arrived to a date in fixed metal braces - there was no sign of those in his profile pictures. Jean Benoit looks, well, French. Isn't it funny how French men look so French? I can't even explain what that means; it's just a general air of cosmopolitan-ness and it's sexy. He has kind eyes and a funny, lopsided grin and he over pronounces everything.

We take the elevator to the top of the Heron Tower, I love this quirky and cool venue and we chatter partly in English and partly in French. We reach the fortieth floor and we're getting on well - a good job since as I hate long elevator silences. The Duck is the highest restaurant in the UK and better still it's open 24/7. I love the architecture and I'm glad I'm with someone who gets it. The restaurant has this beautiful porcelain-tiled floor, *hmm that would so great in my kitchen,* and gorgeous oversized light fixtures. Jean Benoit has booked us a circular booth looking right out at the spectacular London skyline. This guy has class and style and more than a little *je ne sais quoi* so far. I'm already perusing the cocktail menu, and am so tempted by the sound of the Chocolate and Blue Cheese Martini. Jean opts for the Roasted Cosmo - thank god he's a drinker. I get bored when a guy says he's teetotal, not sure what that say's about me, but hey 'horses for courses' an all that.

Jean turns out to be the perfect gentleman. He has impeccable taste in wine and is witty and funny. I think he appreciates the fact that I'm trying out my French; men are so easily pleased compared to women. If you're attractive and polite and make an effort, then they are happy. But that may be because all men only see dating as a pre-cursor to sex. In fact, they see it as something they have to do to get sex, but it pains them to have to go through the process. Although, you can't make massive generalisations, of course. Some men I'm sure enjoy courting a woman, the more cultured fellows at least, but they still want to get laid at the end of the night. That whole whether to sleep with a man on a first date thing or not is a grey area. After the age of eighteen, there are few reasons or excuses not too, (i.e. my parents are at home, I have to be back before 11pm curfew, etc.). When you're an adult you can pretty much do what you want. So is it okay to sleep with a guy and still have him consider you as a prospect? Well, yes and no. Generalising a bit there though, I'd say if you sleep with a man on the first date, he'll forever label you as a good-time girl who's not up for anything serious or worse still he'll write you off because he assumes you sleep with everyone on a first date and he doesn't want to marry 'that girl'. Yet the relationship can go on to lead to something serious, trouble is, you never quite know which way that particular cookie will crumble.

Adult or no adult, there won't be any such decision for me tonight. I like him and I've had a good time, but I'm not gagging to be thrown over his shoulder and taken to bed. So at the end of the night, he pays the bill while I'm in the bathroom (impeccable date behaviour) and then waits till the lift doors close and then goes in for a kiss. I wouldn't normally entertain PDAs, but I'm a little tipsy from the cocktails and all the wine - and really, there's no harm in a little kiss is there?

It isn't a bad kiss, but there isn't a whole lot of urgency there. I'm not sensing a bucket-load of passion and there aren't any fireworks, but maybe he's a slow burner. Some men are - they get better with time like a fine wine. *Uff Dylan, enough with the alcohol analogies.* The cold air hits me when the doors open and I feel quite drunk.

'Would you like to come back to mine for coffee?' he enquires casually - worth a shot, can't blame the guy for trying.

'No, I have an early start tomorrow, but I've really enjoyed tonight, Jean Benoit'.

He looks disappointed, but gracious in defeat. 'Dylan, *ai passé une excellente soiree*'.

'Me too', I smile as I hail a passing black cab. I plant one last kiss softly on his lips with a '*Bonne nuit*' and I'm gone, Cinderella style.

"Agreeable Symmetry"

James is a case that needs wrapping up swiftly. It's been a week now since I linked him up with the seductive Irina and so far he hasn't bitten - yes, he liked some photos and followed me back, but I think it's time to up-the-ante. Later today I'm planning to follow him on a night out; Erin called me earlier to tip me off that he was going out on a stag do. I think she may be enjoying this a little too much; whenever I speak to her, I get the distinct sense that she's enjoying all the covert spy stuff. I wonder absentmindedly if the idea of James sleeping with other women is some kind of kinky turn on - *oh god, I do hope not.*

So, I decide to push it a bit and send him an Instagram message. I write it in broken English and come on all sweet: 'Hi James, I'm quite new to "the London" and I was wondering if you would like to show me around? Kisses'. I'm aware that I'm entering honey-trapping territory, but I really want to see if there's anything for Erin to worry about. I've been checking his Instagram feed and monitoring the patterns of who's photos he likes and vice versa. I've located his ex-girlfriend - that was easy enough as he still has the old photos on his profile - but they no longer follow one another. *Hmm nothing unusual about that.* Although men, social media and exes do puzzle me slightly. Does leaving photos of your past relationship mean that you're still hung up on them? On the other hand, if a guy deletes them, does it mean he's still bothered and can't bear the reminder? The last man who broke my heart waited till he met someone else and then deleted all trace of me; I assumed he was told to by his new and clearly-threatened girlfriend; he always was a bit of a pussy bitch that one.

Nothing happens with the Instagram message, so I decide to head over to his workplace in Covent Garden and scope out what he does on his lunch hour. This case feels a bit flat to me; I just don't get the vibe that there's any great mystery to solve but I want Erin to feel like I've covered all bases. She's got him pretty sussed out I reckon; she's given me his typical lunch hour and what he's most likely to do.

'Come on, Sherlock' I shout to Cassie, 'We're going out'. I reckon this impromptu stealth mission could be the ideal teaching opportunity, plus following someone is always easier in pairs. It attracts way less attention. She appears in the doorway, massive trench in hand, dressed in another classic outfit topped with a tweedy trilby. 'Okay, lose the hat, or the coat, or both!'

Cassie is rather excited by this sudden turn of events and she's talking at 100 miles an hour as we walk down the street. The sun is shining and everything, including the pavements and the buildings, look shiny and new. James works as the manager of a watch shop just off Neal Street, so we decide to walk and soak up the lunchtime sights of Leicester Square, plus the Covent Garden Tube is just too much hassle with its 193 steps and slow lifts. Trust me you only make the mistake of climbing the stairs at Covent Tube once; it's the bloody equivalent of fifteen storeys. No, I'd far rather make the fifteen-minute walk from my office through China Town - besides, I've got my Louboutin Roller Ball studded loafers on, so I'm all set for a stylish quick hike. We stop at the Hummingbird Bakery down the road in Soho and grab a piece of Red Velvet cake. I love to snack and stalk. I have the weirdest feeling today like I'm being followed, which is kind of ironic. I keep the occasional check over my shoulder.

'You alright, Boss?' Cassie asks, observant as always, 'is this part of my training?'

'No, no it's nothing just being paranoid, ignore me'.

'Righty-o', she replies amiably.

We reach Covent Garden at 12:45pm, having had my ears burned for the entire duration by Cassie - this might not have been the best idea, I really do work better alone.

'Right we are going to do a little drive by of his store first, get our mark and make sure he's there'. As we walk past, we both glance inside, and I see him behind the counter talking to a customer. Then after we pass the doorway, I stop Cassie and say, 'Right, describe to me what he looks like'.

'Uh, what?'

'Give me a full description of our target - everything you can remember'.

She looks momentarily stumped and then her god given talent a photographic memory kicks in. 'Okay, well he's approximately 5'10". He has mousy brown with flecks of blonde hair cut into a classic crew cut. He's muscular like he works out at the gym a lot'.

'...and?'

'And...oh I know he has a half-sleeve tattoo on his forearm. I couldn't quite make it out, but I'd know it if I saw it again. How did I do?' She looks pleased with herself.

'You did great actually'. She's not a bad kid, and despite her obvious ditzy-ness, she's actually super smart and has one of those 'techno' brains which is great. There are two sides to any PI's job: the surveillance and the physical act of following, interviewing and the gut instinct part; and then there is the technological computer forensics work. The latter has never been my strong suit. I frankly don't like technology, but I don't have to like it, I just need to know how to use it to my advantage.

Following someone is quite an amusing experience, because you always feel they are going to catch you, and turn around and say 'What the fuck do you think you're doing?' But in reality, if you are a complete stranger, why would they? I've followed ex-boyfriends before and literally been caught red-handed. I was once surveying an ex's house in my car when he pulled up behind me. When I saw him in the rear-view mirror, I panicked and drove off with him chasing me down the road, flashing his lights. That was quite a pickle to try and get out of. I explain to Cassie how the fact that we are in a busy area in central London at lunchtime will make this a very easy task.

'So where would you suggest we wait?' I ask her.

'Well', she pauses to scope around the immediate area, 'I think we should wait across the street by that bus stop, so we can see the doorway, but he can't see us from inside'.

'Perfect, let's do it'. I check my watch. It's five minutes to 1pm, so hopefully we won't be waiting long. Sure enough, a few minutes later we see James walking out the store and putting his coat on. As he emerges, he's straight on his phone and it looks like he's replying to a message. He turns left and walks down the street, head in his phone. Silently, we begin to move.

'Always give yourself space between you and the target'. Fortunately, the street is busy, so that's easily achieved, I see him put the phone to his ear.

'Right Cas, we need to speed up. Let's have a listen to what that call is about'. We up the pace until we are almost right behind him. He's stopped at the pedestrian crossing, so we can a good earful as we wait for the traffic to stop. He's talking pretty loud, too. 'Alright matey, just checking what the plans for tonight are, we still on for Camden?' pause, 'Cool, cool. Yeah get the pints in. I'll be there at 7'. And that's it. I love how men's phone conversations are short and straight to the point; he crosses the street and we follow at a safe distance. James stops suddenly to greet a woman on the street warmly. We almost bump right into him; I grab Cassie and pull her back and we pretend to be chatting about where to go for lunch. I can't exactly make out everything, but they seem to be old friends. I notice she's wearing a wedding ring and the body language isn't screaming suspicious, they chat for five minutes and he moves on with a smile and a wave.

He's goes into a local coffee shop and sits down; I gesture to Cassie that we are also going in. I have an ulterior motive: I want to check Tinder. So we sit down, making sure James has his back to us; I give Cassie a £5 note and tell her to go grab some drinks. I open Tinder set the distance to the minimum it allows - 2km - change the settings to James's age group 27-29 and start scrolling. Now whether I find him or not concerns two main factors: 1) If he actually has an account and 2) If he has location settings turned on and is logged in. I've already flicked through thirty profiles by the time Cassie gets back with the drinks. The sheer number of flipping men on Tinder in Central London is crazy. I'm looking at names and photos, in case he's using a different name like 'bigboy88' - *actually he's hot*, I think for a second looking at a shaved-headed Jason Statham look-a-like before composing myself. I can't match with him anyway as I'm logged in under Irina's profile, so I keep scrolling.

James is busy on his phone as he eats and nothing is coming up, so I'm thinking he doesn't have a Tinder profile or at least an active one because I know lunchtime is prime Tinder scrolling hour for bored men. Yet in a twist of fate, I get an Instagram message notification from him! It's so weird to be sitting less than five metres away from a total stranger and get a message from them. I show the new development to Cassie, who's finding the whole situation very exciting. His message reads:

Hi Irina, thanks for your message. Would love to have showed you around London, but I don't think my girlfriend would be too happy lol, but if you need any tips or advice feel free to give me a shout ☺

Well that's unexpected. It's a rare man indeed that won't take the opportunity when it's presented so blatantly to them. And to openly admit to the existence of a girlfriend? Well, I'm actually speechless. Okay, so yes, he did leave the conversation open but reading between the lines, I think it was more a friendly gesture than a come on. I finally get to the end of Tinder matches and it notifies me there is 'no-one new around'. It's ten minutes to 2pm and I see James clear away his lunch and get up to leave. I don't see any point following him back to work, so we watch him go and once he's gone, Cassie literally explodes. Having to stay so quiet for all that time must have been a stretch for her.

'Oh-em-gee Dylan that was so crazy. I can't believe he actually sent a message to us while we were sitting right there. So what's next?'

'Next, we are heading home, my dear. Your adventure for the day is over'.

'So what do we think: is he a love rat?' she says dramatically.

'Actually, I don't think so. He hasn't taken the Irina bait, he most likely doesn't have Tinder account and he seems to do nothing on his lunch hour other than well, eat lunch'.

I'm half wondering if Erin is going to be disappointed. Women are weird like that: their desire to be right often outweighs their desire to not have a cheating partner. I'll phone her later, outline everything and ask if she wants me to continue with the plan to follow him tonight.

Apparently, as we've gleaned, James and his mates will out in Camden tonight at the local boozer for a stag do. Generally, it's a perfect cheating opportunity. *What an annoying tradition stag dos are*, I think crossly. I mean they actively promote cheating and I've heard from many of my male friends that the groom in question cheated but 'it didn't mean anything'. Although, to be fair, I think a lot of 'hens' also cheat that night, too. Women are certainly getting ballsy these days, rewriting the rulebooks and basically saying fuck you to men.

We head back to the office. 'Cas, don't disturb me for the next half hour, okay? No calls - nothing'. I quietly close the door, check my reflection in the mirror and give my hair a good rustle - bed head style. Sitting down at my desk I open Skype on my iPad, scroll down to my New Yorker and hit call. I'm nervous and I fiddle with my hair, winding a strand round and round my finger while I wait for him to answer. It's only 10am in NYC, but I know he'll have been in the office for a few hours.

'Baby', his strong, gravelling voice is unnervingly familiar but unknown all at once, an intoxicating conundrum, 'You just made this day start a whole lot better'. His image appears: dark hair, dark eyes and dimples. He's sitting in his big office in the big city and he's smiling broadly with a twinkle in his eyes. That's when I realise that I actually miss him.

What the hell is going on? Dylan Sheriden has a heart of stone and she's untouchable, right? *Hmmm maybe not so much, after all.* I find myself smiling, the kind of smile that comes from the soul and spreads across your entire body.

'Hi honey, seems my afternoon just got a whole lot better, too'. Suddenly I realise that this is something I could do for the rest of my life: look at his face and talk with him about something and nothing all at once. It's so weird I've barely told a soul about him, just the basics; it's like for once I wanted to keep just one thing for myself.

'So what is my little fashionista doing today?'

'Oh, you know, the usual. Just following the trends, researching, doing a bit of social media focus'. *Best not to lie entirely, eh?* 'So you miss me then, eh big guy?'

If anyone could see me now, laughing like a little girl, blushing and flirting, they wouldn't believe it. The ice queen has melted, courtesy of my tall drink of water that hails from the Big Apple.

'Ah little girl, you bring a certain *je ne sais quoi* to proceedings. Without you everything is the same, but with a little less spice and a little less sparkle'.

I swear to god my heart just melted right then and in that moment, I know I'm a goner.

After a very pleasant Skype date, I pick up the phone and dial Erin. She answers after just one ring.

'Dylan, what is it? Did you find something?'

'No', I laugh, 'Don't worry, it's not one of those calls. On the contrary, I'm actually calling to tell you that I don't believe your boyfriend is a cheater'.

'Really, you don't?' She sounds a little deflated for a moment but then (likely immediately realising how ridiculous that is) she perks up. 'Oh thank god! I'm not sure that I could stand another disappointment and he's so great - he really is. Today he just called me to say he's booked us tickets for a West End show and dinner tomorrow night. I feel bad now for even doubting him.'

'Erin, as long as he never knows that you doubted him, it will be fine. You have a right to be wary you know'.

'I know, I know. So did you follow him and check out all his online stuff?'

'Yep. I'm going to put it all into a report and send it across to you this afternoon. Have a read see what you think and then let me know if you'd still like me to follow him tonight. I'll keep the evening free just in case'.

'Great, Dylan. Right now I don't think it's necessary, but let me have a read and drop you a text later on, okay?'

'Sure darling, do that. I'm so glad you seem to have found yourself a good one'.

'Gosh, me too. Who'd have thought it, eh?'

I spend the rest of the day writing a full report for Erin and one for Megan, too. Again what agreeable symmetry that while I unfortunately have to write one damaging report on one man, I also get to write another that pretty much clears another man of any wrongdoing. I'm glad for that; I couldn't take it if my entire job consisted of finding out liars and cheats - and I guess for everything else, there's always wine.

"Self-Sabotagers Anonymous"

Erin texted me earlier, happy with everything and so calling a halt to all future surveillance on James. She decided it was time to trust in love and really believe in this great guy who didn't want to hook up with a Polish model when it was offered to him on a plate. *Boy, James is going to get lucky tonight*, I smile.

As for me, I really need some girl time. As I now don't need to follow James on his stag do tonight, I've made plans to see one of my favourite girls, Ashley. Ashley is twenty-nine and she's a lovely, good-old American gal. She's bubbly and fun and though she hails from the red state of Texas, she's now somewhat of an international expat. I'm so glad she's in town for a while. She also has the best pair of (real) tits that I've ever seen - I mention it because her fabulous rack has earned her a tidy fortune on the pages of lad's magazines the world over. She also has a bloody amazing array of tattoos. Being a tattoo aficionado, I'm always impressed with what I deem good ink. Ash takes one hell of an amazing glamour shot with her full sleeve tattoo, tiny waist, curvy hips and ass - and, of course, those boobs.

She has an amazing life, filled with travel, money and glamour, but she is also completely unlucky in love and used to have a pretty hard-core stalker. We met last year when she appeared at my door at her wit's end because of the unwanted attention of said stalker who was making her life hell. Well, he was more of an internet troll than

160

a full-bodied stalker, because he'd harass her until she blocked him and then just set up another fake profile and start all over again. She's kind of a big deal in the glamour modelling social media world but is still waiting for that big mainstream break. So I think she was still at the stage where she felt she had to be nice to the fans. She'd been to the police, but this guy was clever - and she still didn't know his true identity. The police can't press charges against a guy without a name or an address, can they? I think by the time she came to me, she was just desperate for anyone to take her seriously and help. It took three months of full-on detective work, which culminated in the stalker becoming the stalked...by me. Once I had enough evidence, I went to the police with Ash and he was arrested and charged. Over the next six months, because of my investigations, other people came forward who had also been harassed by the same guy. So he found himself in a whole heap of trouble and Ashley was finally able to walk down a street without feeling like she was being followed by an absolute weirdo.

Anyone who has ever had a stalker will understand that it is a truly terrifying experience - not one to be proud of like some trophy or sign of popularity. I've worked on plenty of stalker cases, some as a contractor for law firms taking private legal action against perpetrators and some for private clients who have exhausted all other options. I can unfortunately also talk about this subject from personal experience, though my stalker wasn't a stranger in a trench coat, lurking in the shadows (although he often did lurk in the shadows) or sifting through my bins (I'm sure he may have done this one, too). Instead, he was a man I'd been in a relationship with for six long years.

Often the most dangerous stalkers are the ones who have had a personal relationship with their victim. They are already two steps ahead of the game: they know intimate details about you, your friends, your family and where you work; they know where you go out, where you shop for your groceries, the passwords to your laptop, phone and other accounts; and they also often have a key to your house. There are also some fairly frightening statistics regarding stalkers who perpetrate violent crimes against their victims - around 85% are someone you already know and as many as 60% are specifically ex-partners.

My stalker, let's just call him Tom in the interests of protecting the guilty, had been my long-term partner for more than six years. It was a relationship that started when he was unhappily married to someone else - and I said before, a relationship that begins in an affair, ends in a kind of agreeable symmetry. I can sum up in one word the perils of dating a married man: shitstorm! Married men are off limits for so many reasons aside from the moral implications. Mostly, they are totally fucked up - and if you spend enough time invested in one, you will be, too. You can't get involved in that level of shit and come out shiny white at the end of it; if you play in the mud, you will get dirty. But it's amazing how easily you can justify any behaviour to yourself until it doesn't sound so bad anymore; we all have the innate ability to take the events of our lives, reorder them and give them a little polish and recall them in a way that better suits your character. I also believe that for most of us, the human desire for thrill and drama is high. But seriously, there are better ways to get your kicks. Unfortunately, in my line of work, I meet way too many women who only date married men. I would suggest to these individuals that therapy might be a better option. Maybe they are just women who've been burned one too many times and don't want to put themselves in a situation that can ever threaten their fragile hearts. Plus, I think it's a major power play: these women love the control. But affairs spiral quickly out of control and the women who thought they were in control find themselves massively on the back foot. I'm pretty sure some of these women turn into stalkers, too.

Anyway Tom: one day after a standard argument, which happened all the time and was part of what had kept the fire burning all these years, I ordered to go stay with his parents for the night, but never came back. He cleared out of the house two days later while I was at work and disappeared into thin air. And so began the two months of hell, where I tried to deal with what was now looking increasingly like a proper breakup as well as trying to find out where the hell he was. This experience is coincidentally another key life moment that led me into amateur-investigation; I was a pretty poor detective then, especially in in my seriously incapacitated state, but I did have a running joke with my mom about what we termed 'Recy-ying', which is a made up name for doing a 'Reccy' (i.e. checking something out covertly). It's now what I call completing surveillance on a suspect. Side note: Bless all the mothers in the world that will do anything to help out their children - even in the most ridiculous of situations.

Cue much 'reccying' outside of his workplace, his parent's house and the gym, all to no avail; he had vanished into thin air. The case was cracked with the help of my mom, who rather wonderfully waited outside his office for hours and kept lookout while I waited down the road in my car. I was parked in an open driveway, so when she called me to say he had just driven out of the car park in a strange car with an unknown woman driving, I was so high on adrenaline that I didn't care about the woman. Instead, I waited in that driveway until I saw the car my mother had described drive past and I slipped out two cars behind them. I followed them all the way to the gym, where I watched my partner of six years kiss her and get out. She then turned around and drove off and I followed her in hot pursuit. I caught a glimpse of her as she passed me and I laughed out loud. She was plain as fuck and dare I say even ugly? After following her for more than half an hour on the motorway, it finally clicked as to why I hadn't been able to find my boyfriend: he was holed up in some two-bit terraced house in a town thirty miles away - one which

I had a good old look at the following day thanks to the wonder of Google Earth.

A few more good bits of reccying over the following days and I saw them buying their dinner in M&S, holding hands just like a regular couple. It is in moments like this that you really understand the coldness of a person, the complete disassociation with their former life and their disgusting lack of moral code. I had cried a river over those two months; I became scarily thin and my mental state was in severe question, but something happened after I saw that - after I saw them holding hands - I just let it go. It had also helped that I'd been chatting to a gorgeous male model Kieran and his daily messages and the prospect of sex with a hot new man had changed my perspective enormously. Seriously since Tom, I've always subscribed to the idea that you should *'put as many cocks as possible between you and the person that hurt you'*. Or in a less vulgar sounding way *'the only way to get over someone is to get under someone else'*.

My ex-boyfriend deigned to face me a week later. After all, I wanted to have the final say. I remember the clarity with which I prepared for that meeting; I felt sinisterly cold, calculating and surprisingly devoid of emotion. I put on my gym clothes and I filed down my nails, because I fully intended to punch him in the face. He sat there in the house that we'd shared for more than five years and talked a whole lot of shit about how they were just friends and were not involved in a 'sexual' relationship. I was surprisingly calm. In fact, I couldn't even muster up the aggression to hit this rather pathetic creature who I finally saw for who he was. But as he was leaving, he said something that made my blood boil about how 'it wasn't her fault (the other woman), she was the innocent party in all this' and taking the only opportunity I was going to get, I hit him square on the jaw with a right hook Tyson would've been proud of. Then I grabbed my golf club, a five-iron sitting casually by the front door - a weapon for any wannabe intruder - and chased him down my driveway. He ran as fast as his legs could carry him like the little bitch that he was. I walked back into the house, placed the golf club by the door and closed it. The last word on the subject had been mine.

Now I suppose you're wondering what this has to do with stalking. Well, a few weeks after that, I was at work and already looking and feeling much better. I was still chatting to my hot male model and also enjoying a few dates with a nice guy from work. It was a quiet, unassuming Thursday afternoon when I looked up to see my ex-boyfriend sidling towards me from the escalator; my blood went cold. I honestly never expected to see him again and I'd made my peace with that. As bold as brass, he walked right up and announced: 'I've made a terrible mistake. Will you give me another chance?'

What unfolded after that day was months of hell. He was everywhere I went. He would arrive in the middle of date I was on, pull up a chair and sit down menacingly; he would follow me everywhere in his car; he would stand outside my front window in the dark looking in; and he would phone non-stop - once fifty-seven times in one hour. He would send letter after rambling letter and text after text. The behaviours only escalated the more I refused to entertain him and after one unfortunate incident everything got much worse....

Now we are all wired to want revenge for the poor way in which someone has treated us, and we often want it right away - the instant gratification of serving someone what they deserve - but it almost never works out like that. I can say, hand on heart, that revenge is a dish best served cold. I got my revenge that day without even planning it. I had received an impromptu house visit from my model and after spending rather a lovely day together, we had ended up in bed. Let me tell you - it was good. In fact, it's one of my favourite memories, Kieran is still to this day the best thing I've ever had wrapped around me: twenty-three with a boyish grin and the body of demi-god. As I was kissing him goodbye on my front porch dressed in only a slip robe - a regular little Mrs Robinson, I was - I saw the ex's car coming up the road, slowly doing his recon. I'd seen him do this many times, but glimpsing me in the arms of a six-foot-two hunk of a man, wearing practically nothing, had him swinging his car towards the house. To this day, I don't know how I got my guy into the car and away in time before the ugly scene I knew was coming, but I did. As he pulled away from my driveway, I slammed the front door, locked and bolted it, and stood in the hallway waiting for all hell to break loose.

Tom started by hammering on the door shouting like a man possessed, but when it was clear I wasn't answering, he rather unbelievably tried to take the garage door off by the hinges. I knew in that second, I would have to let him in and when I did, he crumpled down onto the floor and cried like a little baby: that's the thing about revenge though, it never feels as good as you think it's going to. This was only the beginning of a terrifying set of behaviours, culminating in him eventually letting himself into my house, using a key I didn't know he still had. He rearranging my stuff around; photographs of him and I kept appearing in random places. Worst still, my underwear had been moved around, and stranger still, he always seemed to know where I'd be and when - now I figure he hacked into my laptop. The police were eventually called by my dad, who had a personal hatred for this man - a man whom hadn't just tried to ruin his daughter's life once but twice now. The policemen who visited my house were kind and took everything seriously. They told me they'd visit him and warn him off, coincidentally one of them was my 'thunderbolt' moment. Talk about bad timing. At the time, I was adamant that I didn't want to press charges because I felt sorry for him. In hindsight, that was a mistake - never feel sorry for a stalker who makes your life so miserable.

That wasn't the last time the police were called and it wasn't it the last time I'd hear from them about him. In fact, I received a call from them some months later as the girl he'd originally left me for had pressed charges for stalking. Turns out she had gotten herself knocked up by another man and this was in fact the reason he had popped up again in my life so vehemently. He had been stalking us both, hedging his bets. She had no such qualms about pressing charges, so he was now on the police radar and wanted in at least two counties. The stalking never stopped and neither did his persistence. He refused to accept what was plain as day: I had moved on, but more crucially, I had lost all respect for him and he was making my life hell.

It also caused a lot of stress with the new guy from work I was seeing at the time. As I tried to keep much of what was going on to myself, I had started to act really strangely as a result. Isn't it sad how even a pathetic man like that can still control your behaviour? In the end, I had to move to another country to make it stop. Fortunately, (for me), he attached himself to a new girl and I didn't hear a peep out of him for at least a year. I did, however, hear from his new girlfriend who shared tendencies with him. I heard from my mom that she had started driving past my house and waiting outside, even though I lived thousands of miles away. Then I received a call from yet another police jurisdiction back in the UK, asking me to help them with a current prosecution that was underway. They didn't tell me much, but from what I gleaned his current girlfriend was pressing charges for illegal entry into her house and assault. It seems some behaviours once adopted become a pattern that's hard to break.

If you have a stalker, I beg you to take it seriously. There is a vast difference between what I do for a profession, following people and monitoring their behaviours, and someone who invades a person's life to inflict actual harm and distress. I've worked on enough stalking cases to be suitably fearful for the victims. Relationships make people crazy; they do that to the best of us, but for some people they are just too inherently unstable to cope with it. These people are not well and the kindest thing you can do for them is put them out of their misery. Don't entertain them or feel remotely flattered by the attention, stalking is never about the victim; it's about the perpetrator. As with much of life; people's behaviour is rarely about you, people will only ever see the world from their own perspective and their actions are driven by a motivation and reason within themselves.

I'm still thinking back on this now distant memory as I walk the short distance to Soho to meet Ashley. The streets are already buzzing; the early Friday evening happy hour is in full swing and I breathe in the vibrant air and I feel invigorated. I love Soho and how it spills into China Town. The air is always full of chatter, traffic noises and people standing in the streets enjoying an after work pint. It's already getting dark: a crisp spring evening, not too cold, and thankfully dry. London in the wet is a miserable place; the tube becomes a damp sweatbox and the streets become much less busy as people stay indoors. Us Brits are used to the bad weather, but our culture is still fairly Mediterranean. We like our after-work drinks even if it means sitting outside and freezing our asses off - damn the smoking ban, it's a pain in the ass, as it relegates us smokers to doorways and fenced off pens at least fifty feet away from a venue. Give me a warm terrace in Europe where I can sit, relax, smoke and people watch any day.

I head towards the welcoming doorway of Wahaca, my absolute favourite Mexican Tapas Bar, and there's already a queue for a table so I leave my name and head down to the basement bar, where Ashley is standing at the bar with a margarita ready and waiting for me. She waves excitedly and I think again what a knockout she is. I can see men checking her out from all directions and the arrival of a blonde friend is only encouraging further attention. She engulfs me in a big hug and thrusts the margarita tumbler glass at me, saying, 'Drink up, honey. I've got so much to tell you'.

Some friends are just easy to be with and our conversation is effortless and our laughs are many. We make quite a terrible-twosome: both blondes, tattooed and carrying mildly innocent doll-faced looks that have just a hint of a wicked glint. Ash has a more obvious sexuality in her fitted t-shirt and skinny blue jeans. Her new razor-cut blonde hair, which falls just below the chin, has also given her a real edge. I'm more of your standard rock chick: JBrand leather-look skinny jeans tucked into black Isabel Marant Otway ankle boots and pared with a simple black shirt, unbuttoned to show just a glimpse of my Agent Provocateur Mercy bra with a Balmain leather biker jacket thrown on the top. I take a sip of the margarita, a Wahaka speciality, and savour the hit of the Tequila as the sour of the salt tingles on my tongue. I glance around the busy bar, occupational hazard - like a hawk, I always like to suss out my surroundings.

'Oh don't bother; I already looked. There are no hot men', drawls Ashley, rolling her eyes. 'And that one over there?' She jerks her thumb over her shoulder to a proper geezer all suited and booted, 'Already hit on me with the worst chat up line ever'. Ashley, like most women, is used to being hit on, and she will tell you as I will, that there's not a guy in the world who makes a good job of it. Chat up lines are cheesy at best, cringe-worthy at worst and you have to really like the look of a guy to put up with one.

'So tell me, how was your date last week?' I assume she's referring to the guy who's giving me the ick big time with his Whatsapp message assault, so I roll my eyes.

'Ah, enough said. Well how about the other one you were chatting to?' I roll my eyes again before giving her a full response.

'Well, a quick Facebook check showed me his wife and two kids!' I place two fingers to my temple and pull an imaginary trigger - one of my favourite and most appropriate gestures. 'But I did meet up with the French guy and he was actually okay - a bit timid but nice'.

'Nice? Honey, you don't want nice, you want hot and heavy'. *Hmmm she has a point.*

I can tell Ashley has something she wants to tell me. People are so easy to read once you spend your days reading behaviour. 'Go on then, tell all'.

'Well', she starts with a self-satisfied smile on her face, 'I met a guy. Don't worry, he's a good one. We've been on two dates and he's already taking me to Thailand next month and talking about what trips we will take next year'. *Oh god*, I think silently. 'Now now Dylan, don't be so pessimistic. I know what you're thinking' she laughs, 'You think he's one of those guys, don't you? The ones that make all the plans and then disappear?' Well, at least she's got it spot on.

I have something against the 'we men and women'. You know the ones - *we* should do this together, *we* should go there, *we* should travel to the Seychelles together next summer....yadadadada and all of this after chatting online for a few hours or days. Rather inexplicably, the 'we' planners fall in the same category as the guys who just disappear. They simply stop messaging or calling or they just don't call as often and suddenly all the 'we' vanishes. And you're left scratching your pretty little head saying *'what the fuck'* that was all about. The 'we' guy has always been around and he's a pain in the proverbial ass. But he does give me a fair bit of business that sneaky little promiser, because some women (those with the cash and the time) actually want to know where he went, not satisfied with just writing him off as another chancer, they either: a) believed all the hype and feel something terrible must have befallen him, or b) just want an answer as to what the bloody hell happened. It is a strange world we live in now. Gone are the days when I used to have to go to the phone box round the corner to call a guy who'd given me his home number in a nightclub. Ahh what a simpler time when no one had a mobile phone; when no one had Facebook or Instagram and people gave out their home numbers.

But anyway back to my original point: how strange it is that we have days of intense messaging with another person, we talk about our hopes and dreams, laugh together and make plans and then suddenly, there's nothing. One stops messaging and the other, wishing to keep pride intact, doesn't message either - a total impasse! I do it all the time, I'm far too wily to ever chase a man and so this would-be liaison never comes to fruition.

Ash continues. 'He's twenty-eight and works as a photographer. We met on a shoot'. *Oh blimey*, I think to myself, *this just gets better and better*. A young, hot guy who photographs models for a living, there's a recipe for disaster if I ever heard one. 'We hit it off right away and *momma* is he a cutie', she drawls, becoming all Texan, 'This morning he sent me flowers to the hotel, a dozen black roses - it's symbolic I think? And he's taking me out tomorrow night to a red carpet event in Leicester Square and afterwards I'm thinking I road test him in the bedroom' she laughs, she has a great laugh, booming and dirty.

'Are you sure you want to sleep with him so soon, Ash?' It's uncharacteristic of me to be so chaste, but she seems to really like the guy and we all know once you've given up the farm they tend to disappear into the ether. 'I mean he's a photographer; this is standard territory for him. He likely frequently picks up models at shoots - make him work for it, I say'. She pouts like a five-year old who's been told she can't play in the sandpit.

'Well I hear ya, but I'm only in town for another week and I want to give him something to remember me by when I'm gone, don't I?'

'Okay, okay, I concede, but don't let him stay the night. Kick him out as soon as possible, just so he knows you're not a pushover'.

'Dylan did you ever consider that this may be your problem?' she smiles to soften the blow, 'If you keep kicking guys out, not calling and pulling tight on that rubber band you're always going on about, maybe these guys just don't think your serious'.

She is right and I know it; she's not the first friend of mine to make that observation. I think I may just be racing around meeting guys, hooking up but too scared to get involved or commit. I'm sending out silent signals to them that I'm a woman who uses guys for sex and then callously abandons them. It's a funny idea that there's a ton of guys out there feeling used and discarded. *Oh well, about time the cosmic balance was returned.* I mean god knows there are a million women out there in the city feeling the same. 'Dylan Sheriden, righter of the wronged' could be my new superhero name.

'So D, have you heard from he who shall remain unnamed?' Ashley interrupts my little daydream. She always remembers to ask me about him, the ex I always think of even when I don't want to. The hateful ex-boyfriend, who turned my world upside down.

'No, not a word in a long time, babe'.

'Good cos you know I think he's kind of a wang'. I burst out into spontaneous laughter; I love her American expressions and she's right, he is a wang.

'Although his new goldigga is still stalking my social media', I add.

'Honey, that's just the way it should be. Haters gonna hate, that's the way of the world baby. You gotta keep your focus, cos at the end of it all, it's just about you and nobody else got nothing to do with it and you gotta make your peace with that'. She is so right on this one.

Just today, I was sitting at home at my kitchen table and was struck by sudden inspiration. I jumped up wrote down my thoughts and stuck a post-it note to my duck-egg blue Smeg fridge door. It was my goals for this month: 1) Look into setting up the LA office, 2) clear out your shoe closet, and 3) (most crucially) forget about the people that have hurt you. *Hmmm that last one is a tricky one though. Can we ever forget the people who've hurt us the most?* There are some hurts that can't be easily forgotten, they cut too deeply and shake your confidence something fierce. The 'ex' hurt me like that - and I've never forgotten it, although it seems he has forgotten all about me.

Sensing that I'm about to enter a dark pit, I shake my head as if to vanquish the demons and focus on my stunning friend. Her modelling career is rocketing; she tells me she's just hit 500,000 followers on Instagram - no mean feat in today's fickle world of the internet. But she's also living proof that no matter how gorgeous, successful and got-your-shit-together you are, finding someone to love is still a tricky business.

'Dylan, do you even know what kind of man you want, like a type? I'm reading *The Secret* again and it says to be super specific when asking the universe for something'.

'Hmmm', I think for a second, 'Okay, I want a man who writes songs for me and plays them on his guitar with a gravelly voice and facial hair. A man not intimidated by a strong, beautiful and feisty woman - oh and I want one who can cook and who smokes occasionally', I add as an afterthought.

'Well I heard that Bryan Adams cooks a mean lasagne', she laughs 'No seriously, Dyl, I hope that guy is out there somewhere for ya, I really do'.

'I just keeping fucking everything up though, doll. I meet a guy I like and I can't just be happy and see where it goes. I over-think it and then I trash it, because I'm scared of liking someone more than they like me'.

'Well you do have a history of sabotaging shit, honey', she laughs affectionately.

'True story, baby girl'. I pause before taking the leap. 'But, well, I may have kind of met someone'.

'Whaaat!' she screams a little too loudly, 'and you've waited this long to tell me?!'

'I've barely told a soul. He's just good to be true and I think the phantom sabotager is about to strike again. I'm freaking the fuck out Ash'!

'Hi, my name is Dylan and I am a sabotager. I sabotage potential new relationships in the name of self-preservation'

'Hi Dylan' responds Ashley dutifully and throws her head back in deep laughter.

This would be my introduction if they ever invent an AA for self-sabotagers and I imagine I would not be alone in that group. On the contrary, I suspect the room would be full of 'Type A' women (because let's face it, us Type A personalities break things). We'd all be thirty-plus, single, successful career women - smart women - who are probably head-turners and are all unlucky in love. At least in part, because our biggest failing is the need to destroy something good, because we are so goddamn scared of being hurt. Vulnerability: the most terrifying word in the English dictionary, yet it's the one thing we all need to succumb to in order to fall in love. If we can't show one other person who we are, flaws and all, then what chance do we have forming lasting, trusting and meaningful relationships?

The problem is, if your single, then all you know for sure is that in the past, showing someone your vulnerable side has backfired. It left you feeling hurt and heartbroken…and if we are all supposed to learn from our mistakes (i.e. if you put your hand in the fire and it burns you, don't do it again), then why would we ever be vulnerable again? Ah, it's one of life's greatest conundrums. A professional sabotager like me doesn't take the risk. As soon as we feel even the most remote feeling of loss of control, we are out of there like a shot.

Self-sabotage takes many guises, though showing a little bit of your crazy too early will always do it, as well as jealous fits, stalkerish behaviour, accusations, mood swings and coming on too strong too soon. All of those things are standard for any woman in a new relationship, but for a self-sabotager, these things are done deliberately and even in a calculated move. Alternatively, we just stop calling, start playing it cool, disappear or become offhand and distant. We secretly hope the guy will chase us and prove us wrong, but they hardly ever do.

We all have a voice at the back of our heads, whispering 'Don't do it! He could be the one; this one has prospects,' so we will keep a lid on it as long as our inner control-freak will allow, possibly two to three days max. I think any sane woman will eventually be hurt one too many times. My last relationship bled me dry and I literally had nothing left to give. Who the hell puts themselves up for that again without a fight?

A slight problem with this philosophy is that you sort of have to resign yourself to being alone and having very meaningless dates and one-night stands forever; it's a crapshoot. I suppose there's the hope that one day some striking character will come in tell you to cut out your bullshit and cut you off at the pass. He'll dismiss your sabotage efforts and make you love him. Maybe Self-Sabotagers Anonymous could also run some kind of networking system; they source these strong, no-bullshit kind of people, hook you up and that's how they break you free of the habit. I might actually have to look into this as a viable new business venture.

If I'm honest, I think us sabotagers are the most intensely vulnerable people in the world. We are the ones who are so easily disappointed and we feel that disillusionment to our very core, every day. Have you ever met a person who just radiates happiness twenty-four-seven? The kind of people that live in their own little worlds, unfazed by the people and behaviours around them? I'm so very jealous of those folks - what a lovely life they must live and how well they must sleep at night. It's our thoughts that do us in, the incessant thinking, questioning, wondering, round and round in your brain, as you struggle to figure it all out. What a blessing to not think and just *be*. The search for inner peace must begin with controlling your thoughts as I've heard gurus often say; I just wish they'd make a pill for that.

All of dating life is a power struggle and it continues throughout the whole of any romantic relationship. It's the battle between two people for control, yet regardless of whoever is ahead and whoever is behind, the real battle remains inside yourself. You're fighting with no one but your own mind, your own expectations. There is no person in the world that can make you feel better other than yourself. Until we recognise this, we will forever be unhappy, forever beholden to the behaviour of others, and what we all know about that: it's a big disappointment.

The standards we set for others will never be achieved, because no one other than you knows what it takes to quiet the pain within yourself; what your soul really needs to achieve inner peace. We can never accurately convey it to another, no matter how well they know us, because they will never understand the vibration of your very being. The world only exists inside each individual's mind as your experiences and feelings are only yours. We make the mistake of thinking that others share them and know what we think and feel, but they can't. Life can be a series of miscommunications. Relationships are rife with these between two people who think they are sharing the same emotions, while most often those feelings are worlds apart. They might be on the same chapter and sometimes even the same page, but never the same word; we simply never experience the same thing as another it's not the way of the world. Best we can do is fix and unconditionally love ourselves and hope to find someone who is also at peace with who they are, maybe then, dealing with miscommunications becomes much easier.

Phew. I really need to get out of my own head. So I fill Ash in on 'the New Yorker'.

'Oh my god', Dylan. He sounds like Mr Big'.

'I know, right? He's great and holy shit the sex was amazing. We just clicked, but it's long distance and after the last disaster with that, I'm just not up for it again. I need someone I can touch and be with…at least once a week', I add laughing. After all, I am still an independent woman who likes her space.

'He sounds kind of perfect, doll, when are you seeing him again?'

'Well, that's the thing. I don't know and it bugs me, and the fact that it bugs me, bugs me even more'.

'Hon, I may have drunk too much tequila, but that statement has just floored me'. Ash bats her big eyes at me, looking puzzled. She's an eternally hopeful romantic, and she, despite a lot of disappointment, has yet to enter full-on cynic mode. 'Why don't you give it a chance? I'm not sure if you realise this, but when you talk about him, your face lights up. You seem different and I, for one, am pretty damn excited for you'.

I can't stop the smile that comes across my face then. Being given permission to be hopeful about a man from someone who really knows you, let's a control freak like me let go of the reins for a moment. And I realise that deep down I am happy albeit scared as hell. We wile away another few happy hours, drinking too many margaritas and engrossed in our conversation. We don't notice men and that's just the way it should be. I haven't gone out with a girlfriend 'on the pull' in years; it's not my style. Sometimes it's just nice to catch up with your mate with no agendas and no master plan.

I rather excitedly tell her about the call I got from the Sheikh who wants to aid my plans to go set up a branch of Lipstick Inc. in the City of Angels. It's something I'm seriously considering, you really should 'never look a gift horse in the mouth' - strange expression that one I ponder momentarily. I need a change of scenery and I've always loved LA - it's something about the way the light hits the palm trees and its one place in the world I've visited that looks just like it does in the movies. Yes, I'm seriously considering the idea and having Ashley there for at least half the time is a big plus.

'Honey you have to! Think of all the fun we'll have if you were in LA'. By the time midnight rolls around, we are drunk and merry and call it a night.

*"Sometimes true love will
wait for you to catch up"*

Sunday morning starts bright and sunny. Today, I'm going on a road trip. I'm heading to Brighton to meet with Elliot, the guy who wants to find his long-lost love. I wouldn't normally travel to meet clients, but I offered, because I haven't been down to Brighton in forever and I really fancy the drive. I take the elevator down to the basement garage and admire my car for the millionth time; she is a beauty - an Aston Martin DB9 Vantage in gun-metal grey. She doesn't get taken out nearly enough, a disadvantage of living in London - it's not really a city of drivers, at least not compared to somewhere like LA, where no one gets public transport if they can help it. No, in London, millionaires sit next to paupers on the tube every morning, all having the same thing in common: the desire to get somewhere quickly.

I'm always one to dress for an occasion. I have, after all, always felt like I was living my life in a movie and dress accordingly to what my character has to do that day. As Shakespeare famously wrote: 'All the world's a stage, and all the men and women merely players'. Today's look is early 70s glamour, so I choose a coffee-coloured vintage Halston micro-suede shirt dress with oversized Gucci tortoiseshell sunglasses and Zara tan suede knee boots matched with my tan leather driving gloves. The weather is good for a drive: crisp and bright and crucially dry for once.

Once I've navigated my way through the thankfully quiet London streets, I get onto the motorway and press my foot on the pedal, enjoying the surge of power. I've always been a bit of a petrol head. I grew up reading my dad's car manuals as a way of falling asleep. I couldn't exactly fix a car if it was broken, but I sure know a lot about driving them. When the business started to make real money, the car was my treat to myself. I have always been an independent kind of gal, so I like to have my own money and buy my own things. As much as I loved being treated like a queen and showered with gifts in the past, I always found it came with a cost that far outweighed the benefits.

A good drive does wonders for the brain. I have chance to really think things through and organise my thoughts. I grab a coffee from the Starbucks drive-thru on the motorway and I happily drive the hour and a half drinking coffee, smoking and talking to myself. I've always done that, talked to myself that is, in the often mistaken belief that I make the most sense. Internal dialogue or chatter has a lot of power: be careful what you say to yourself as 'you' are listening and all that.

So I decide to switch to fairly pointless metaphorical questions like 'If I could have a super power what would it be?' I know the answer to this one; I reckon it would be the ability to read minds, which is surely a blessing and a curse. Imagine walking past a person in the street and being able to hear exactly what they think of you - yikes. Though there would be no more trying to figure out why that guy isn't calling, just read his mind and you'd save yourself a whole heap of hassle and brainpower.

Anyway, I always have this kind of internal chatter going on; I can't stop it, not the daydreams, not the metaphorical questions and just barely can I stop the dreaded darkness. Whenever I feel that one coming, I instantly pick up the phone and dial Sasha. Sash is my emotionally-dark person; she is the one person I can say things to I wouldn't say out loud to anyone else. She allows me to reveal my gloom in a way that other people might be frightened or alarmed by. As such, she has always been my emotional sounding board. If I'm really screwing about something, she's the first person I'll pick up the phone and call to rant about it. Putting the world to rights is one of our favourite pastimes. I believe everyone needs a friend like this; this bloody world is a difficult place and I've never been one to pretend it isn't so. Sasha is also off men for the time being and I often hope for her it stays that way - her life is a lot less complicated for the absence of these idiots.

Hitting dial, I wait for her to pick up. 'Sash, hey, it's me'.

'Baaabe - what you sayin'?

'Heading to Brighton, kiddo, got a meeting and a bit of shopping'.

'Good good, I'm coming down next week to see you - just decided today, that okay with you?'

'Absolutely. You know I love a bit of Sash and Dylan time'.

'Anything to report?'

'Actually not much, just the usual nonsense, you know. Crazy busy exposing liars and cheaters, been on a few dates and had a bit of hot sex'.

'Ooh the fitness guy?'

'Yep that's the one'. Sash knows the intimate details of all my liaisons.

'And that cunt, any developments there? I checked his Instagram account this morning - I really wanna punch that motherfucker every time I remember how he treated you. He's still posting the same shit about how fucking happy and in love he is…and that new bitch he has? Man, is she a weird looking ho'.

I burst out laughing, because this tickles me on so many levels. Sasha knows everything about everything and she was the one who was there when I was on the floor, heartbroken, and she's the one who picked me up and set me back on the straight and narrow. She hates my ex and with good reason; I generally forget that the last time I saw him he slapped me across the face, but she never will. I honestly believe that if he ever crosses into UK waters again, she'll be there with her Chinese throwing stars and a baseball bat. Everyone needs a friend who's totally got his or her back, no matter what. I love her big time.

'I can finally say that I don't give a shit, babe, but I still hope that karma comes back around for that asshole'.

'I was telling someone the story yesterday about the time you called him a "pussy bitch" and he didn't talk to you for like three weeks; they thought it was genius'. *Hmm, not my finest moment.* Word to the wise: unless you're absolutely done with a guy and never want to see him again, it's probably best not to call your boyfriend a pussy bitch - even if he absolutely is one.

'Oh lord, well I'm glad that someone was amused with that story'.

'Hell, it amuses me every day, my love'.

'Right, kid, I'll get off as I'm almost there. Gimme a shout during the week about your visit'.

'Will do, love ya' and with that, she's gone, and I feel that everything is right with the world. She has that effect on me.

* * *

The coastline of Brighton comes into view; us Brits love to see the sea. I'm meeting Elliot at the Tempest Inn, a lovely little cavern of a bar with a terrace and sea views. Brighton is so different from London; It's so laid-back and cool and I can't wait till this afternoon when I can have a good mooch around the vintage shops and quirky fashion boutiques in the North Laines. Sometimes you just gotta get out of London; the city can get you weary. Just the smell of the sea air makes me feel like I'm a million miles away from the traffic and the smog of the big smoke.

I'm digging the whole vibe. Between my outfit and the car, it's like a frickin holiday. Well okay, that's an exaggeration, but they do say 'a change is as good as a rest'. Sunday afternoon in Brighton is a great time of the week; everyone is doing brunch and because the weather is pretty nice, not hot but warm and dry, everyone is outside along the sea front. I decide on a seat outside, even though the inside is so cool - tiny little natural rock coves form the booths - because I really want to make the most of the gorgeous weather. I look around. Elliot isn't here yet, so I order an espresso martini from the ample cocktail menu and enjoy a quiet smoke, happily observing my fellow drinkers. Elliot arrives not long after. He's quite a striking guy; he's mixed race with gorgeous caramel skin, tall and has a bloody great smile. I wave and he strides over extending his hand warmly. I like him instantly and I'm glad. I try to only work with people I genuinely like. The amount of time I have to spend waded into their private lives means that we have to be able to get along and I, more crucially, want to *want* to help them.

'Dylan, it's a pleasure. Thanks for meeting with me. Would you like a drink?'

I like him even more, I think playfully, 'No no, I'm good with this, but please go grab one before we get started'.

'Great, I'll just grab a pint', he smiles amiably.

So there we find ourselves on a sunny Sunday autumn afternoon in Brighton chatting like old friends; he's very cool and there's something inherently soothing and easy-going about him that I like very much. It's so refreshing for once not to be hearing a tale of deception, but instead a tale of good old-fashioned love, although as it turns out there was a bit of deception in there, too.

Elliot had met Selina at the age of fifteen when she had moved to his comprehensive school in East London from up North. She was a good old Geordie girl and had immediately fitted right into her new life despite joining secondary school three years in. They had been immediate friends - I laugh as he describes her as the only girl who loved LL Cool J as much as him - and the clincher had been when they met after school in the Woolworths queue for the new Public Enemy album. In a case of young love, they were inseparable for the next three years, finishing school and going to the same sixth form college.

'I knew back then I wanted to marry her, but circumstances were not to be. After college, I got an apprenticeship in the city and she went on to university in Reading. We spent a lot of time apart and the fact that we were only nineteen caused so many childish arguments on both sides, and lots of tears - though that was all her', he laughs. 'But one night I did something so dick-ish that I have regretted it ever since. I went out to a nightclub with a bunch of mates, drank way too much and well, I guess I succumbed to the charms of another woman'. He shakes his head as he recalls the memory. 'I don't even remember her name or even what she looked like. I just took her home and you can guess the rest'. He has the good grace to still look very ashamed of this act, even all those years later.

'Elliot, you were nineteen. We all make stupid mistakes; you can't beat yourself up for that'.

He sighs and continues. 'Selina decided to surprise me with a visit for the weekend and, as the old cliché goes, she walked in to find her man in bed with another woman', He winces at the memory. 'I can still see the look on her face, the absolute shock and disbelief - and then the rage'.

'Selina was inconsolable and refused to ever speak to me again. I tried so hard to fix it, but my efforts were always in vain; she moved, changed her phone number and moved on her with her life. I didn't see her again for almost six years. We met briefly at a high school reunion party - she was there with a new boyfriend, and I was with my girlfriend, who would later become my wife'.

'Seeing her face again, it had been like seeing light for the first time after years of darkness. But we only exchanged pleasantries and nothing was mentioned about what had happened or the love that we had shared. We were like two total strangers who had once known each other very well. I only stayed at the party for an hour, maybe less - being in the same room with her was just too hard, and that was the last I ever saw of her...' he trails off and just looks plain sad.

And here we are, almost thirteen years later, and he's asking me to track her down, so he can make one last attempt at righting a wrong.

Here's a man who has reflected and accepted total responsibility for his actions and I sense he has suffered many of these years with the burden of regret. The way he speaks so eloquently about her and everything that has happened renews my faith in men, a least a little while.

'I tried to forget about her, I really did. I was in love with someone else. We had kids together, a whole life, but you know what? I never felt the same way I felt when I was with Selena. I guess I just want to know - I need to know - if she's the one. I figure if you track her down and she's happy with someone else, then I'll just put it to bed once and for all'. He stops talking and looks bashful, 'Do I sound like an old fool?'

'Not at all', I reply, and I mean it, sincerely.

In fact, talking to Elliot, I find myself thinking about my first love. Before you get your heart broken for the very first time, you are a different person entirely. It changes you in a way that you don't even realise for a long time; it leaves an indelible scar and blueprint for which all other relationships will be directly related. It seems like such a long time ago now, I don't really ever think about him and I doubt he thinks about me. But for some men, one woman really sticks in their mind. My first heartbreak changed the woman I was; I think to some degree I became the woman my first boyfriend went off with. She was a cold bitch, but boy did she know how to play a man the right way. My innocence was lost at the age of twenty-two. Heartbreak makes you suddenly aware that people can be cruel and the most unexpected ones can hurt you.

Elliot's story gives me a bit of hope though that maybe true love does exist and those who are meant to be together will eventually find a way. Perhaps love can remain. Aren't we as women guilty of presuming too much? Assuming that we have been forgotten and never thought about again? Or is it just easier that way for us to close the door and move on?

Elliot goes on to tell me how his marriage eventually broke down, due to neither deceit nor cheating, just time. 'We just outgrew one another; you know? We have two great kids, now eight and eleven. Our divorce has recently been finalised. My wife met someone else and I've been rather unsuccessfully trying the dating scene for about six months, but man, I know it isn't for me'.

I tend to find divorced men have a harder time adapting to single life than women, men crave stability and habit and they really miss the home comforts of being part of a family.

'Honestly, I don't know how anyone meets anyone serious these days. These women, they blow hot and cold. Sometimes they message like ten times a day and then nothing for a week - it's exhausting'.

I can't help but laugh at his obvious confusion, 'Elliot, trust me, the women are out there thinking the exact same thing. There's just too much choice and too many opportunities now'.

He nods and continues, 'I want to meet someone and be happy again, you know? Can I ask, Dylan, are you single? I'm not hitting on you, I promise, I'm just wondering how you find it?'

'Actually, yes I am, but that's the way I prefer it. I don't have the patience for it all or the time right now, but one day, maybe, if the right one comes along'.

The right one? God, we hear about him all our adult lives: 'the one'. You'll know when you meet him and all that blah - I guess never having met *the one*, I can't substantiate these claims where there is a moment of epiphany, when you just know it's right. That being said,

I've never heard a real life story of the thunderbolt. Instead, all my friends who are happily ensconced are so because they work hard at it, because they met someone and decided that was a person they could happily wake up to every day, forever. It isn't all rainbows and sunshine, but they make it work. I just never met anyone who didn't drive me crazy or who I didn't live to drive crazy. I've known for a while that I'm not an easy woman to love.

I try not to relive the worst heartaches of my life, except of course when I'm reflecting for a greater analysis or to offer advice to another person. When the heartbreak first happens though, I wallow long enough at the time to hit the all-time lows: I obsess, I cry, I stop eating, I talk incessantly about it all to my friends and I don't sleep, because I hate waking up. I do it all and it hurts, but over time, the pain does go away. Over time, you meet new loves and new things hold your attention and gradually you forget. Generally, only when dispensing advice, do I draw on some of my more colourful experiences in detail to offer guidance, counsel or just plain empathy.

I wasn't always a PI, not at all. Once, I was just a normal young woman who thought that love was always within her reach - that it was only a matter of time before I'd find him. In fact, I'd found *him* at least four times by that point, only to be disappointed - and the last one was the final straw. I've finally accepted certain inalienable truths about myself. Sometimes there isn't someone for everyone. Soul mates exist, but it seems they are rarely for keeps. Maybe most of those smug married couples actually envy us singles - did many simply get bored of looking for 'the one' and accept the next best thing? Not the man who made their heart race, but the man who'd race home every night put his feet up, watch TV and fall asleep next to her night after night. I'm jaded and cynical, no doubt about that - too many failed attempts at love will do that to a person, but marriage is still something that I want, very much so. I just want it to be right.

I look over the notes I've been writing as Elliot talked, there's not a whole lot to go on. 'Sorry I can't give you more information', he says, as if reading my mind. 'Twenty years ago, I could have told you everything about her - her favourite music, her favourite food, the perfume she always wore, the colour of her lipstick - I knew her so well then. She was my best friend. Now...now I have no idea of any of those things, but in my head she's still the same girl I met at school all those years ago'. A sad smile spreads across his face and I get a lump in my throat before quickly snapping out of it.

'Okay, Elliot, so leave this with me; it might take a while but hopefully I should have something for you by the end of the week. There's no guarantees - she might not want to be found or I might find her and she's happily married to someone else. You just never how these things are going to go and I want to prepare you for that'.

'I understand. That's great, Dylan, really. I'm just hoping one way or another, I can get some closure from something I've been carrying around with me for so long'.

'I've really enjoyed our meeting and I hope I can find her for you, I really do'. It would be so nice to actually bring two people together rather than uncover evidence to tear them apart. As Elliot leaves I decide to start right away while everything is fresh in my mind, so I open my laptop right there on the terrace.

So where was she now, his Selina? I intend to find out. Tracing a person can be either extremely easy or insanely difficult - hell, she might not even live in the same country anymore. I only have two photos of her and a name. This won't be easy, but I do have the name of her school and college and her old address, which helps to narrow things down a bit.

Elliot had already tried the social media avenues, although no offence, but he's a man, so I decide to go over everything again. Taking out my iPad, I open Facebook and search her name - nothing. I'm guessing she's been or is married and probably has a different surname, so I check her first name and enter her school into the search - still nothing. I try just searching through all the Selina's, the FB search does so on location though, so unless she's still in London I'm going to be searching forever. I drop the social media for now.

I take stock again of everything I know about Selina. I know where her family is originally from, where she grew up, her DOB, her school and college - that's a fair bit to get me started. I run a Google search and then search Bing and Ask as well; it's always worth checking your search on different engines as they all throw up different results. I get a bit of a hit when I run her name and the city of Warrington where she grew up; I find a local news article in Google News Archive written about twelve years ago titled 'Local Girl Does Good' that recounts a prestigious award she'd been nominated for in the sciences. Registered PI's have access to professional grade databases, such as Merlin and Accurint, which compile public records. I need a surname, so I try the DVLA and hit gold: Selina changed her name ten years ago to 'Wright'. Now my job is a lot easier. I decide to check Court Records in the UK and cross-check them with her DOB - bam! I find court records filed in 2008, they are a petition for full custody of two children, ages two and five. Divorce, custody? This is looking promising for Elliot, I think, unless she has remarried in the eight years that have passed, of course.

I run her name through Spokeo and get quite a few hits: a Facebook profile (not active in quite a while), and a LinkedIn. The LinkedIn isn't exactly up to date, but it shows her work history for the past eight or so years. It seems like she has been working in pharmacology since graduating and has moved around the UK a lot for work; her last position is showing in Oxfordshire, so I pick up the phone and call them, despite it being a Sunday.

'Hello, Marcy speaking, how may I help?'

'Yes, hello Marcy'. I always make sure to address people by their names if I can, it has the effect of making them feel special and much more liable to help. 'I'm looking to speak with Selina Wright, I believe she works there?'

'Oh Selina, no, I'm sorry, she's not with us anymore; she left last year'.

Damn it. I decide to appeal to the receptionist's better nature, 'Oh that's such a shame. She's an old family friend and I very much needed to get in contact with her about some family business, do you have any idea where she may have moved to?'

'Well, actually, I did hear she took a job in France. I can't remember the town, but somewhere near the sea - Marseille, maybe?'

'Marcy, thank you so much, you've been a great help. There's nothing else you can remember that might help me, is there?'

'Well she had all that terrible business with her ex-husband and I got the impression she just wanted to get away. He wasn't a nice person in the end, that one, or so I heard anyway'.

I'm getting the sense old Marcy is the office gossip. 'Marcy, I'm going to leave my number, if that's okay? If you think of anything else, please do give me a call'.

'I certainly will, dear. I hope you find her'.

It's amazing once you start to build a picture of someone's life in your head; it's also a good idea to gather all the facts before you go hammering in there with a message or a call. I've also got a more up to date photograph now too from the LinkedIn profile, so I run it through Google's reverse image search. It occurs to me that Selina might have other reasons for not wanting to be found - marital problems and child custody battles do account for a large percentage of missing person's cases.

I close my laptop after a good hour's session; I'll start again later when I get home. Once I'm immersed in a case, especially one involving locating someone, I like to keep the momentum going, but for the next hour I'm going to have a look round the shops before they close at five. I still like the tradition of shops closing early on Sunday's. life has so little traditions these days, it feels good to know this one still remains - although that does give me only about two hours to shop. I head straight to one of my favourite vintage shops in the North Laines: Beyond Retro, which is housed in a converted bus depot and it's crammed full of vintage treasures, but I have to work quick as I also want to pay a visit to a great little furniture shop that sources antiques, furniture and decorative items.

I bloody love vintage shopping, finding that perfect item that no one else is going to have, rummaging through charity shops and thrift stores, too, although long gone are the days when you can happen across a Chanel boucle jacket. No they are all too smart for that now; the high price items go straight on eBay and never see the light of the shop floor. I quickly find myself with a ton of items slung across my arms and I haven't even looked at the accessories yet. I'm a demon shopper when I have the time, which I pretty much never do; my shopping activity is pretty much relegated to late night sessions on Net-a-porter at the moment. I love shopping but I hate trying on, so I don't do it. I'm just going to have to select what I think will work - hell, I should know my own style after all this time. I'm definitely in the market for a new faux fur; I can't abide real fur or the people that procure it. If bloody Karl Lagerfeld, the king of couture, can dedicate a whole Chanel collection to the wonder of Faux Fur, then there's no excuse for people using real fur in the name of fashion. Some of the best faux furs were made in the 50s, and if they had the technology back then to create divine furs that look real but are totally cruelty free, then I'm not buying any spiel about how faux doesn't look the same.

I head towards the coats rack and look for XS; I spy a cracking camel colour fur with panels and a nipped in waist, oh how I would have loved to have gone to Studio 54 in its heyday: 70s glamour at its very best. I can just see me strutting around in a white batwing jumpsuit and lots of gold with this coat slung around my shoulders and massive heels - what an era. *No time for daydreaming, Dylan.* Time is a ticking, so I skip past the racks of denim - I absolutely cannot buy any more jeans! So I decide to look for jumpsuits and playsuits; I'm obsessed with rompers and all-in-ones - don't know why really when we hardly get the weather in England to get your legs out, but I'm already thinking about LA and the possibility of opening a branch of Lipstick Inc. there. Oh, just imagine if Taylor or Khloe hire me to do surveillance on a high-profile boyfriend or a corrupt movie producer - and think of all the sunglasses I can wear! I'm obsessed with shades. Not to mention, I can drink peanut butter and blueberry protein shakes every morning after a brisk jog around Runyon Canyon Park and then maybe spend afternoons at a Malibu Beach house. *Okay, okay Dylan, getting carried away again.* But still, what a perfect excuse to load up on vintage seventies high-waisted denim shorts and cute playsuits. The faux furs soon lose my focus as my head and my wardrobe is now firmly in Los Angeles.

Driving home, I'm totally focused on Elliot's case, so I'm barely through the front door and the laptop goes on, an ice cold glass of Chardonnay is poured and I'm engrossed. So far I know that Selina may be in France, possibly Marseille, so I'll start simple with the *'Pages Blanches'* - France's version of the White Pages. I can cross reference her name with the possible cities and hope for a hit. She may not have been so careful with data protection in France, where personal privacy laws are overseen by the CNIL. Theoretically she could have contacted them to remove her details, but it's unlikely. There's also the *'Pagesjaunes'* phone directory to try. I'm hoping I can track her down myself, otherwise I'll have to outsource the job to one of my contractors - I have a few of these in Europe. They are other PIs who I subcontract to if the work is international and can't be done from here, they, in turn, do the same for me.

Every PI wants to think that they are the best and can work it all out on their own, but it just isn't practical sometimes. I wouldn't usually be on top of a case so quickly, but missing persons is totally different to cheating partners: that takes time and study and patience: online stalking, following the suspect, social media patterns, hacking even. Don't get me wrong finding a missing person too, can take months, but I'm already halfway there with this one and when I'm on the scent of something, I'm a proper little Basset hound, or some other such dog that keeps its nose to the ground.

Marseille brings up no hits, so I pull up a map of France and running a pencil around the coastline, I look for other likely suspects. I type in Avignon - nothing; Cassis - again nothing; Montpellier - *hmmm how about the Riviera*...all this French research is making me think about cheese. I have a block of Comte in the fridge I picked up in Montelimar recently that will go down very nicely with this wine. Amazing how I can be so easily distracted by cheese, I think absentmindedly, as I return from the fridge with a generous chunk. Cannes and St Tropez are also no-goes, but finally with Nice, I get a hit and most importantly a phone number for a Selena Wright. Surely there can't be too many Selena Wright's living in the South of France?

I dial Elliot, putting him on speaker, and I light a cigarette, inhaling deeply. 'Elliot, hey, it's Dylan'.

'Dylan, hi, wow, I didn't expect to speak to you so soon. Missing me already?' he laughs loudly.

'Ha, quite. I have some good news. I've been working on the case since I left you and I believe I may have located her. At the moment, it's not confirmed and I just have a phone number, but I wanted to see what you'd like me to do from here'. There's such a long pause that I check the phone hasn't disconnected. 'Elliot?'

'Sorry Dylan, you caught me off guard there. I didn't expect this so quick and well now, to be honest, I'm a bit terrified'. Poor guy. He's made this huge gesture and focused so solely on finding her that he didn't consider what he'd do if he actually did.

'Look, I was thinking, since we don't even know if this is the right person, how would you feel about me making contact first? If it's not her, then no harm, no foul. If it is then I can try and pave the way for you to then follow up. It might take the pressure off both of you?'

'Wow, yes I'm liking that idea. Thank you, Dylan. I don't even think I'd know what to say if I had to call her right now'.

'Then let me deal with it for you' I say firmly, 'I'll be in touch soon, okay? But don't get your hopes up just yet we don't even know if we're onto the right one'.

As I put the phone down, I ponder the efficacy of searching out a soul mate. Surely if we are destined to be together, won't fate bring us thus? Or does it need a little helping hand these days? It's quite an idea that two people will be together regardless of their choices or the turns that they take down roads less travelled. I'm not entirely convinced on that one - I'll have to see it to believe it. For now, let's take this particular little experiment to the next step. I take a slug of wine and a final drag of my withering cigarette and dial the number. France is one hour ahead and I'm sure no one appreciates being called at 10pm on a Sunday evening, but it's one of the few times a week that most people are at home. *Here's goes nothing.*

The international dial tone rings out six times and just as I'm thinking no one's home, she answers out of breath and thankfully in an English accent. 'Hello?'

'Hi, yes, I'm wondering if I can speak to Selina?'

Her tone is instantly sharp in response, 'What's this regarding?'

'Well this might sound a little strange, but I'm a friend of Elliot's, Elliot Harper'. I hear an intake of breath then absolute silence. 'Have I got the right person?'

'Er no, I'm sorry, you haven't. I have to go...' and the line goes dead. *Shoot,* she's on the run now. I sit there for almost a minute wondering what to do next; I'm almost totally sure now that it's the right Selina - man, she sure is a jittery sort. I figure she can't call me back as my number is withheld so I reluctantly redial. She answers on the second ring.

'Hello, is that you? I'm sorry I panicked but I just haven't heard that name in a really long time. You caught me by surprise. God, I'm so glad you called back'.

Phew. I'm a little relieved to hear this. 'I'm sorry. I know it's late to be calling, but let me introduce myself: I'm Dylan. Elliot contacted me to ask for my help in finding you, I sort-of find missing people, I guess. He tried to find you himself, but like a typical man, he needed a woman to do the real work', I laugh, trying to release a bit of the tension.

'Sounds like the Elliot I used to know', she replies ruefully, 'but why? Why is he trying to find me?'

'Well I think that's probably a question best answered by Elliot himself: would you be open to speaking with him? I can give him your number or I can give you his?'

'I suppose, I would yes. I think about him a lot, but my situation is messy. I just don't know...' she trails off and I fill in the blanks: Selena got burned, definitely with custody issues and god only knows what else, and sometimes the prospect at a second chance at love is scarier than a life without it. Us women have strong constitutions we can close ourselves off to love if necessary; it's a form of self-protection that we are instinctively born with, something that only heightens, I believe, when you become a mother.

'Listen Selina, take some time and think about it. I'm going to leave you both my number and Elliot's number. I won't give him this one unless you tell me it's okay, but please consider giving him a call. I know it would make his day. The way he talks about you...well, it's quite something. I can only hope there's someone out there who thinks so much of me'.

'Is he...is he still married, I heard he was?'

'No, don't worry. I'm not in the habit of aiding and abetting married men', I smile, 'But why don't you let him tell you all about that, okay?'

'Yes, okay, and thank you; this is the most random thing that's happened to me in a long time, but I suspect one of the best'.

'Absolutely, remember life throws us many opportunities and sometimes all we have to do is reach out and grab one'. *Wow, quite the philosopher today, Dylan.* 'Be well Selena, *bonne nuit*'.

I sit back, take a sip of wine and fire off a text to Elliot. I don't want to speak another word tonight; I'm mentally exhausted: 'Expect a call, I don't know when, but it will be coming, I'm pretty sure of that, D x'

Today was a good day. I started and wrapped up a case in twenty-four hours - a new record, I also possibly engineered the reunion of two soul mates. I saw the sea, I drove my car and I bought three bags of vintage clothing that I'm going to have fun trying on right now. The only thing that would make this day complete is a fine man to crawl into bed with at the end of it, funny because I have just the one in mind, getting him here from New York in the next hour might be problematic though...

"The Mushroom"

Before I know it, it's the start of a new month. I'm dead-set on calling it an early night tonight, which for me will be 1am instead of 3am. Tomorrow will be a long, ear-burning kind of day, because I've started a new service, which I'm trialling for clients who can't afford my full fees. It's kind of like an advice line, call me an 'impartial friend', if you will. I will do a phone consult with a client and offer no nonsense advice - and I won't tell you your boyfriend is an asshole and tell you to dump his ass because it's hardly constructive when your well-meaning friends tell you to do that. Because the thing is with friends, however much they may love and care about you, they also have an agenda.

For example, a single girlfriend might want her wingman or her Saturday-night movie buddy back and stand to gain from you being single again; some (not so good) friends may be secretly envious of your relationship and act in a way that is destructive, if you listen to them too much. Ultimately, you have to act for yourself, by yourself, and like Baz Luhrman says in one of my favourite songs. 'Wear Sunscreen': 'Be careful whose advice you buy, but be patient with those that supply it, advice is a form of nostalgia, dispensing it is a way of fishing the past from the disposal, wiping it off, painting over the ugly parts and recycling it for more than its worth'. True Story Baz, true story.

The majority of calls I've had so far have been in the 'I think my husband/boyfriend is cheating on me' genre. It's hard for me to say conclusively what signs to look out for if you think your man is cheating, but there are behaviours that are consistent with deceit. For example, major changes in daily routines is a big one, especially if working hours suddenly become extended or trips away become more frequent. Cheating partners can become distant and detached; they may become critical of you or cause stupid arguments, just to get out of the house or, even more cowardly still, to get you to end the relationship, so they don't have to. They may become more concerned with their appearance: buying new clothes, changing their hairstyle, general grooming, etc. - all things that become more important when you're trying to impress a new woman or man in your life. This is a big one: if your long-term partner is suddenly making a real effort with their appearance for a day at the office, you can be sure that some new hot colleague has rolled into town. People rarely start tarting themselves up for no reason; new underwear is also a dead giveaway for men and women, because, let's face it, everyone gets lazy in the underwear department after enough time with the same partner.

Onto the physical things you can check for. The old favourite of mine is to check for receipts in their wallet - places they didn't mention visiting, checks for dinner for more than just one person. Condoms in the wallet are dead giveaway if you've been married for years. Also check gym bags and washbags as this seems to be a new hiding place for such things. Check their phone call log, depending on how many calls he/she receives in a normal day, you might find there are way less than the maximum number of entries because of deleting received or made calls. You can play at-home PI by purchasing key-logging software and installing it on your partner's laptop or phone that way you get access to their passwords. I find that although a lot of affairs start on Facebook or Tinder, the way they communicate is often via email as most people assume a suspicious partner won't look there.

The thing about snooping through someone's phone is that you leave footprints everywhere you go. If you check a profile on his Insta, it comes up on a separate list of profiles you've viewed (that one got me). Facebook has a last device log in menu, and some people have notifications set up when anyone accesses their profile from a new device. Email accounts have a last logged in the timestamp and Skype has a recent contacts menu for anyone's messages you've opened. You can't open unread messages on Whatsapp or even texts. You have to think and then double think every step.

I've always struggled with the battle of intuition versus paranoia: where does intuition and gut instinct end and paranoia begin? Should you ever ignore your intuition? Women are especially guilty of supreme jealously and we love to create stories in our heads. Yet more often than not, I've been right and the times I've trusted someone and not even thought to check, have been the times I've been royally screwed over and shocked by the actions of another person.

I guess this is what I'm trying to balance with this new phone service idea; I want to tell people if they sound crazy or if they are on the right track. One thing I will say is that if you sit quietly and pinpoint exactly what moment it was, what action made you feel uneasy, you will strip away all the other inane thoughts running through your mind. What tips you off to something shady is a gift from the gods - you're meant to see something that doesn't quite fit. Intuition is a powerful thing but you've got to listen to it carefully, and keep your eyes wide open. Take emotion out of the equation and look at the facts, look at what actually happened and remember actions always speak louder than words.

My private phone rings, interrupting my thoughts and Ava's face flashes up - it's a Whatsapp call, *For Fucks Sake* this is not what I had in mind for phone advice day. Ava has Persian roots, she has the most insane mane of hair ever and men just swoon at her feet.

'Hi sweetie, do you have a minute? I need your advice'.

'Sure, for you babe, anytime. Although I should tell you I've put my rates up to 50p a minute'.

'Oh that's fine doll, I'll happily pay you a tenner a minute if you can tell me what to do'. She knows I am joking. Though if I did charge my friends for my well-dispensed advice, I'd be a bloody millionaire.

Ava is kind of fiery and more than a little crazy when she wants to be. She has a tendency to get an idea into her head and then run with it. So whenever she meets a new man or decides she wants an old one back, she creates a narrative in her head and when it doesn't follow to plan, she gets all stalker-ish and well weird. 'Okay, I've got five minutes, so shoot'.

'Well you know the guy I've been chatting to for ages - the young one?' *Not especially.* But then all of Ava's men are young; it's how she likes her men served up. 'Well, we met up last night and it didn't go so well; he didn't seem interested. He didn't make a move or anything and he seemed nervous and massively intimidated, unless,' she pauses, 'Dylan, am I ugly?'

'Ava, I don't have time for stupid questions. Of course, you're not ugly. It's perfectly fine for two people not to like each other on a first date; there's no wrongdoing or harm in that - and it's also not a reflection on you. Honestly, he does sound intimidated. You're a strong character, you know', I say, laughing.

'But seriously Dyl, he wasn't even that hot in person and I feel like it's an insult that he wouldn't even try to put it on me.'

There is a worrying new breed of men in town, served up to initially make you feel fabulous and quickly make you feel awful about yourself. These guys are mostly young - twenty-five or twenty-six maximum and they are very cocky when hiding behind a cell phone, but when you meet them in person, they ain't got no game, especially if you are any kind of a strong woman. They shrink back and run home like little bitches. It's baffling if you ever find yourself in this situation.

'Well anyway, I got sort of annoyed and affronted and worked myself up all day at work, so I sent him a message that may be a little aggressive'.

This doesn't sound good. 'What did it say?'

'Well in a nutshell, it said he needed to grow a pair of balls and not be so intimidated by a beautiful woman - and what's his problem, can't he get it up?'

'Oh good god Ava, you didn't! Did he reply?'

'Yep and he got nasty and said personal stuff about my age and now I'm raging'.

'Ava, he's just lashing out, because you made him feel stupid. You know what male pride is like, once you knock it, they will hit back with the nastiest shit they can think of. Plus, he's young, maybe it's time to date men over the age of thirty, honey?'

'Should I apologise for the outburst?'

'No, I don't think there's much point in that - and you probably shouldn't contact him again. At least walk away with a modicum of self-respect'.

'Shit babe, I really thought I was gonna like him, too. What a waste of two months of chatting'. Nothing new about this story, my new rule is: as soon as you start the chat, arrange a meet within a week - that way you won't waste time this way.

Ava's dilemma has got me thinking about pride. Pride is more than just a five-letter word; it is the most relevant facet to understanding and therefore manipulating a man. Manipulating - yes I said it! Because after all, it's what we all do on some level in romantic relationships. Strategic manipulation done well is a work of genius; done wrong it's a fool's errand. Failing to understand the role of male pride in a relationship or dating is the key reason most men cheat or leave the relationship or decide not to start one at all. If you make a man feel foolish or less than a man, he'll act out and go elsewhere to get his ego fix. I should know; I've made this grand mistake countless times through being a smartass, who had to be smarter than them. A friend of mine told me she can tell when her husband has had no female customers that day (he's a tattoo artist), because he comes home bloody miserable. He's had no-one to massage his delicate ego and make him feel like a man. But back to pride, any time you do anything to threaten his pride he will most likely go to work that day and flirt with one of his female colleagues or message an old girlfriend on Facebook. It's kinda like tit for tat; this silent action rights things in his mind and he can come home feeling better - it's super passive aggressive and super annoying. Problem is if you're always trying to be one step smarter and constantly nagging or making him feel stupid then this is a slippery slope, I've lost every man I've ever loved this way. I'm not saying you have to dumb it down to have a happy relationship but you have to bear it in mind, guys like to feel smart and in control so think before you act if he's someone you want to hold on to.

I can never think about male pride without thinking about one of the proudest men I ever dealt with, known affectionately as 'The Mushroom'. I no longer think of men I've been in love with as being 'the loves of my life', even if I did at the time. But if there was one guy out of all the disasters that came close I'd say it was The Mushroom. It was a name a friend of mine gave to my Arab boyfriend, because we'd break up every second day and he'd always 'pop' back up like a mushroom a few days to a week later. He really screwed me over in the end, but boy did I give that guy hell in the year and a half we were off and on again. I was an out-and-out nightmare. He was younger than I was by six years, but because of his childhood and his culture there was a major immaturity issue that reared its head a lot. But I think it was also his innate childlike manner and enthusiasm for life that was infectious - I always liked acting a child with him. We ended up having a chemistry that wasn't initially there, that's for sure. Oh no, my initial thoughts on him when I met him on one fine party-filled day in November on his family's yacht moored for the Abu Dhabi Grand Prix was that he was kind of a geek and *so* not my type. Yet we had the most fun together that day and a friendship blossomed, and that friendship somehow turned into love after he pursued me with a purpose and a vigour that was undeniable.

We had a weird fucked up situation. We would have the most unbelievable sex and spend days in bed, drinking, smoking and laughing, and then we'd have a fall out and have the worst fights. Following the fights, I'd go out with friends, get hammered and hit up his phone with crazy shit at 4am. One memorable night after one such argument, I went to the bar of a friend of mine - don't believe anyone who says you can't have fun in the UAE; it's one of the craziest places I've ever lived. My friend Logi was (and still is) a crazy son of a bitch and ran a happening bar on the waterfront; it was always my go-to place for a lock-in after a big fight with my man. That night we sat in the bar drinking and smoking till 7am, and after hearing me rant on about 'the mushroom' for hours, he simply went behind the bar, took a bottle of Baileys straight off the optic, put a straw in it and handed it to me. That's the thing about good friends - they always know just what you need. The night ended at the crack of dawn with us sitting in the middle of a roundabout trying to hail a cab #roundaboutsarecool is still a viable and much used hashtag to this day.

So, back to my Arab. Multi-cultural relationships can have interesting challenges and there was always plenty of fireworks. I think that's what always brought us back together - plenty of passion and a genuine friendship - but man did we drive each other crazy. We were never happy for more than five minutes, yet the five minutes we were happy it was bliss. But he was one hell of a proud man. Many fights of our fights happened because I couldn't just let him be the smart one; I had to always impress my superiority somehow. Regardless, we made it through a lot of tricky situations and he stood by me when I lost my job. He walked around that town proudly resplendent in his dish-dash, hand-in-hand with his little white chick. We made a good go of it and for a while I really believed I would spend my life with that crazy little fucker, but then, as with all things, sometimes life has other plans. He was posted offshore - it's true that most Arabs do work in oil! for two weeks at a time and then three weeks at a time. Now, I wasn't opposed to this set up; I've always valued my freedom and let's face it: what was he going to get up to in the middle of the Arabian water surrounded by nothing but ocean and a hundred guys?

As it turns out, he could get up to quite a lot. One quiet evening at around 1am, I was working away at my laptop and that little Skype notification popped up to say that my Arab was online. *That's weird,* I thought. He worked in shifts and he'd said goodnight three hours earlier as he had to be awake at 4am to start work and all. The private detective in me, a PI instinct that I didn't even know I had yet rang a little bell in my head. It's important to remember this: the main event of a betrayal is always preceded by a small warning sign; by some little piece of the puzzle that doesn't quite fit. Most people don't notice it or dismiss it as nothing. That's easy to do as it won't seem like much at the time, but if you're hyperaware, then the universe always sends you a little sign. It's your choice if you acknowledge it.

This little sign didn't escape my attention. I fired off a Whatsapp message along the lines of 'How come your online?' He shot back (a little too defensively in hindsight) that he'd left his Skype online when he'd had fallen asleep and didn't take too kindly to being woken up. So I let it be and forgot about it for another few weeks.

Then on another idle day, we were spending a fun afternoon at the shooting range. Hell, I still love firing a Sig Sauer 9mm - turns out I'm a crack shot, too. At the shooting range, I always liked to imagine I was Kelly Duquesne from CSI Miami. She was a cute badass bitch with a revolver. Anyway, I asked to borrow his Blackberry to send an email and just before he logged out of his inbox I saw a social-media type of notification for a website I'd never heard of called 'Tagged'. Again, it was something I noticed in my peripheral vision and it was filed away for later perusal. So when it popped back into my head later when I was cooking dinner, I asked him 'Babe, what was that website I saw on your email? Tagged, I think it's called'. You know that moment, right before your world caves in around your ears? You almost know it's going to happen before it does, right? But even so, I just wasn't prepared for what came next.

When questioned about something that they are guilty of, a generally decent person will pretty much give up the farm straightaway. Other unsavoury characters that I've had the misfortune to deal with, lie and then cover up that lie with another lie, His story came tumbling out without too much effort at all.

I think he knew straightaway that he'd made an almighty mistake.

'Oh nothing, it's just a social gambling website my friends use at work', he said.

Gambling is still illegal in the UAE so this made some sense, but his face gave the game away. He opened the website right there on my iPad to show me it was nothing - just a fun game where you 'buy' and 'sell' people and try and make as much fake money as possible. Upon further interrogation, he logged into his account to attempt to prove it really was nothing - what a big bloody mistake to make.

When he logged in, what I saw was plain as day. It was a seedy dating site. His profile picture was a topless (and headless) shot of him and worse still the site had a Private Message function. Taking my iPad off him, I clicked on the private message inbox. By this point, I had gone icy cold from head to toe and had that horrible fuzzy feeling on my skin - the feeling that accompanies shock and horror, just before the numbness sets in. I read the streams of messages he'd sent to other 'players' in the game - all women. I really only remember flashes at that point: 'nice rack' sticks in my mind, and other shit talk I'd never associated with my respectful guy before. He sat there for fifteen whole minutes without saying a word - and neither did I. Not one word lefts my lips as I just kept scrolling and reading, scrolling and reading. Finally, he muttered: 'Is this over yet?' Not long after that, he got up and left. I don't think he could stand the silence. It was so unusual for his fiery little British girl to not say a word, neither good nor bad. Plus, I think having the person you love read that kind of trash talk is never going to make a man (or his pride) feel good is it?

The phone rang not long after that.

'You're still looking at it, aren't you?' Then came the apologies and the tears and the pathetic excuses. 'It's nothing. I got carried away. Everyone at work uses it. It means nothing, I love you. I'm sorry, please say it's okay'.

But it wasn't okay and it never would be again, I didn't entertain any of his excuses, no way, but I kept on looking, because I knew that as soon as he could he was going to change the password. So I did it first, that sort of quick thinking that makes me a bloody good investigator today. I made sure that I got all the information I needed. When you're in it, you're in it and you might as well find out exactly how bad it is.

I never answered any of his calls after the first that night. Instead, I sunk into the seedy world of Tagged. I traced all the people he'd been talking to; I read and reread all the messages. I figured out how long this been going on and when he'd been doing it, then I cross-referenced everything with our own timeline, recalling where we were and what were we doing.

Turns out if you put a bunch of sexually-repressed men on a rig in the middle of the ocean with little to do, they find ways to entertain themselves. This bunch had passed round Blackberry Messenger pins for women who were up for chat and had also shared all manner of new social sites, dating sites, and ways of passing the hours of boredom. Every message and log in was recorded - it seemed that he only used the site when he'd been on the rig. There was a gap of a few weeks since he'd last used it, and I grudgingly felt grateful for that.

After the shock passed, I got seriously angry, and then I was absolutely raging. I'd given him everything, including the best sex of his life, so I did what all scorned, smartass women would do: I set up a profile on 'Tagged' and spent some bitter hours sending him texts with all the messages I was getting from equally seedy men. Now I wasn't the only one who was raging, but now he also wasn't the only one in the wrong. It didn't take him long to flip that one on me; his great pride just couldn't swallow the fact I'd played him at his own game and it drove him crazy.

I'd love to tell you that that was the end of it, but my personal quest for vengeance took on a life of its own. I was convinced there was more to the story that just what I had seen. So after a two-week break, I forgave him for two reasons: 1) I still loved him and 2) I needed to get him in my apartment face-to-face to figure out what was what.

When I get a sniff of something, I'm like a crack whore looking for a fix. So as New Year's Eve rolled around, I took my opportunity and plied him with a ton of alcoholic pops (yes, Bacardi Breezers, it's funny to me even now). He was such a lightweight that it didn't take much; he passed out right there on the sofa. I then proceeded to take his Blackberry, a bottle of wine and a packet of cigarettes onto my balcony to settle in for what would be an exhaustive analysis. He wasn't so smart; he kept notes of his passwords for everything and other notes with lists of BBM pins. But it was his Skype that would prove to be his downfall. Because beyond the family names I was familiar with, there were several entries I didn't recognise. These entries had no photo, but the name 'BesaHoti' stood out just a tad. I mean who the fuck is called BesaHoti?

It took all of my investigative powers to track down who she was, but I knew the answer lay within Tagged. and After a few hours, I found her and sure enough she had a Tagged profile. What I wasn't expecting was that she also had an Adam's apple. I'd swear up and down that she was or used to be a guy. I requested her on Skype and sent her a message when she accepted. She played it down, said she'd spoken to him but only as friends as she had a fiancé. *Yeah, right love, how does he feel about you skyping random men you've met on a fucked up dating website?* I kept the information I'd found out to myself until the right moment presented itself.

My boyfriend, meanwhile, got himself all wound up about some guy on my Facebook he thought I was chatting to and at that point I'd just about had enough. Who the hell was he to have a go at me? The cheeky fucker. At that point, I was ready for the fight.

'So do you want to tell me about the Skyping?' I asked him. I think at that point he was way past being sorry. Men, I've learnt, will only grovel so long and then they expect you to forget the whole thing and never mention it again. So he was angry rather than scared when I brought this up.

He admitted that at work he'd sex-skyped BesiHoti, a woman he'd met on the site, but he hastened to add that he'd kept the camera off - *like that makes it any better you freaking moron.* So he nearly died when I brought up a picture of her on my iPad and screamed, 'Are you fuckin' insane? Look at her. You had sex-Skype with a total fucking stranger just for kicks?' I knew he wasn't sticking around for this one; he'd been made to look as stupid as anyone could look and both he and I were done.

I don't know why he did it. I can't explain his motivation - perhaps he had desired something 'new and exciting'. God only knows. I don't think he even realised BesiHoti was a 'she-male' and pushing fifty. He fucked it all up for a two-minute seedy-ass Skype conversation with a complete stranger. I do not and ever will understand men.

So, it's not the best story. After everything, I spent three weeks sitting on the floor with packets of cigarettes and endless bottles of wine beside me. My friends back home would Skype me. Sometimes they would play music and chat about nonsense, sometimes they'd say nothing at all, offering their silent companionship. This is a fact for which I am beyond grateful. For those three weeks, I couldn't sleep, I couldn't eat - I was but a tiny shadow of myself. I just felt so heavy; the disappointment and the let-downs of a lifetime weighed too heavily on my chest then. People can be so cruel to one another. I was tired of hearing that 'Karma's a bitch and they'll get what's coming to them', because I never saw it happen. I was forgotten once again, and, in the act of being forgotten, I slipped quietly away, becoming more and more of a shadow until there was hardly anything left.

During that break up, I developed my own strategy and I called it 'one day'. It goes like this: you have to stop yourself from contacting that person, so tell yourself firmly that 'today is "day one" of not speaking', and then, when you get to the end of day one, you pat yourself on the back. You'll feel a tiny bit stronger for your resolve so that the next day when you wake up and desperately want to make that call, you'll say 'no' to yourself; you'll say, 'Today is day two and I've made it this far, I'm doing good' and so on. Maybe you'll make it till day five before cracking and making the call; maybe you'll make it to day seventeen. Whatever day you make it to, something good is happening; you're training your brain to take back control one manageable day at a time. And as it often happens, if you wait long enough, the guy will break first; he'll panic that he's lost you forever. If he doesn't, then you know he didn't care that much about you anyway. Either way, every day you win is a personal victory. 'Day One' is my pride kicking in because I'd rather be the girl that never called again and just slipped away quietly than be the crazy bitch hitting up the phone of a guy who's gone into his cave and may never come back out.

But time and space heals. My 'day one' turned into my 'day 1,260' or thereabouts, and here's the funny thing: certain men, no matter their betrayal, left me with a certain trait that stuck. My funny, quirky

Arab taught me to drive on the wrong side of the road, educated me on another country and gave me another world perspective - until this day, I still have a great respect for this culture and religion. He even bought me a car and presented me the keys with a key fob, one Irish charm and a charm of the UAE Flag. He never *tried* to change me but somehow he did.

It took a long time to forgive his betrayal and a helluva lot of Kelly Clarkson, but now, not that many years later, I do forgive him and I always think of him fondly. His childlike qualities and his often-gentle air was both endearing and intoxicating. I thank him for what he brought to my life and also for the quiet unobtrusive way in which he removed himself from it. He never rubbed my nose in anything: no stupid social media displays that paraded bravado or new ho's, I never saw or heard a word from him. The Mushroom never did pop up again. Instead, he disappeared like a thief in the night, a thief who for the briefest moment of time had completely stolen my heart.

I realise suddenly that I'm still on the phone to Ava, whose been politely and unusually quiet for the past minute while I took my trip down 'mushroom' lane.

'Ava honey, I have to run. I have another call scheduled now, but I'll catch you later okay? Stay away from the phone!'

'Sure sweetie, I'll keep you posted, mwah', and she's gone, most likely off to terrorise another poor young guy who won't see it coming.

My work line rings almost straightaway after I put done my personal phone. 'Hi Dylan? It's Sophie. We emailed the other day'.

'Yes, yes. Hi Sophie, thanks for calling', I mentally run through my mental checklist; Sophie emailed asking for a phone consult about her boyfriend who she suspects is still pursuing his ex, 'So tell me how I can help?'

'Well, as I explained, I wanted some advice and some pointers. I've only been seeing this guy for three months and it seems to be going well, but the ex-girlfriend is still on the scene from what I can tell. I've seen her name come up on caller ID a few times and he hasn't answered the calls - at least not when he's with me anyway. They were together for ages, like six years or something, ever since university anyway. So I'm thinking that maybe there's some unfinished business. What do you think?'

'Okay', I pause, 'So any other signs that he's actually cheating on you with her or is it just a hunch?'

'Well, we only see each other twice a week at most and that's totally his idea. I've met none of his friends and I haven't been to his place either. He always stays at mine...but then again, it's only been three months. We're exclusive though so maybe all this isn't as bad of a sign as I'm thinking?'

'Do you live in the same city?'

'Yep, both here in central London'.

'Okay, well given that you live in the same city, then I'd have to say that I'd expect you to have been to his place by now. I'd also expect you to have met at least a few of his friends. But only seeing one another twice a week makes that less likely', I pause for a breath before the plunge, 'Do you have a name for the ex?'

'Just a first name, but I know where she works. He mentioned something about it in one of our first conversations'.

Funny, isn't it? I think to myself. Men give away so much information in the early stages, then as time goes on, they quickly learn not to share too much. We women jump on every morsel and they eventually stop dropping them. Personally speaking, I prefer not to open the 'ex-files'; I don't want to know anything about it as there's far less probability for paranoia and stalking that way. The less you know, the less tempted you are to look. I snap back to the advice I'm about to give Sophie.

'Right, great. So first thing you need to do is look into the 'ex'. Enter her first name and her company's name into Google. Most likely you'll get a hit on LinkedIn, which will then give you a surname and, if you're lucky, a photo. Then once you have that basic info, you can search all the most likely social media sites - Instagram is the best bet as it's more likely to be public, Twitter too. What you're looking for is any photos or mentions of your boyfriend. You want to build a timeline, so obviously anything recent is a bad sign. Have you tried looking through his social media?'

'Not much point there, really. He said he used to have a Facebook, but he closed it after his breakup, because he was getting too much hassle from "the ex"'.

'Hmmm, how long ago was this breakup?'

'Not sure. I didn't want to ask too many questions and look like a typical woman', she laughs.

I glance at my watch. Each of these appointments is scheduled for fifteen minutes and I've got to keep on top of it. After all, time is money.

Sophie jumps to another question before I can respond to her. 'So Dylan, can I ask you how long you've been a PI?'

'Sure. I've been working in the business for almost three years'.

'That's great. I bet you have a ton of women just like me calling all the time with our neurosis, right?'

I chuckle in response. 'Yes, something like that...', I trail off.

'I'm kind of interested to know about the whole honey-trapping side of things. Do you do that yourself? Do you try to entice all those cheaters?' she laughs.

Blimey, I think. *What is this, twenty questions?* 'We take on quite a diverse range of jobs for clients, but I'm afraid all that's confidential'.

'Of course, of course', she mutters. 'So can I ask what percentage of men are cheaters, do you reckon? Or is that confidential too?' she laughs again.

At this point, I'm getting a bit suspicious. Who pays for an advice call about their boyfriend and then spends most of it asking about my business? I swerve this last question entirely. 'Very hard to say, cheating is such a subjective thing, but anyway, back to your boyfriend. Is there anything else you wanted help with?'

'No, no that's all. I think I'm just being paranoid, maybe. I'll do what you said though and investigate a little myself and get back to you if I need any more help'. Her tone has changed to a rushed speech. She's in a hurry to get off the phone suddenly.

'Okay, great. I'm not sure what help I've been, but you have all my contact details, so if you need anything, get in touch'.

Strange one, this one. Then again, I suppose there's a reason this phone thing is a trial. I suspect PI work should be done face to face.

I don't have too long to think about it though before the phone rings again.

Three hours later and I can definitively say I'm not enjoying this 'advice line' day. I've had possible cheating enquiries, plus one woman who suspects her husband is gay and one man who wants to get rid of his girlfriend, who he says is, and I quote, 'a pain in the arse'. He wanted to pay me to pretend to be his wife and scare her off (I suggested he hire an actress or an escort as I don't do amateur dramatics, while in my head I silently suggested he should grow a pair of balls and tell her directly). If advice line is becoming a new fixture, then I think Cassie is about to get a promotion. Maybe it can be her pet project, she loves to talk on the phone, getting her off it might be a problem though.

I decide to head to the nearest bar and have a glass of wine. Screw it, I'm taking tomorrow morning off; I need a lie-in. I fire off a quick email to Cassie telling her I'll be unavailable till 12pm tomorrow and ask her to 'hold down the fort' - she'll like that. Realising I'm close to 'Yo Sushi', I perk up considerably. Ooh a glass of wine and a Tofu Katsu Curry will make this day a whole lot better. They know me here and greet me accordingly. It's empty as the lunchtime rush is long over and it's that afternoon lull before the city's office's close. I slide into a booth and order a large class of Pinot, a tofu curry, cucumber maki and finally do what I've been looking forward to all day: check my personal messages - with a special emphasis on looking for one particular sender, my New Yorker, of course. Happily, I read: 'Baby, it's crazy here, but I'm missing you, little lady. And your hot ass too'. *Such a charmer.* I roll my eyes but I'm grinning at the same time, which must look odd to any passing observer.

"Who is Dylan Sheriden?"

At 7:42 the following morning, my personal phone starts ringing and beeping with all manner of calls and messages - which, though I don't know it at the time, will be a trend for the next ten hours of my day. Now, I'm not an early riser. I like that my job gives me the relative freedom to clock my own time. And everyone who knows me well knows that I don't like to speak a word before 10am if I can help it. I'm decidedly not a morning person. So the fact I'm being rudely awakened suggests that there is a problem significant enough for everyone to risk awakening the wrath of Dylan Sheriden.

I roll over and pick up my iPhone, which is ringing again. It's Sasha. I murmur 'Hello' in that husky tell-tale voice that tells her I was fast asleep.

'I'm sorry to wake you, honey, but I thought it was best to give you a heads up...you've been outed'.

'What?' In my half-asleep state, I'm totally confused by this, but as Sasha continues, I feel my mind becoming sharper and what she's saying becomes clearer.

'Dylan, there's a huge article on you in the newspaper. There's a picture and your name with the tagline, 'Who is Dylan Sheriden? The Private Investigator becomes the investigated'.

'Holy crap', I say, sitting bolt upright and trying to gather my thoughts. 'Which newspaper? Is it bad?'

'Well, you look fucking hot if that helps, but it would appear some reporter has been following you for a while. She sounds like a fucking twat!'

I manage a smile at Sasha's usual forthrightness, but I'm still processing that several hundred thousand people are sitting on the tube right now, reading the daily free newspaper and digesting a puff piece about a day in the life of a private detective - a day in *my* life.

'It's possible they may have also intimated that you're some kind of *Belle de Jour*, too'.

Sasha's latest revelation snaps me back to reality. 'Seriously?! What the actual fuck?'

I hear the call waiting pinging, I take a look and see it's Cassie. 'Sash, honey, I've got to go. I'll call you back'.

'Okay babe, remember fuck these cunts, okay?'

I switch over to Cassie, while my brain is still travelling 100 miles an hour, trying to run through all the implications of this.

'Dylan, I'm so glad I got hold of you. The phones haven't stopped ringing. It's mayhem her and I'm freaking out. Are you coming in? Oh and I'm in the newspaper, too. Thank god I'm wearing my hat though'.

'Cassie', my tone comes out a bit sharper than I intended, 'Are you seriously more concerned with your fifteen minutes of fame right now than the actual professional mess we are in?'

'No, no course not. What do you need?'

'Right. What's been happening?'

'Well all the email enquiries have crashed the server. We literally have a ton of people wanting to hire you'. *Well, that's good*, I think. 'There's also been quite a lot of calls from the press asking for interviews. And you should check your inbox, because I think a few of your clients are freaking out about confidentiality'. *Hmmm, that's not surprising given the secrets I'm privy to.*

'Ok, so the article - I haven't seen it. Tell me, is it damaging?'

'Well...' I don't like her pause much, 'It's not exactly damaging. They've kind of painted you as some kind of glamorous exposer of the dark truths of love', she states this last bit rather dramatically and I roll my eyes.

'An exposer of the dark truths of love?', I ask slowly and deliberately, 'Cas, you need to read less fantasy romance fiction. This isn't frickin' *Twilight*, okay? Just handle everything until I get there. I'm on my way. Listen, no quotes to anyone. In fact, don't answer the phone or anything till I get there'.

I scroll thought the many messages bombarding my inbox, noticing that strangely there's one from Peter Day, celebrity latex lover and serial cheat. "Hon, I'm so sorry I think I may have dropped you right in it. Shit got out of control with this latest tabloid frenzy and somehow your name came out. They hacked my phone. Fuck, let me know what I can do to make it up to you'.

'Fucking Peter Day' I say out loud, addressing the quiet Kensington street below. Everything I've worked so hard for…anonymity is the key to my business. 'Lipstick Inc' has been outed. Hell, we just went public but without the bloody stock options. *So the jig is up, eh?*

All those non-disclaimer agreements that my clients sign and my relatively private existence just hit the crapshoot.

Oh god. I hadn't even thought of the personal implications; the guys I've been dating are gonna know exactly what I do for a living now. Geez, as if finding a decent man wasn't hard enough before, it just got a whole lot harder. For fuck's sake, I'll probably never get a boyfriend again. Who's going to date a bloody private detective? It's every man's worst nightmare. I walk onto my balcony, light a cigarette and take a moment to collect my thoughts. A lot of realizations come to me at that exact moment and for some reason Cassie's 'dark truths of love' comment is sticking in my head: a surprising plethora of thoughts about life, love and the future - but mostly about fucking men - are spiralling through my brain.

Dark, that's me I guess, if I could collectively sum up everything I've learnt personally and professionally up until this moment, it is the following: The world is fighting a losing battle. People have a deep lack of appreciation for what surrounds them - nature, animals, the precious environment and most of all, the sanctity of love. The world has become superficial at best and a lost cause at worst. So let's dispense with this myth now: there is no magical fairy tale. There is no amazing man who will swoop in and make everything perfect. First, *you* have to be perfect, be okay with your flaws, change what needs changing and then really accept who you are, because there is only you, then maybe fairy tales can happen, at least I hope....

Life is hard. Relationships are tough. They take everything you have and they often leave you with nothing - your memories can't keep you warm. A person can take everything you have to give and after it's all over they can tarnish even the treasured memory of true love and piss all over it like it meant nothing, like you meant nothing. Everything you keep sacred and true can be cast aside in a second.

There is a sorry truth to be faced here when it comes to the end of true love: those things you hold so precious and dear exist only inside the deep cave of your own mind. Because your ex, your love, will not go there, at least not that you'll ever know. It will feel as if they don't remember your smiling face as you looked at them with utter adoration, the times you laughed together till you cried, what it felt to touch your skin or to feel you writhing beneath them looking into their eyes telling them that they were your everything. They will make you believe they don't remember any of it, not one moment: what it felt like to love you and what your love felt like to them, they will fight like fuck to make you believe that.

Keep those feelings just for you, because you know them, they are imprinted onto your heart, they meant something to you and they changed you. Your ex will probably move on and it will likely be as if you never existed. Accept it, deal with it, and move on, it is your only choice, I've had to learn to do this time and time again, maybe I've become a little too practised at forgetting or at the art of 'pretending' to forget. Relationships will probably never meet your perfect ideals and neither will your ex; they were simply not enough, and it just wasn't right, if it was they would be here with you now. Exes are 'Ex' for a reason: because they cease to EXist.

In such a moment of utter clarity, standing on my balcony about to face an utter shit-storm, I am suddenly confronted with so many thoughts and I feel the strange sensation of a few cracks involuntarily appearing in my tough outer shell. The first man who wanted to put a ring on it was when I was eighteen years old. Do you think I said no to the other three and waited a whole lifetime to say yes to any old piece of crap? No, I've waited for the right one, and I'm still waiting, still searching. I only want to get married once and I want it to last forever; I want it to be as if we had met in the 1950s - I want it to last a lifetime. For me, marriage is the ultimate commitment and not one entered into lightly. I want a man I can proudly call my husband. A man I know deep in my heart will never cheat, never stray, will be devoted to me for the rest of my life.

Am I unrealistic? Maybe so. But somewhere in this big old world is a man who will love me for my flaws, not despite of them, someone who will love me for who I am - including the fact that I am bloody selfish and insecure at times. I am a person looking for true love and for me there is no other kind.

The notion of romance throws so many of us through a loop and the blinding effects of 'pair bonding' do nothing to help clarity. We become so easily enticed and distracted by passion and chemistry that we forget the most important things. Life is hard it's full of disappointments, sacrifices and hardship, we must choose to love someone who makes us feel safe and who allows us to be entirely who we are with no front and no armour. When you find that person, hold on to them tight, because real love burns deep in your soul - it is a feeling of complete certainty that you are home. It cannot be replicated and there is no disguise for real love that can last for very long. Choose the man who not only ignites a burning passion in your heart but also the man who ignites a fire in your soul. That's the kind of fire that can never be extinguished. It is he that will carry you through the darkest moments of your life, lift you up when you are broken and give you new wings to fly again. Never settle for less than that. Believe, believe, and believe, despite past disappointments, and choose, when there is little else to do, to believe again.

Don't waste your time on people who are quick to leave, or on wondering how and why they left. I guess that when all is said and done, you should accept nothing less than what you know you deserve. Fight for your right to love, so you can always say 'I may have loved and I may have lost, but at least I was in it - at least I threw my hat into the ring. I said I'm in world, I'm here, give me the best you've got'. You take what life throws at you, you fight the good fight and that's all that really matters. I'm not so worried about those of us with a backbone made of pure stainless steel. We'll be standing long after the weak ones have fallen by the wayside. Surround yourself with good people, especially when you get past your twenties and that time when you want everyone to be your friend. After that, select the people that share your life carefully; remember that good friends will pick you up when you need it, dust you off and set you back on the straight and narrow - and if all else fails they'll get you drunk and hook you up with a hottie for the night.

All the best advice in the world can't get you what you need: peace of mind. Do whatever you need to find it; your mind has its questions and as long as they remain unanswered you won't sleep a wink. Settle your mind first and deal with your pride later.

I sigh and am suddenly jolted with the realization that I should have left five minutes ago, all this gooey-ness is making me feel weird, I give my head a shake and throw back on the metaphorical armour. I have to get to the office and deal with the mayhem - no time to get glammed up. So I grab a pair of large Porsche shades, throw on a crop top and leggings with timberlands and a vintage bomber. As I walk down the familiar Soho Street, I can see a few people standing outside my building's main door. Oh hell, there's maybe two or three photographers outside. I thank god for the entrance to the underground garage just down the street.

This is bigger than I thought. *Why the hell are people so interested in me?* But even as I think it, I know the answer. People are interested in deception and trickery, hooked on conspiracy and paranoia. I seem to represent that to them. I walk past my car and stop for a second, debating whether to jump in and escape, but I know well enough that running away never solves problems for long. Reluctantly I head up the stairs and into my office.

'Oh thank god, you're here'. Cassie is practically on my head before I've barely stepped inside. 'It's absolute pandemonium. There's people outside, the phones are ringing constantly, the neighbours aren't happy either. Mr Constantino from across the hall just stopped in to say he was harassed while trying to go buy his morning coffee. It seems they took photos of him and asked if he was a client'.

'Okay, okay, Cas. Calm down, take a breath, Where's this bloody newspaper?'

'On your desk and I've collated some of the related social media and reviews coming in and sent them to your email'.

I walk into my office, Cassie still waffling in my ear, I pick up the daily newspaper and see the preview on the front page. Opening to the middle pages, I see a double-page spread with a giant picture of me in the centre with the caption: 'Who is Dylan Sheriden?' I'm walking down the street in Kensington wearing a pair of dark glasses just by home. There's another one taken from behind me, the day where Cassie and I were in Covent Garden following James. *Thank God he's just out of the shot.* And there's yet another with me dressed to the nines leaving my office with Kristina. Finally, there's a grainy shot of Peter Day. I scan the text; it's been written by 'Sophie' someone or other and there's a small photo.

'Oh lord', I put my head in my hands.

'What is it?' Cassie demands.

'I know who it is. This bloody girl, she's been following me'. Then all the little pieces fall into place. 'She's the girl who bumped into me that day in Kensington and I ran past her again a few days later outside the bakery. She must have been following us from the office that day in Covent and just yesterday she called me for fake advice about her ex-boyfriend on the new advice line'.

'Wow, she's good. Maybe you should hire her'. My head jerks up at the speed of light and I give Cassie a death stare. 'Yes, quite right, what a fucking bitch', she says in what I see as a much more appropriate response.

I start to read the copy again; it's not particularly well written and is largely supposition, starting off with how I supposedly helped Peter Day get out of his last indiscretion and continues to document a day in the life of Dylan Sheriden, There's quotes from 'ex-clients' - that's a crock of shit for a start., *My lawyer will have a field day with this*, I think grimly. The honey-trapping part has been seriously vamped up just as Sasha described. It makes me out to be somewhat of a 'Belle de Jour' character who sleeps with men to prove that they are cheaters. 'What the fuck?! Arghhhh!'

From the corner of my eye, I see Cassie retreating slowly away from the desk. I don't blame her; I have one hell of a temper under the right conditions. 'Wait, stay right there'.

I keep scanning and 'seedy world of private investigation', 'expose', 'sex scandals' and 'Escorts on demand' all jump out of me, but so do 'female empowerment', 'feminism' and 'women taking control back'.

'To be fair', ventures Cassie, 'she describes you as the "coolly beautiful" Dylan Sheriden. I'm mean that's a nice compliment, right?'

I appreciate her attempts to soothe me and as I finish the piece and again scan over the photographs. I feel a little calmer now. Sure it's not ideal that my fairly undercover business has just been exposed to the entirety of London - and the rest of the UK for that matter - and of course I'm not thrilled at being painted as some kind of sex siren, but the overall message of the piece (albeit slightly hidden under all the intrigue) is that I'm a smart, powerful woman who exposes the liars and the cheats and does so while dressed impeccably (I added that bit). Plus, according to Cassie, we are being bombarded with people wanting the services of Lipstick Inc.

My phone rings; it's Jacob. 'Not a good time darling'.

'I'm sure, little lady. You're quite the talk of the town, but you sure look hot in that red dress'.

Bloody men. I'm in the middle of a crisis and he's focused on how much he'd like to fuck me right now. This is probably a great example of the differences between men and women.

'Seriously Jacob, not now. Go take a cold shower and I'll talk to you later'. I cut the call before he has a chance to reply.

'Wow boss, I gotta learn how to talk to men like that'. Cassie looks at me with admiration in her young eyes.

'Don't worry, young-un, you'll pick it up soon enough. Life has a way of teaching us women how to deal with such things'.

'Noted. Also, Peter Day has called quite a few times, too'. *I bet he has.* I could wring his bloody neck right now. That's another lesson right there: only deal with normal people, not sex-mad celebrities who can't keep it in their pants.

I scroll down the missed calls on my personal phone: Ashley, Jay, Harry and, *oh crap*, Brogan. Shoot, I forgot about him. There's a few messages from my mom asking if I was aware that I was in the newspaper - err yeah, Mom, it has cropped up.

I can hear the office phone ringing off the hook. 'Cas, go answer the phones. if it's a new client, take all their details. if it's an old client, put them through. And if it's the press, say we have "no comment", okay?'

'Sure boss'.

I reach for my cigarettes and pour a whisky straight up. Then I lean back in my big chair and gaze out of the window. There's a few people still milling around outside the front door. I inhale deeply and consider the new curve ball the universe has thrown me. Maybe it's a sign that it's time for a change of scenery. The business will continue to bloom and this bit of unexpected publicity won't hurt it. Maybe I'll source some good people to run this office and go out there into the world and see what the 'craic' is. One thing I know for sure is that wherever I go there will always be plenty of liars and cheats to keep me busy - it's as predictable as the sun and the moon. There will always be the love rats, the broken hearted, the hopeful and the downright suspicious.

By the end of the day, it's been one hell of a long one, but thankfully the photographers have moved along onto their next big story. As I lock the door to my office, my phone rings. It's Sasha. She doesn't even bother with a greeting.

'You need to check your Instagram - I mean you need to check the cunt's Instagram'. I still find it funny how she never stopped calling him that.

'What? No way. I'm done with seeing that bullshit'.

'No seriously, babe, trust me. Look at it'.

'Okay, hang on' I say slightly irritated and just a little bit scared.

I put her on speaker and I open up the Jad's Instagram, a profile I stopped looking at a long time ago. There's just one picture I see stand out straight away. It's an old photo of me and him lying in bed, blissfully happy. I'm cupping his face in my hands and he's smiling.

I'd had it framed for him as a present and here it was again, after all this time, right in front of me and for the whole world to see. I slowly click on the picture and underneath is the simple caption: 'you really do get only one true love in your lifetime, and she was mine' and there's just one hashtag: '#regret'.

'Uhh Sasha, I'll call you back'.

I stare at the photo for the longest time after that - maybe an entire minute. My mind is racing and the weight of years of sadness falls off my shoulders right there in the middle of the busy London street. People are walking past, going about their lives, with no idea of the magnitude of what just happened to me.

I take one last look at the image, the words, then I close the page and drop the phone into my bag. I walk down the busy street, strutting like Heidi Klum on the VS runway minus the million-dollar bra, because I feel as light as a feather (unexpected validation will do that) and because I know that as long as I live I will never ever look at it again. Finally, closure.

I'm heading to LA or possibly even New York next and I'm going to take a huge bite out of this big old world. No regrets and no more baggage.

A few moments later, my phone is ringing again. When I see the name, a smile lights across my face and possibility once again tingles in my soul. 'Hey baby, how you doin?'

Epilogue

Karen finally moved on; Richard did not. He's still calling everyday asking for a second chance, but he won't get it. Karen's new boyfriend is a singer in a band, has long hair, tattoos and a penchant for penning songs inspired by her. Richard is a middle-aged singleton office worker, a fact that makes single women run for the hills.

Ashley is still single; she now has 1 million followers on Instagram and more stalkers than ever. But no matter what, she never gives up on love.

Megan met with my hotshot divorce lawyer armed with all the evidence and he wrangled almost all of her fortune back from Mark. She let him keep the watch.

Jacob is now dating another suspected gold-digging 'model'. He still texts me at least once a week, and occasionally, when drunk, proclaims his undying love and devotion to the woman he describes as 'impossible to pin down'.

Erin has moved in with James. They are totally happy, but she still checks his phone from time to time - I taught her well. Forewarned is forearmed.

Elliot and Selina were reunited and after a few dates decided they were meant for each other after all. Elliot is moving to France soon and he plans to propose at the first opportunity; he's never letting her go again.

Irina is still successfully ensnaring guys online; she may be the happiest of all of us, perhaps because she doesn't actually exist. As the Tin Man said: 'Hearts will never be practical until they can be made unbreakable'.

Harry has not gone vagina again; his experience only further cemented his affiliation to cock.

Kristina is dating a footballer from Real Madrid; she's been gracing the tabloids in dark Tom Ford glasses and giving good face. I give it a month tops. She needs a man, not a boy.

Brogan is still proving a great bootie call from time to time when I have an itch that needs scratching; he is, after all, very pretty to look at. A girl's gotta eat, right?

Jean Benoit lasted about two months. He was very nice and my French improved to no end, but ultimately, I can't get on board with a man that won't go down.

Jay is still keeping Whatsapp in business. I can guarantee her online status 24-7. But hey, at least there's always someone there to talk to, no matter what time of day or night.

Sasha is still permanently 'off' men; she is possibly the sanest person I know for the absence of the nonsense that comes from fraternising with the opposition.

Cassie is still talking about her photo in the tabloids and continues to come to work in all manner of obscure outfits. Her technical mind is proving invaluable. Last week she hacked into the Bank of England after I bet her a fiver that she couldn't.

As for me, well, I gained minor celebrity after the whole tabloid exposé and am now called upon to give no-nonsense dating advice on TV and in glossy magazines. Hollywood is calling. The New Yorker (sadly) turned out to be just another pillow-talking loser: impossibly arrogant and easily swayed by the attention of a certain Polish Model. I'm still looking for my gravelly-voiced rock star. I'm sure he's out there somewhere…

So honey, I'll leave you with one final piece of advice: Don't ever give up on real love.

Disappointment will set you back; it will tell you to stop trying, but the soft voice of love will always whisper 'try again'. What's the worst that can happen? You get to the end and you never found the holy grail we hear so much about? At least you can say you tried; you gave it your all and had a hell of a lot of fun in the interim. It's surely better to be the person who believes in love and never settles for less than the best, than to miss out on all the adventures you can have along the way.

> *'People don't forget girls like you, they try. But they*
> *will never forget what your love felt like'.*
> *(unknown)*

Printed in the United States
By Bookmasters